BLOOD OFFERING

The prime minister turned away, striding over to one of the girls hanging from the wall. At first he didn't notice anything—except the girl was dead. Her skin was as white as the cleanest kerchief, even in the yellowish light of the torches. The stink of blood and death filled Rakoczy's nostrils, and he turned away. Then he saw *it* and returned his attention to the girl. A small puncture on the inside of the thigh had almost escaped his notice. He had seen men die when that part of the leg was cut in battle. There was no stopping the flow of blood once a wound was inflicted there.

"You have bled these girls to death, woman?"

"Not all of them. Some of them. Some are still alive, alive and ready to serve my mistress."

Other Leisure Books by John Tigges:

VESSEL

John Tigges

LEISURE BOOKS ✖ NEW YORK CITY

*For Tim and Jay, both
of whom might get around
to reading this.*

A LEISURE BOOK

Published by

Dorchester Publishing Co., Inc.
276 Fifth Avenue
New York, NY 10001

Printed in the United States of America

VESSEL

PROLOGUE

Hungary

December, 1609

Globular clouds drifted slowly through the dark night sky, on occasion blotting out the small half moon. Chilly air swept across the rocky landscape, embracing the crouching Magyar warriors as they awaited further orders. When the moon seemed to glide behind a particularly large cloud, the signal was given, and the soldiers stood, following Janos Rakoczy, the Prime Minister of Hungary, up the hill toward the foreboding, shadowy outline of Castle Csejthe.

"This is asking for trouble," Petöfi muttered to his fellow foot soldier.

"It is all right. The Prime Minister is with us," Bocskay said quietly. "And he is a relative of hers."

"What of the cries and screams that come from the castle? Why should he be impervious to harm? He's only a human like we are. I say we are going to our deaths."

"Coward! Go to the back of the ranks where you'll be safe," the taller of the two snapped.

"I live in the village below, and I've had relatives taken by her." Petröfi nodded toward the wall that increased in height and breadth with every step the company of Magyars took.

"So? You've been spared, haven't you?"

"You fool! My two cousins were taken a year ago. No one has seen or heard of them since. They're dead and she killed them."

"So? We'll kill her. It's that simple. Then your village and the countryside will be safe once more. Is that not so?"

The smaller man fell silent for a moment before looking up at him. "Her death will not bring back anyone, will it?"

"Of course not, but vengeance will be extracted from her. What would you do to her if you had the opportunity to judge her and be her torturer and even her executioner?"

Petröfi pursed his lips. "It would be difficult. She has caused much pain and heartbreak—as well as much death. Of that I'm positive."

"Listen." Bocskay placed a huge finger to his pursed lips.

The file of soldiers stopped as one. A

cold wind wrapped itself around the company, and each man shivered. Off in the distance, from the castle, a high-pitched, maniacal laugh carried on the wind and stabbed the warriors with a white-hot fear none had ever known in the heat of battle.

In the lead, Janos Rakoczy motioned for them to follow once more when the shrill laughter drifted off, carried away on the breeze. A sick gnawing chewed at each man approaching the arched entrance in the wall. The heavy oaken gate stood open, defiantly suggesting that no one was brave enough to enter. They did not know how many adversaries they would encounter, and the Magyar warriors warily approached the enclosed fortress of Castle Csejthe.

When the prime minister stood in the doorway, the cloud that had filled half of the sky swept aside as if to allow the cold, blue-white moon the opportunity to view the macabre scene below.

Without a word, Rakoczy motioned the warriors to hurry through the gate and into the courtyard. Each had been told to stand guard at the first window or door they encountered, thus blocking all chance of escape.

By the time the first floor's doors and windows were manned, sounds of revelry reverberated through the courtyard. The same high-pitched laughter that had frozen their souls before, rang out once more, winding its way through the semi-darkness.

The prime minister approached the main door, followed by his entourage of 40 warriors and other dignitaries to assist in the arrest and capture. In the rear was Father Miklos Hunyadi, the village priest who finally had drawn enough attention to their problem, finally getting his message through to the king.

Rakoczy boldly grabbed the huge ring and banged it against the heavy wooden door. The ensuing explosive knock echoed through the night. Overhead, another cloud blotted out the moon, and an inky blackness washed over the raiding party.

He tried knocking again, but when no one responded, he pushed on the door, and it slowly swung inward. A sole torch flickered from its place on the stone wall, faintly illuminating the interior and a distant staircase.

"The impudent bitch!" he said quietly, stepping inside. "It smells of death here. Where is the priest?"

The question passed along the line, and the cassocked man hurried to the prime minister's side. "Yes, Your Excellency? How may I be of assistance?"

"Do you know this place?"

"No, Excellency, I've never been here."

"It reeks of death, wouldn't you say?"

Father Hunyadi raised his head, inhaling deeply. His eyes grew large as he turned his head from one side to the other.

"It is as the graveyard when a body is interred, Excellency."

Rakoczy nodded brusquely. "Follow me," he said without raising his voice.

The priest dutifully fell in behind him, and the warriors followed, entering the huge hall. Dust and filth from years of inattention covered everything in sight.

The prime minister stopped, peering at the priest in the gloom. "For how many years has your village been plagued?"

"Eleven, Excellency. Eleven terrible years."

"It is apparent that more attention was given to kidnapping, and God only knows what else, than to maintaining the condition of the Bathory property. Come, we'll go upstairs, for surely no one uses this area other than as an entranceway." Pointing ahead, he strode toward the wide stone stairs winding upward along one wall. The soft soles of the soldiers' feet barely sounded in the gloom. As they passed the single burning fagot, the soldiers touched their grease-saturated torches to it and slowly, a foreign, almost cheery glow filled the high-ceilinged room. Following their fearless leader, each warrior vowed to himself that it was nothing more than a mere woman for whom they searched. A mere woman would not be able to harm them, and if she tried, their swords would taste her blood.

When the last soldier stood on the second floor, Rakoczy motioned for them to be still. As he took one step, a piercing scream filtered up from someplace below. Had they come to the wrong floor?

The familiar laughter cackled through the darkness close by. Had the scream prompted the laughter? And who was laughing?

The king's representative strode down the hall into the pitch-black maw at the end. A crack of light seeped through beneath a closed door toward which the official hurried. Without hesitating, he threw open the door, and the warriors spilled into the room behind them.

A tall, thin woman, completely naked, whirled around to face the intruders, stepping between them and a bathtub behind her. Her slight breasts barely moved when she swung about to confront them. Unashamed, she glared at them without making a token gesture to cover her nudity.

"Who are you?" she asked hoarsely.

"I am Prime Minister Janos Rakoczy, emissary of King Matthias II. What are you to Countess Elisabeth Bathory Nadasdy?"

"I am Ilona Joo, her lady-in-waiting. This," she said, dramatically stepping aside and gesturing with a sweep of one thin arm, "is my lady, Countess Elisabeth Bathory Nadasdy."

The Prime Minister stepped back. A

woman, radiantly beautiful, reclined in a huge ornate bathtub—a tub filled with blood. Her long blond hair swirled across the sanguine bath. When she stood, a spray of gore showered the surrounding floor. Crimson trails forged their way around her full breasts, running down her body. Droplets fell from her erect nipples.

"How dare you come to my home without invitation and without reason." The countess stepped from the tub, making no effort to cover her bloody nakedness.

The prime minister looked about the room. The two women seemed harmless enough as far as being able to resist arrest was concerned. Just as he was about to speak, another scream wove its way up the wide stone stairs, down the hall and into the room.

The Magyar warriors rolled their eyes, half-expecting a monster to leap at them from some hidden nook or corner.

"What is that sound, Madam?" Rakoczy demanded.

"That is none of your business, cousin. You fool! Get out. You have no reason to be here. Are you not aware that I am of the noble gentry? I will notify the king of your horrendous actions."

"It is by request of King Matthias II that I am here, my lady. You are under arrest."

"For what reason? Bathing?" She threw her head back, and the men immediately recognized the high-pitched laugh pouring from the woman.

The prime minister turned, motioning for his men to leave the room, and ordered the captain to search the castle. He gestured at the same time for two of them to remain with him and the priest. Father Hunyadi, his back to the naked woman, remained, spastically fingering the rosary beads hanging from his waist.

When the soldiers had left, Rakoczy stepped closer to the women. "Dress yourselves. You both are under arrest for kidnapping if nothing else."

The countess haughtily lifted her face and stared over the head of the man confronting her. "Never."

"My lady . . ." the other woman began but stopped when the countess continued.

"The king should remember how many times the Bathorys and the Nadasdys have helped him in time of strife and war. Is this the way he shows his gratitude?" She stamped her bare foot on the stone floor, flinching when the expected clap did not sound.

"Dress, my lady, or I will dress you myself." The prime minister took another step toward her. "Regardless of our distant relationship, which I now deny, you will be punished for your deeds."

The countess turned to her lady-in-waiting, a look of panic crossing her oval face.

Ilona Joo stepped between the intruders and the countess. When Rakoczy fell back several steps, Ilona turned and, picking up a gown, draped it around the countess. After donning one herself, she said, "Perhaps the prime minister would withdraw along with his henchmen and the priest while we dress properly."

The prime minister crossed the room to the two windows, peering through them into the inky night. The ground was at least 50 feet below on this side of the castle, and the windows were the only way out, other than the door to the hall. "Very well. You both may dress. My soldiers will be right outside the door."

He gestured for the men to leave, and the priest, crossing himself, hurried out. Rakoczy closed the door and took a deep breath. Before he had a chance to recollect his wits, the sound of running feet came out of the darkness, and he saw a torch bobbing toward him.

"Excellency, Excellency! Hurry! Come with me. You must see this. Mother of God, it is awful! Hurry!" The soldier stopped when he stood in front of the official, panting. The man's countenance was twisted in anger and pain, fright and indignation.

"What is it?"

"I . . . I cannot tell you. You must see it."

"See what? What are you talking about?"

"In the cellars. I cannot say such things. I have been in battle countless times and have seen men killed and blood flow like water. I have watched heads chopped off, but all of it is nothing compared to what we have found below."

The prime minister knew the man by reputation and was aware that he was not prone to exaggeration. Turning, he said to the remaining soldiers, "Stay here. Do not let the women come out. Do you understand? Even if they are dressed and ready to accompany us, they are to stay in the room until I return or send this man with orders to bring the countess and her lady-in-waiting to me. Is that clear?"

"Yes, Excellency," the men chorused.

"Come, Father." The prime minister took the priest's arm, guiding him down the hallway behind the soldier.

After passing through the great entrance hall, the trio made their way to the back of the castle and through an arched doorway. They immediately started down a course of stairs that seemed to lead to the bowels of the earth. Four times, the casement turned, following the wall as the steps descended. When at last they stood on an earthen floor, the soldier spoke for the first time since they began their descent.

"Through here, Excellency." He went through another archway and entered a room lighted with several torches leaning out from the wall. At first, it seemed an

ordinary cellar room, but then the prime
minister saw the naked bodies hanging
along the walls. Young women, most in
early pubescence, hung from spikes driven
into the rock walls. Ropes cut into their
wrists while their feet barely touched the
dirt floor.

Rakoczy slowly walked along the line of
girls. Some appeared dead while others' eyelids fluttered from the unaccustomed
brightness.

"Excellency, over here," the captain of
the soldiers said, stepping forward.

"What is it, Zanic?"

"This woman will not tell us her name."
Zanic stepped aside and roughly shoved
forward a woman who was clad only in a
leather apron. The force of the push
brought her to her knees at the prime
minister's feet.

Glaring up at him, the woman snarled.
"Filthy animal, get out of here. This is my
domain. The countess has given it to me.
You have no right—no business being
here."

Rakoczy bent as if to help her to her
feet. Her long, black hair whipping about,
the woman struck out at him, biting his
hand.

Screaming from the pain and indignation, the prime minister pulled back.
"Who are you, woman? Tell me your name,
or I'll order your head chopped off this
instant."

The woman slowly stood, adjusting her leather covering. "I'm Szentes. Dead, I am of no use to my lady, nor would I be able to milk my little lambs here." She laughed softly, turning to look at the girls and young women hanging from the walls.

"What do you mean by 'milk' your lambs?"

Szentes laughed again, louder. "It is for my lady's bath and her special drinks—to keep her young and beautiful. She *is* young and beautiful, don't you think?"

The prime minister turned away, striding over to one of the girls hanging from the wall. At first he didn't notice anything other than the fact the girl was dead. Her skin was as white as the cleanest kerchief, even in the yellowish light of the torches. The stink of blood and death filled Rakoczy's nostrils, and he turned away. Spinning away, he saw *it* and returned his attention to the girl. A small puncture on the inside of the thigh had almost escaped his notice. He had seen men die when that part of the leg was cut accidentally or in battle. There was no stopping the flow of blood once a wound was inflicted there.

"You have bled these girls to death, woman?"

"Not all of them. Some of them. Some are still alive, alive and ready to serve my mistress." Szentes cocked her head to one side in a way that seemed to plead with the prime minister that he should understand.

Her triangular face assumed an innocent, pouty look.

"Beast!" he shouted. "Is this all of them? Are there more?"

The woman turned away, a snarl on her full lips.

"This way, Excellency," Zanic said, moving toward the back wall. He pushed aside an animal skin that covered a small doorway and entered. A single torch protruding from the wall lighted the chamber. More girls, chained to the wall, peered at the men as they entered.

"What is this place, Zanic?"

"I'm not certain, Excellency. I think these are being fatted for the milking that goes on in the other room. One of the girls said they are fed well, and when they are robust, they are taken into the next room."

"Good God, this is hideous. The people of the village are to be pitied."

"Not only the villagers but people for miles around. There have been reports for a long time of young girls and women being kidnapped at night and being taken away in a black coach, never to be seen again by their families."

"And for what reason, Zanic?"

"I believe what the woman in the other room said—for the countess to bathe and to drink. She's a vampire, sir. A *vampire*."

"Perhaps, Zanic, but that hasn't been proven yet. The priest can give her a test by exposing his blessed cross to her. If she reacts, she is a vampire and must be destroyed. How many of the girls are alive in the next room?"

"Perhaps six or seven. I counted twelve dead girls. These four in here are all well, I believe. But you haven't seen the third room."

Rakoczy stared at him. He'd had enough for one night. What else could there be?

Seeing his superior's consternation, Zanic said, "This way. You must see in order to prosecute." He turned and left the room, the prime minister immediately behind him. After giving orders to free the girls in the second room and to release those who were hanging from the wall in the first room, Zanic strode from the area.

Crossing the vaulted room, he opened a door set into the wall. A stench rolled out, gagging the Prime Minister who quickly threw a muffler across his face. Zanic, who had failed to warn the official, held his arm across his nose. Thrusting his torch forward, he entered.

The deeper they went, the stronger was the stink. When Zanic stopped, he said, "There are hundreds of dead women here. We can't stay long for the smell will surely render us ill. However, each one looks as though they were bled to death or . . . or bitten."

"What?" the prime minister exclaimed.

"Bitten, sire. Look for yourself." He held the torch down to one gray cadaver, a girl

who once might have been considered
pretty, even beautiful. Countless teeth
marks marred the decaying flesh. The body,
the neck, the arms and the legs had been
ripped by teeth shaped in the form of a
small crescent, not more than an inch and a
half across. Human teeth! Both breasts had
been torn from the girl's chest.

"There are rats in here, Excellency. They
ran the first time I came in, but I hear them
coming. Hear their squeaks?"

Rakoczy stood erect. His eyes widened
farther when he heard the undeniable
squealing of rats coming toward them. As
he turned to leave, Zanic stepped in front of
him to lead the way. The rats closed in on
them rapidly, one being smashed in two as
Zanic pulled the door closed.

The prime minister gagged in the damp
air. His stomach heaved before vomiting
out the light supper he had eaten earlier.

"Captain Zanic, dispatch a soldier to
the village to get some help up here. The
Countess Elisabeth Bathory Nadasdy will
pay for her crimes as will her accomplices. I
promise you that."

Captain Zanic turned to do the prime
minister's bidding.

1

Sioux Falls, South Dakota

Monday 3:00 P.M., Today

Rhonda Gordon stared at the approaching car, her best pleading expression spread across her square face. Thrusting out her thumb, she became aware the driver was not going to slow, much less stop. She turned to face the girl with her.

"Do you still think this was such a hot idea, Jude?"

Judy Merton nodded, her strawberry blond hair fluffing up and down. "Hey, look at the money we're saving. Bus fare to Rapid City costs a lot. We can use it when we get there and party earlier than if we have to wait for our first paycheck. Right?"

"Sure, we're saving money, but we aren't getting anyplace either."

Judy stood up, brushing her skintight jeans. "Maybe we should flash a little leg or something to get one of those dudes to pick us up."

Rhonda smiled half-heartedly. "I don't think that'd be such a hot idea. Who knows what sort of nerd would stop?"

"Don't start talking like that again, Rhon. Christ! I didn't think you'd ever go along with the idea of hitching all the way to Rapid City. I thought you'd come out with: 'It's dangerous.' 'We could get raped.' 'We could get killed.' Bull! Not if there's two of us. There's strength in numbers, right?"

Rhonda shrugged. The one thing that bothered her was simply, what if there were three men in the car that stopped to pick them up? Then what? The strength in numbers would be on the men's side, wouldn't it? She hadn't voiced that argument to Judy. Maybe she should have, but Judy was her best friend and Rhonda didn't want her to get upset. They had signed up for work as chambermaids at a large motel in the Black Hills to earn money for their college education. They had two more years of high school, and if this first venture worked and their parents were pleased with the amount of money they had earned, and more importantly with the amount they were able to save, the next two summers

would be already planned for them. "I guess
you're right, Jude."

The sun had begun its descent several
hours before, and while the girls still had
well over five hours of daylight left, both
wanted to make further progress toward
their destination.

"Maybe we should move, Jude."

"Funny you should mention that. I was
just about to. It seems everybody is in a
damned hurry to get up the hill to Minnesota Avenue."

"More than likely there aren't that many
people heading that far west toward the
interstate—too many turn offs."

Judy turned, studying the flow of
traffic. "You're right. Let's start hoofing it.
We'll stand a better chance of picking up a
ride by getting to Highway 42. Then it's only
a short ways to the interstate."

"We could go back to the bus depot."
Rhonda turned away as soon as she had
made the suggestion. That would be ad-
mitting defeat, which neither girl wanted to
do.

"The bus is long gone. What would you
want to do? Wait around until tomorrow for
the next one?"

"Well, we don't know there's only one
bus to Rapid City. We took the first time
suggested by the ticket seller."

"Hey, Rhon, if you want to go home, go
on. I'm going to Rapid City and make big

bucks there. You with me or not?''

"I'm with you." Rhonda sheepishly looked away.

The girls picked up their backpacks and, after slipping into the harnesses, started walking. A police car slowed perceptibly and then picked up speed when the girls continued walking and chatting.

Rhonda turned to her friend. "This is going to be a great experience for us. When we get to college we'll know what it's all about—being away from home and handling our own money."

Judy grinned. "You know it. And don't forget the boys we'll meet. Or should I say men?"

Ignoring Judy's boy-craziness, Rhonda said, "How far from the motel is our rooming house?"

"Just a few blocks. Why?"

"If we work as hard as our parents said we would as maids, I don't want to have to walk very far, to or from work."

"As I understand it, the motel and the rooming house have a deal, and most of the summer help from out of town live at the same place. Who knows? There might be some good looking guy with a car who'll fall madly in love with me and take me to work. If that happens, I'll insist that he give you a ride, too. Deal?"

Rhonda laughed. "God, you're generous, Jude."

The girls continued up the hill toward

Minnesota Avenue, then crossed the busy intersection. They walked without speaking much, and once the hill was completely behind them and the street and sidewalk leveled off, they picked up their pace.

"What time is it?" Judy turned to Rhonda, who glanced at her watch.

"3:30."

Judy frowned. "Shit! We wasted too much time trying to hitch downtown. We should have known better."

Overhead, the cloudless June sky canopied the world, and the sun, although shining brightly, did not yet have the power to bear down in the hellish way it could. Once there had been three or four days of continuous sunshine and no clouds or rain to cool the air, the temperature would climb into the high eighties and nineties.

"One good thing about our going to the Hills is the fact that it should be cooler there than here."

Judy shook her head. "When it gets hot, it's hot all over the goddamn place."

As the girls walked, one would turn around, walking backward, to keep an eye on the street in the event they saw some likely driver who might stop and help them reach Highway 42. On occasion, the one walking backward would thrust out her thumb and look pleadingly at the driver. The wide, one-way thoroughfare seemed suddenly bereft of traffic on the right side and the girls crossed to the other as quickly as possible once they realized the traffic was bearing to the left to negotiate the "S" curve that would lead to the highway and eventually to the interstate ramps. Once they were on the left side, the cars seemed even less likely to pick up a hitchhiker since it would mean stopping on a dangerous curve.

When Judy and Rhonda realized they wouldn't get a ride, they continued walking.

"Christ!" Judy said suddenly. "If we don't haul ass out there pretty soon, we'll be sleeping under the stars if the drivers are as generous on the interstate as they are here."

Another patrol car passed them, this time not paying much attention to them. When they reached the small hill that dropped the roadway into a wide valley of sorts, they hurried to the bottom and walked several blocks, passing gas stations, drug stores and fast food outlets.

"Let's try here, Jude." Rhonda ran a hand through her short, auburn hair and slipped off her backpack, leaning it against a trash barrel.

Judy laid hers next to Rhonda's. "We gotta get a ride now. Most of the people going this way should go at least as far as the interstate."

Both girls stuck out their thumbs and waited, each hoping and mumbling a quick prayer that someone would stop.

"Back off," Judy said curtly, turning to

step onto the curb and sidewalk.

"What's the matter?" Rhonda had automatically pulled her own arm back and followed her friend.

"Cops!"

"Where?" Rhonda started to turn around to search out the patrol car.

"Don't look. If they stop, let me do the talking. All right?"

"Fine. Just stop acting like we've committed some horrible crime."

The car slowed, pulling in toward them, and stopped. The officer inside leaned over the empty passenger seat. "You girls hitchhiking?"

"As a matter of fact, Officer," Judy said, staring at him with as much innocence as she could muster without being obvious, "we're waiting for some friends from school. We were supposed to go on an overnight hike, and we have no idea what might have happened to them."

"Where are you girls from?"

"Sioux Falls."

"Do you go to school?"

"Sure."

"Where?"

"O'Gorman."

The policeman's face softened a bit. Apparently believing the girls were from the city because of their adeptness in naming their school, he nodded. "What're your names?"

Judy glanced at Rhonda. "Why?"

"Well," the officer said, "let's just say I'm curious."

"You do believe we're from the city, don't you?"

"I do. I just want to make a note of your names for my daily sheet."

Judy leaned down to peer into the car. "My name's Anita Small, and this is Dinah Waldowski."

The policeman dutifully jotted the names down.

Rhonda turned to keep from laughing. Anita and Dinah were children both she and Judy had babysat occasionally throughout the school year.

"I hope your friends show up soon, Anita," the officer said, moving back behind the wheel.

"I'm sure they'll be along pretty soon." Judy stepped back from the Dodge.

The patrol car eased away from the curb.

"Rats." Judy kicked at the dirt.

"You said it. If he checks, he'll be back and we'll be in deep shit with our folks. What'll we do?"

"Let's hustle our buns to the interstate. I don't think the cops go down there to patrol."

"I hope you're right."

They walked hurriedly along Highway 42, heading west, toward the interstate.

Monday, 9:41 P.M.

The sun had set over an hour before and Judy and Rhonda shuffled along Interstate 90. Sioux Falls lay behind them some six or seven miles, and they had no idea what they should do.

"It was a good idea to come to the interstate, all right. The thing I don't understand is how come no one has stopped to pick us up yet." Judy looked up at the sky. In a matter of minutes, it would be dark. Then what could they do?

"Maybe there aren't enough tourists on the road yet. After all, school just ended on Friday."

Judy stared ahead. "I think we've messed up, Rhon. I really do. Maybe we should have taken the bus the way we were supposed to. After all, it left around noon. What time is it now? Nine? Going on ten? The damned thing is probably four hundred miles away by now—and here we are all of six or seven miles away from town. Real good planning, eh?"

"What should we do?" Rhonda peered into the night. Off to their left cars and trucks zipped along the eastbound lane while the westbound, along which they walked, carried an equal amount of traffic. Still, no one was willing to pick them up.

"You know, it makes you wonder, doesn't it?"

Rhonda turned to Judy. "What? I don't follow you."

"You're an attractive girl, and I think I'm all right. How come none of those lonely, horny truck drivers have even slowed up to ask us if we'd like a lift?"

Rhonda shrugged. "I don't know. Unless it's those newspaper stories about the people who were murdered by that hitchhiker in Minnesota last month."

"Oh, shit, you've hit it, Rhon! No wonder. God, we're stupid."

"So what do we do? Go home?"

"You want our folks to really come down on us, don't you?"

Rhonda shook her head.

"If we went home, they wouldn't let us go. In fact, they'd probably never ever treat us like adults again. Then, too, we're supposed to be in Rapid City tomorrow afternoon for job orientation at the motel. If we're not there, we don't get the job. If we go home, we're as good as dead."

"What was it the guy said in the movie we saw last Saturday night? Something about being caught between a rock and a hard place?"

"That's us, all right." Judy bit off the words, turning automatically when she heard a car or truck approaching. Thrusting out her thumb once more, she said, "Even my thumb hurts from all the hitchhiking we've tried. I—Hey, it's stopping. Geez! Look at the length of that pile."

Rhonda turned, gasping as the stretch limo eased to a stop. Other than the windshield, the windows, were darkened for privacy.

The girls hurried up to the car and stood next to it. The moon, just rising in the east, reflected brightly on the dark surface of the automobile. Afraid to even touch the magnificent vehicle, the girls bent down to peer at their own shadowed reflections in the smoky glass.

Both jumped when the window in the front door quietly opened, and the chauffeur leaned over a bit.

"Would you girls like a ride?"

"You bet we would." Rhonda wanted to ask how far he was going but elected to let Judy do the talking once more. Even if it were only a few miles, it would be that much closer to their own destination.

"Madam?" he said, turning to the dark interior of the passenger compartment.

The girls heard a muffled voice, and then the chauffeur got out of the car. Moving lithely around the front, he stepped to the rear door and opened it. He bowed slightly from the waist, gesturing at the same time with his free hand that they should enter.

Judy picked up her backpack and started to put it in.

"Allow me, please," the man said, taking the pack. He picked up Rhonda's and, after the girls got into the car, closed the door.

After they heard the trunk open and close, the front door opened and the chauffeur got back in. The door shut with a muffled thud, and the car glided forward.

The two teenagers peered about the blackness of the passenger compartment. They waited patiently for their hostess to speak, and when she didn't, Rhonda coughed in an embarrassed way.

No response of any sort.

Judy peered into the darkness. "Hello?"

No answer at all.

"I . . . I'm Judy, and this is Rhonda. What's your name?"

Still no answer.

Judy turned to Rhonda and squealed softly when she could not see the driver. A panel of the smoked glass separated the driver's seat from the passenger compartment. Turning, they stared intently through it, barely able to make out the pinpoints of light that came toward them from the opposite lanes.

"Hey, what's going on?" Judy cried out.

"What's the matter, Jude?"

"I don't like this one bit, Rhon. Something fishy is going on. Who are you, lady? Come on, speak up. We know you're in here. We heard you."

No answer.

Rhonda groped for the door handle and tried it. "It's locked," she wailed. "Try your side."

She could hear Judy moving to the far

side of the jumpseats in which they sat.
"Damnit, so's this one. Come on, lady.
You've had your little perverted joke. How
about turning on the lights so we can see
you?"

Nothing.

The lights suddenly went on, and they
found themselves in the luxurious back seat
alone. There was no one with them.

Then they heard the soft hissing.

Terrified, Judy and Rhonda stared at
each other. Before either girl could speak,
their heads began feeling lighter and lighter
until both fell forward into a deep faint.

2

Hangary

January, 1610

A hush fell over the large gathering. None could believe the story unfolding during the trial. Countess Elisabeth Bathory Nadasdy stood, quietly listening to her deeds being recounted by Prime Minister Janos Rakoczy.

"The bodies of your daughters, your granddaughters, your sisters, your cousins and your friends were heaped in a pile in a room of death and carnage, deep within the bowels of Castle Csejthe. All had been bled to death. Some, if not all, had been bitten viciously during their waning moments of life. Those still alive were being robbed of their life's blood by this woman, Szentes." Rakoczy dramatically stopped for effect, allowing the sordid facts to sink in.

A ripple of murmurs flowed through the crowd. They had known for some time that their loved ones, their young women, were being kidnapped and taken to the castle, which stood on the low mountain, ominously towering over their small town. For years, the Bathory family had watched over them, protected them when necessary, and taxed them constantly—but this was something altogether different.

Rakoczy coughed, clearing his throat. He had waited but two days, until the bodies were counted, and then commenced with the prosecution of the countess and her fellow female conspirators. Outside, a cold wind from the north channeled through the streets, caressing each building with its icy touch, but no one on the inside seemed to feel the drop in temperature. Those unfortunate enough to be standing outside, ignored the elements. Their moment of revenge was at hand.

"This murderess," Rakoczy proclaimed, "this fiend, performed her bloody work for the benefit of this woman, the Countess Elisabeth Bathory Nadasdy, your protectorate. More than six hundred young girls and women suffered and died as a result of her mad desire for blood. Your priest, Miklos Hunyadi, Captain Laszlo Zanic and several soldiers caught her reclining in a tub of human blood—blood drained from her poor, innocent victims."

Elisabeth stood transfixed, listening to

Rakoczy's damning statements. A smile crossed her lips as she ran her tongue across them, recalling the delicious taste of the maidens' blood. It had worked. She remembered how it had happened. How long ago had it been? At least 11 if not 12 years had passed.

The dining hall had been sparsely peopled by the nobility who had come at her request to mourn the death of her husband, Count Ferencz Nadasdy. While serving food, one of the servants, a young peasant girl from the village, had spilled grease onto the hand of her mistress.

"You clumsy animal! Get away!" The countess had leaped to her feet, lashing out with her open palm to slap the maid across the face.

Her hand had struck hard, and when part of the girl's inner cheek slashed against her teeth, blood spewed out. The countess held her hand closer to one of the candles lighting the table.

"Beast!" she screamed. "You dare bleed on me as well?" Wiping away the crimson dots, she stopped again and touched the back of her hand where the blood had been. "My word, it is softer," the countess whispered.

Dismissing her guests, the countess went to her room. After summoning her chambermaid, she dispatched her to fetch Thorko, the sorcerer with whom she was in love and who had been employed by her husband to conjure up spells. It had been Ferencz who had introduced her to the black arts and the worship of Satan. It had been Thorko who had brought her mind to the keen understanding of the nether-world's inhabitants and the practices used to further their desires and gains. She had toyed with the idea of dismissing Thorko when her husband had been killed in battle, believing she should perhaps return to the graces of the church. Now she had questions to ask the sorcerer.

When the tall, thin man arrived in her chamber, he bowed deeply and raised his angular, cadaverous face to stare deeply into her eyes. "You have a question concerning blood, my lady?"

Not taken aback by the man's knowledge without being apprised of the reason for his visit, the countess said, "Will the blood of a young maiden, rubbed into the skin, restore it to its youthfulness?"

Thorko smiled evilly. "Of course, my lady. If drunk as well, the recipient maintains a youthful vigor far beyond the years alloted to one. I know these things."

"Then I have found the secret of perpetual youth."

"And that is?"

"Here," she said thrusting her hand out. "Touch my hand here."

Thorko rubbed the skin. "It is indeed soft, my lady."

"Do you know what happened?"

Thorko shook his head. "No, my lady."

"I slapped a clumsy maid. In so doing, I struck her hard enough to draw blood, some of which fell on my hand. It immediately became softer. How can I utilize this magnificent discovery?"

"Bathe in it. Drink it. You shall remain forever youthful."

"Must I deal with Satan to attain this?"

"You already have, my lady. You are his. and you are mine—for all time. This is merely another of his munificent gifts to you."

"Then fetch me the necessary people from your circle to perform the deeds vital to this enterprise."

"It shall be done, my lady." Thorko bowed deeply, backing out of the room and her presence.

The single word "Death!" screamed at her had brought Countess Bathory Nadasdy back to the room wherein she was being accused of murder. Wincing at the proximity of Rakoczy's face to hers, she leaned back to escape his foul breath.

"Death to them all!" the peasants chanted.

Fearful that he might lose control, Rakoczy held up his hands for silence, and slowly the cries ebbed and died. When no one spoke, the prime minister stepped to the middle of the room, away from the accused noble lady.

"I am empowered by his Royal Highness, King Matthias II, to render justice in this case. My decision is—"

As one, the crowd leaned in, afraid the sentence passed would not be heard.

"—death to Szentes, the beast who actually killed the women and girls. She shall be burned alive immediately—this very day. If she wants an audience with Father Hunyadi, such shall be allowed and perscribed. We are not vicious killers such as she."

A cheer went up from the gathering. Word of the impending execution filtered through the crowd and outside where the villagers and peasants waited.

"Death by beheading for Ilona Joo, Countess Elisabeth Bathory Nadasdy's handmaiden. She, too, shall have the opportunity to save her immortal soul from the clutches of Lucifer by confessing her sins to God, the Almighty."

Another cheer went up. The crowd, thirsty for revenge, clapped their hands at the prospect of two public executions.

"Before I pass judgment on you, Countess," Rakoczy said, "will you tell me where your magician is? Where is the man, Thorko?"

Elisabeth remained silent.

"It will do you some good perhaps to tell us. Is he not your lover?"

She said nothing.

"Where is he?" Rakoczy snarled the words. He knew he had her in his power and that with a word he could snuff out her life. "Are you in league with the devil?"

A stony silence fell over the room as the people awaited her answers.

Glaring, first at Rakoczy and then at the throng of people crying for her life, she shook her head, the ruffled collar of her dress trembling like a leaf in a strong gale. "I am of the noble gentry. I do not answer to peasants." She folded her arms, the great sleeves of her gown billowing out as she moved. Defiantly holding her chin up, she widened her eyes even farther.

"You are a disgrace to the nobility of this country. Your family has always lived on the edge of decency, at times spilling over into the realm of indecency with their actions and behavior." Rakoczy leaned closer to her as he shouted the words.

"My family has always been faithful to the Holy Crown. Even from the time of King Stephen, we have been faithful. As members of the nobility, which was gained for us by Stephen Bathory, we have served Hungary and Transylvania well." She stamped her foot and turned her head away from her prosecutor.

"Killing young girls for their blood is hardly in the best interest of the Crown. You will not tell us what we want to know?"

"What is it you want?"

"The whereabouts of Thorko, your lover

and sorcerer. The whereabouts of Ujuvary,
your alchemist. The whereabouts of
Darvula, the forest witch who has lived at
your castle for the last seven years."

"That is not for you or any of these
common pigs to know."

An instantaneous hissing burst from
the crowd at this remark.

When the anger subsided, he held his
hands up for quiet. "You have nothing more
to say, my lady?"

Her hair, pulled back into tiny curls,
bobbed as she shook her head.

"Very well. With the power vested in
me by his Royal Highness and Serene
Majesty, King Matthias II, ruler of Hungary, I
sentence you, Countess Elisabeth Bathory
Nadasdy, to first watch the deaths of your
accomplices. I wish I could bestow the most
vile of deaths upon you, but I must use a
certain amount of discretion because of
your noble station, though not because of
any favor for you because of our common
blood. It will be much worse for you to live
than to die a death similar to those already
meted out to Joo and Szentes. I sentence
you to life imprisonment—"

The response was immediate from the
crowd. They wanted blood. They wanted
the noble blood coursing through the
countess's body to flow freely and her flesh
and bones to be burned until nothing
remained. For 20 minutes, the peasants and

villagers screamed their displeasure at the
lenient sentence.

The Magyar warriors, strategically
positioned around the hall, stepped forward, creating a wall of spears and swords
to separate the indignant citizens from the
countess and the prime minister.

When the furor died down, Rakoczy
shouted, "Life imprisonment, walled up in a
small room in her own castle, without
attendants other than someone to bring a
single meal to her each day with a cup of
water. No one will speak to her or serve her
in any way. If one does, that person's life will
be forfeit instantly by the captain of the
guard who will be stationed there until such
time that Countess Elisabeth Bathory
Nadasdy dies."

After a few moments, the impact of the
sentence struck home and the throng
erupted into cheers and prayers of thanksgiving.

Ilona Joo peered evilly at the people surrounding the hastily built platform. Dózsa,
the executioner, stood nearby, stripped to
the waist, his huge chest bulging. A gray
leaden sky hung overhead like a giant tent.
Regardless of the somber day, the people
laughed and sang, relieved that their reign
of terror was finally at an end.

The prime minister mounted the steps
in a slow, deliberate walk. When he stood on

the dais, he held out his arms. "This woman cared for the countess. Bring the countess up, so she can witness the death of her chambermaid."

Two soldiers roughly urged the countess forward and up the steps. When she reached the top, she closed her eyes. "You cannot make me watch if I don't wish."

Rakoczy nodded to the men and each grabbed her, one by the shoulder and the other by her head. The prime minister stepped closer and positioning his hand on her forehead, opened her eyes with two fingers. "The sentence says you are to watch and watch you shall!" He nodded to Dózsa.

The giant stepped closer to Ilona Joo and muttered, "Forgive me. It is my job."

Joo ignored the traditional apology, and when he placed his hand on her shoulder to force her to kneel, she shook it off and dropped to her knees. Without a word, she laid her head and neck on the roughly trimmed tree stump.

Dózsa raised his huge battle axe and with it poised for only a second at the peak of its flight brought the blade down in a wide arc. The keen edge cut through the skin then the flesh before severing the bones of her neck. Without any resistance other than the woman's neck, the blade finished its flight, splitting her windpipe, arteries and veins.

Ilona Joo's head bounced once before

rolling to the edge of the platform where it came to an upright position, the eyes serenely staring at the crowd.

The countess did not make a sound, and Rakoczy looked at her face. The icy blue eyes had watched everything, but the expression on the lovely oval face remained passive, untouched by the death of her handmaiden. When she saw the prime minister's face close to hers, she shifted her attention to him and said, "Interesting."

"We shall see how you react to the screams of Szentes when she burns." Rakoczy waved at soldiers in the back of the crowd and they lifted the murderess to their shoulders, carrying her not unlike a log over their heads.

The crowd fell back when the prime minister, the soldiers attending the countess and the executioner stepped from the platform. Like a stream of water flowing around a sunken sand bar, the people fell in behind the entourage, heading for the pile of brush and logs at the end of the street. A stake set in the middle waited for Szentes.

When she was tied to the pole, Dósza again stepped forward. "I am sorry. Forgive me." He dropped the torch he carried into the tinder at the woman's feet. Grayish smoke wound its way upward, caressing and enveloping her.

Again Rakoczy ordered the soldiers to hold the countess' head and moved in to hold her eyes open.

"It really is not necessary," she said
haughtily and fixed her whole attention on
the burning spectacle before her.

The flames leaped and danced from log
to log, fanned by the breeze, and the people
fell back as the heat grew in intensity. When
the tongues of fire lapped at her feet,
Szentes moved them, but when her gown
caught, the fire streamed upward, eating at
her bare flesh. When the garment fell away,
a cheer went up from the spectators.

Fire cavorted about the nude Szentes,
slowly roasting her. Her skin blistered,
peeling away. When the muscle lay exposed,
it browned not unlike meat on a spit.
Szentes raised her head to the dark skies
overhead, screaming, long and loud.

Her hair caught fire before her face
blazed up in a sheet of yellow-orange. Her
large breasts bubbled momentarily before
bursting, their fat running down her body,
feeding the fire even more.

Dósza continued stoking the fire,
heaping brush and logs onto the bier until
the flames grew so thick that the body of
the woman could no longer be seen. For four
hours, almost to the hour of the Angelus,
the fire continued. When Father Hunyadi
turned away to go to the church, most of the
townspeople and peasants followed, to pray
for the damned, demented souls of the two
women they had just watched die.

"I have chosen this room as your

prison, my lady," Rakoczy said, gesturing with his arm toward the small room.

"I should have expected it," she said softly. "Your sense of justice is confining to say the least."

The prime mininster smiled at the intended joke she made. "I would, my lady, grant your wish to select any room you wanted, but as you can see, this one already has had the windows walled up. One thing I can do for you is give you one candle. When it is gone, your remaining days will be spent in total darkness except for whatever light comes through this double door which I have had installed."

She fixed her attention on the man's outstretched hand, pointing to a small door that had been added to the wall. When he pulled it open, it tipped outward to show a v-shaped interior.

"When it closes on this side, it opens on the other and vice-versa. I believe you'll find that it will keep you isolated from even the most casual contact with the person bringing you your daily ration of food."

"I must compliment you on your ingenuity, Excellency. I could not have thought of better myself."

Rakoczy bowed from the waist, clicking his heels in a form of gratuitous salute. Walking partway down the hall, he took a candle from its holder and returned, lighting it on the way from one of the wall sconces.

"It has been a busy day," she said simply. "I have watched two dear friends die. I imagine the idiot priest and the pigs who live at the foot of my castle are praying for them and me this instant. Am I right?"

Rakoczy half-nodded, half-shrugged. "If they are, it is more than you or the others deserve. I will ask you once more to tell me the whereabouts of Thorko, Darvula and Ujuvany."

The countess turned away. "I will not."

"What difference does it make to you? They cannot help you or seek revenge on you if you tell me. I implore you. I appeal to your sense of decency, if you have any, to tell me in order that I might rid the country of them."

Turning to face him, she threw her head back and laughed.

Rakoczy shuddered. It was the same laugh he had heard when he and the soldiers had assaulted the castle and taken the countess and the other two prisoners. It was the laugh of one demented, the laugh of the village idiot. He was dealing with a mad-woman, trying to get her to do something logical.

Motioning to the soldiers, they stepped back and allowed the stately woman to enter her cell. When she was in, Rakoczy stepped forward handing her the candle.

Without a word, she took it and turned, entering the darkness.

Rakoczy nodded brusquely to the stone mason who stepped forward.

Row by row, the stones were set in place and held there by mortar. When several feet remained to be filled, the prime minister stepped closer to the new masonry work.

"Once more I ask you tell me where I can find Thorko, Darvula and Ujuvary."

His answer came in the form of the high-pitched, maniacal laugh. Turning away he stepped to the far side of the corridor while the mason stepped forward to finish the job.

Rakoczy walked down the hall of the tower to an opening that looked out over the valley below. Lights in the village huts flickered in the dark distance. At least they could sleep well tonight, knowing that the scourge of their existence would no longer harm them. He turned, peering into the darkness from which he had just come. The torches flickered brightly here and there, but his attention was riveted to the shaft of weak light coming from the walled-up door-way where one more stone remained to be set in place.

He hurried down the hall and motioned for the way to be clear. Standing on tiptoes, he leaned as close as possible to the opening. "May God forgive you, my lady."

The laughter peeled out and rang through the night. The mason stepped forward to finish his task.

3

Sioux Falls

Tuesday, 1:16 a.m.

Judy opened her eyes. Darkness. Had she actually opened them? She made a conscious effort to widen her eyes. They were open but she couldn't see anything. It was as if she might be blind. Was that possible? How had it happened? What had happened? Her head hurt a little; ached was a better description. Why? Where was she? Was she alone? Where was Rhonda?

"Rhonda?" Her voice squeaked, and her mouth seemed almost gritty from the dryness. Running her tongue over her lips in an attempt to wet them, she tried again. "Rhonda? Are you here?"

A soft moan sounded, growing louder from someplace in the murkiness surrounding her. Thank God, at least she wasn't dead. *Dead*? Had that thought even entered her mind? She might have been dead and in her place of eternal rest, perpetual nighttime without any sort of light. Was hell like that? Didn't they promise that heaven was a place of bright light and God's face beaming on those who had made it? Hell must be like this dismal black pit in which she found herself. But she wasn't dead. She couldn't be.

"Rhonda? Answer me. Are you here? I can't see anything."

Another moan. "What? What did you say?"

Judy could hear someone smacking their lips. Probably Rhonda was doing the same sort of thing Judy had done when she first awakened.

"Are you near me, Rhonda? Is that you? Come on, answer me."

"Oh, my head hurts."

It was Rhonda's voice. "Yeah, I know what you mean. Mine does, too."

"What happened? Where are we? What's going on?" Rhonda stopped and smacked her lips again, to create more moisture in her mouth.

" 'I don't know' just about answers any question you can come up with right now," Judy said, moving her legs. She was sitting on a hard surface. Reaching out with her hands, she rubbed what felt like concrete or stone. Uneven and yet level enough to

be a floor or platform of some sort, it
seemed to slope away sharply on either
side.

"Judy, I'm scared. I really am."

"Hey, so am I, but let's not get panicky.
All right? That won't get us anyplace."

"I guess you're right. But I sleep with a
night light on all of the time. This is the
darkest I've ever seen."

"That's sort of funny, you know."

"Funny? What's so funny? I think we're
in deep trouble of some kind, Jude."

"I didn't mean that. You said something
about this being the darkest you've ever
seen. What are you seeing? Nothing. Right?"

"That's not very funny."

"I guess you're right."

"What the heck happened, Jude?"

"All I remember is getting into that car.
When the lights came on and we found that
we were in the back seat alone, I . . ." She
paused, recalling the sound of the hissing.
"What was that strange noise?"

"Strange noise? I don't remember any
strange noise."

"Yeah, sure you do. The hissing.
Remember?"

No answer came out of the darkness
until Rhonda said, "I *do* remember it, now
that you mentioned it. Yeah. What was
that?"

Judy coughed. At least her mouth was
moist now, and she could swallow without it
hurting. "You've got me, but I think I passed

out right after that. Maybe it was a gas of
some sort."

"Who'd want to gas us like that?
Besides, it didn't kill us."

"It probably wasn't supposed to. I don't
know. Maybe they've got other ideas for us."

"Other . . . ideas? I don't follow you."

Judy bit her tongue. She shouldn't have
given voice to the thought that had suddenly exploded in her mind. Someone had
kidnapped them and was probably going to
rape them. God, why hadn't they taken the
bus the way they had planned? Now they
had no idea where they were, who had been
driving the car or anything. Had the driver
been responsible? What was he going to do
with them? Was he working for someone
else? Maybe that was it. Maybe he worked
for an international ring of . . .

"Jude?" Rhonda's voice whimpered the
single word.

"What?"

"What other ideas are you talking
about?"

Judy thought for a moment. Rhonda
was pretty level-headed. Perhaps she should
tell her everything she was thinking.
"Rhonda?"

"What?"

"Don't get scared but listen carefully to
me." She launched into her theories of their
abduction. After finishing with her thought
of an international ring of white slave
traders, she waited.

Rhonda didn't answer immediately. "In Sioux Falls? You gotta be kidding. You are, aren't you?"

Judy shook her head before realizing Rhonda couldn't see her. "I'm not. It could be, you know. Who knows? I sure don't. All we do know is we were invited to get into a limousine and here we are."

"Hey," Rhonda said, her voice lifting excitedly, "I just thought of something. The woman."

"The woman? What woman?"

"You remember, Jude. You leaned down and looked into the car. Right before the driver got out to put our back packs into the trunk, he said, 'Madam?' Remember?"

"You're right. I heard her say something but there wasn't anyone in the back seat when we got in. I wonder what . . ." Her voice trailed off.

"It might have been a recording the driver activated at just the right moment. What do you think?"

Judy pictured Rhonda, wherever it was she was sitting in the jet blackness, her eyes wide in wonder and filled with fright at the same time, waiting for Judy to agree or disagree. "You're probably right on, Rhon. Well, there goes the job in Rapid City. There goes our chance of being treated like adults by our folks."

"Yeah." Rhonda sniffed.

"Don't start crying, Rhon. We'll get out of this somehow."

"How?" The single word wavered in the utter darkness surrounding the girls.

"You've got me, but there'll be a way. You just wait and see. That is if we can ever see anything in this blackness." Judy moved a bit and stopped. Something held her in check, something around her waist. Gingerly touching her abdomen, she swallowed the cry rising within her. "Rhon?"

"What?"

"Feel around your middle. Are you . . . ?"

"Oh, my God, there's a wide belt around me—and I'm naked."

"Me, too. Try moving." Judy could hear the muffled sounds for a second or two.

"I can hardly move my body—just enough to lie down. I'm being held here in place, but my arms and legs are loose."

"Me, too. Say something and keep saying it. I want to figure out exactly where we're at. We should have done that before."

Rhonda started asking questions. "Where are you, Jude? I'm over here. Can you hear me? Can you see me? Come over here, Jude. Come on. I want you by me."

"I'm to your left and you're to my right," Judy said after several seconds. "Reach out with your left hand and see if . . ."

"That's about the wildest thing—not being able to tell where someone is in the dark like that. For all we know, we could be in a real big place or a real small one."

"What do you think it is, Jude?"

"Well, if it were real big our voices would echo, and they're not doing that. If it were real small, I think we'd know that or feel it somehow. It's probably average."

"What the hell is average?" Rhonda snorted the question.

Before Judy could answer, both girls froze when they heard a quiet moaning coming at them from out of the blackness surrounding them. Neither girl moved. Each held her breath as the moaning grew louder.

The darkness pressed in on Rhonda and Judy in such a way that it became a tangible reality, one they thought they could touch and actually feel. Even though they could not see each other, both knew the other's eyes were widened, desperately trying to find the source of the groans.

"What is . . . ?" Rhonda began.

"Shh!" Judy hissed the admonition.

The sounds came again but didn't seem to be getting any closer. What was it? Who was it? Was it even a person? Were they in danger from whatever the author of the noise might be?

The sounds dwindled to nothing, and the renewed silence joined the darkness in brushing and caressing the girls, squeezing until both thought they would scream from the imagined contact.

"Where are we, Jude? I'm scared. I really am."

"Sh-h-h." Judy stretched until she thought her arm might pop from its shoulder socket, but her fingertips just touched Rhonda's. "I don't know where we're at, but I don't think we're alone. Do you?"

"I . . . I don't know."

"Hey, out there. Who is it? Who's making that noise?" Judy croaked the words in a half-shout, half-whisper. "Who's there?"

No answer.

"I don't like this. It's just like it was in the car, Jude. What the hell's going on?"

"If you did like it, I don't think we'd remain friends for very darn long. Look, Rhonda, we're in deep shit. You know what I mean? We've got some real problems here. We don't know where we're at. We don't know what happened to us after we got into that car. For all we know, we could be in a flying saucer on our way to Mars or someplace."

Rhonda didn't answer. Whenever Judy called her by her full name, she knew her friend was not kidding around. "A flying saucer? You're joking, aren't you?"

"Well, maybe it is going to extremes, but who's to say what happened? I think we've got to keep our options open, no matter what happened."

"I . . . I don't follow you."

"We've got to be ready for whatever goes down, no matter what. Listen."

"Listen? To what?"

Judy shushed Rhonda. Both girls fell

silent, listening intently. Then they heard the muffled snore.

"Hear that, Rhon? We're not alone."

"Who's there?" Rhonda called out, raising her voice to its normal level.

"Do you think that was wise?"

"Why not, for heaven's sake? If it's someone sleeping, it may be someone in the same fix we are."

"And," Judy said slowly, whispering the words, "maybe its some sadistic sonofabitch who's resting up before ravaging us."

"Oh God, no!" Rhonda cried loudly.

"Who's there? Who's talking?" A girl's voice came at them from the dark void.

"Who are you?" Rhonda asked.

"My . . . my name's Coral. Coral Hallop. Who are you? How many are there of you?"

"Two—two of us." Judy ventured the words hesitantly, foreign to her usually bright, snappy way of speaking. "What the hell's going on? Where are we? Who's done this to us? Do you know?"

The sound of someone moving about in the dark startled Judy and Rhonda at first, but then they realized the girl who called herself Coral was merely sitting up or stretching. The sounds intensified then stopped when the girl apparently sat upright.

"I've asked those same questions time and time again. We all have. Nobody's come up with an answer yet."

" 'We all have'?" Judy and Rhonda repeated.

"There's probably six or seven of us in here. At least there was when the gas came on."

"What?" Judy shouted.

"That's right. Whenever they bring in someone new or take someone out, we hear this hissing sound and then we just fall asleep. Truly, that's all any of us know. What're your names?"

"Judy—Judy Merton."

"I'm Rhonda Gordon."

"My name's Coral. Oh, I guess I told you that, didn't I?"

Ignoring the slip, Judy said, "And you say there's five or six more besides you in here? Why aren't they awake?"

"They'll be coming around soon. When they do, we'll take roll call to see if anyone's been taken away."

"How long have you been in here?" Rhonda whispered the question, fearful the answer would feed her fear even more.

"Geez, I don't know. Do you know what day it is?"

The sudden realization that neither Rhonda nor Judy had any idea as to how long they had been unconscious struck home. Had they been out for minutes or hours? Hours or days? Days or weeks? How much time had passed since electing to hitchhike instead of boarding the bus.

"Well, let's see," Judy began slowly. "It was June—"

"June? June, for Christ's sake? It was March when I was kidnapped. What year is it?"

"What year? You've got to be kidding, right? You don't know what year it is?"

"Well, it was 1988 when I was kidnapped."

"It's still 1988—and is that what happened? Have we been kidnapped?" Judy asked.

"I don't know what else you'd call it," Coral said.

"You were just fooling about not knowing the year, right?" Rhonda asked.

"In a way," Coral said. "See, the only thing we ever know is this goddamned blackness all the time. You lose track of everything. Day. Night. Time. Up. Down. The whole thing sort of becomes goofy and unglued. If you're around long enough, you start wondering if you even existed anywhere but here."

"If we've been kidnapped," Judy said, "what's the reason? Why would anyone want to kidnap us? For ransom?"

"I doubt like hell if it's for ransom," Coral said.

"Why do you say that, Coral?"

"Hell, I've been on the road for the last three years. I'm from New Jersey. Ain't nobody around here that even knows me. Why would someone want to kidnap me for ransom that couldn't possibly be paid? I've got no folks. I'm just roaming around the country, seeing the sights. At least, I was."

"Wait a minute, Coral," Judy said. "You said around here. Where are we? Do you know?"

"Your guess is as good as mine."

"Where were you when you were . . . were taken?" Rhonda asked.

"In some little godforsaken spot in South Dakota."

"Where?" Rhonda asked.

"Christ, I don't remember. Wasn't anyplace I'd ever been to before, and I sure as fuck don't want to ever go back there again—assuming I get out of this mess."

"Were you close to Sioux Falls?" Judy said quickly.

"Yeah. I was planning on finding someplace where I could shower and do some laundry."

"What highway were you on?"

"Ah, 38—I think. Why?"

"I . . . that is, Rhonda and I are from Sioux Falls. We were picked up on Interstate 90 west of town. You're not from around here. I was just trying to see if there was any reason for our being kidnapped the way we were."

"Rhonda," Coral said slowly.

"What?"

"Nothing. I was just saying your name.

The town was named something that
sounded like Rhonda."

"Rhonda?" Judy repeated, mulling over
in her mind the names of towns in South
Dakota that might have sounded like her
friend's name. "In which direction were you
going, Coral?"

"I was heading west. Why?"

"Rowena!" Rhonda shouted.

"Yeah, Rowena." Coral's voice
brightened a bit. "Geez, don't think I'm a
flake or something strange. It's a nothing
town and the highway sort of skirted it, if I
remember right."

Judy pressed in with more questions.
"So what happened? What time of day was
it?"

"It was just after dusk. See, I was
getting concerned that I'd wind up sleeping
in some field or under a tree or someplace
like that. There sure wasn't much to look for
in that little dump of a town. I remembered
that one of the last mileage markers I saw
said that Sioux Falls was only about fifteen
or sixteen miles away. I had just left a little
town—I don't remember the name of it, but
it was a pretty little place—and decided that
my luck would hold until I reached Sioux
Falls. It didn't."

"What happened?" Rhonda asked.

"I got a ride with some plow jockey as
far as Rowena, and he said he had business
there. I got out and started hitching.

Nothing. No traffic to speak of at all. When the sun went down, I started looking for some place that would give me some shelter. The air was still brisk, and it looked like it might rain. Then the car came along.''

"The car?" Judy asked. "A long sucker? Black?''

"You got it.''

"And you wound up here. Right?''

"Right. Most of the other girls were picked up by it, too.''

"Nobody in the back seat, right?''

"That's the strange part about it," Coral said.

"What is?" Rhonda asked.

"I swear I heard a woman talking to the driver from the back seat, but when I got in, the car was empty except for the driver. Sure don't make sense.''

"What about the rest of the girls?''

"They heard her, too.''

"It's got to be a tape recording or something like that," Judy said. "Think about it. A girl wouldn't get into a car that big if she thought the driver was alone. At least, she'd think a couple of times before she accepted the offer.''

"What you're saying is," Coral said, "that thinking there's a woman in the back seat makes the girl decide it's all right without hesitating. Is that it?''

"I guess.''

Coral's eastern twang shot through the blackness. "It makes sense to me.''

"To me, too," Rhonda said.

"Which leaves the big question, right?" Coral asked.

"Which is?"

"Why the hell were we picked up in the first place?"

"Yeah," Rhonda said, "and what happens next?"

"I can tell you some of it," Coral said quietly.

"Well, don't hold back. Pour it all out," Judy said.

"We eat well. Very well. You'll develop a lot of strange tastes for food you probably never ate too much of at home."

Neither Rhonda nor Judy said anything for a moment. Then Rhonda said, "Such as?"

"Lots of vegetables."

"Like?"

"Oh, spinach, beans, cabbage, broccoli, peas. At least those are the conclusions most of us have drawn from tasting and feeling them."

"Yuck," Judy said. "No french fries or malts?"

"Do you like liver?"

"No," the girls chorused, and Judy made a gagging sound.

"Beef, tuna, chicken and some kind of meat that was real chewy. One of the girls said she thought it might have been heart."

"For Christ's sake, that's a terrible menu. Anything else."

"Oatmeal, nuts like almonds, I think, and different tasting breads. Not the good old fashioned white stuff you get in a super-market either."

"It sounds like this might be the room in hell to punish people who never ate stuff that was good for them while they were on earth," Judy said.

"Hey," Rhonda said loudly, "what about going to the bathroom and stuff like that?"

"In time you get used to pissing on the floor," Coral said. "There must be a slope to the floor 'cause it never stays around. If you're thinking of taking a good dump, forget it. If you're like the rest of us, you'll probably wind up constipated. When we do manage to have our bowels move, it seems they pick it up whenever they turn the gas on and knock us out. It's really strange."

"Who're *they*?" Judy asked, lowering her voice.

"They?" Coral echoed the word.

"You said 'they pick it up.' I was just wondering who our jailers are."

"No idea. It was just a figure of speech."

Rhonda sniffed the air for a few moments.

"What are you doing, Rhon?" Judy asked, turning in the direction of the sound.

"It smells pretty clean in here. Is that a disinfectant of some sort I smell? I didn't notice it before but I do now. Smell."

Judy inhaled deeply. "You're right. What is that, Coral?"

"I think someone probably washes us down periodically whenever we're knocked out."

"Wonderful. And you've been in here for almost three months or so? Simply fucking great." Judy bit the words in a fit of sarcasm.

During the next few minutes, their voices aroused the other girls and each told their story for the benefit of the two new arrivals.

Sherry Blaine had been walking along Spring Avenue in Sioux Falls during the Memorial Day weekend hurrying to the supermarket before it closed for the holiday. When the car had confronted her, she accepted the story told by the driver that her father's employer had just acquired the limousine. The chauffeur had been dispatched to pick Sherry up and bring her home where her parents were waiting. Something had been added about her whole family going to her dad's boss' house.

"You mean you didn't ask for any I.D. or check to see if the driver knew your dad's boss's name?"

"I was so caught up with the beauty of that automobile, I just never thought, I guess. I wanted to ride in the back seat and pretend I was the owner, even if it was only for a few blocks."

"How old are you, Sherry?" Judy asked.
"Twelve."
Judy bit her tongue. She and Rhonda

had done something just as stupid and they were four years older than Sherry.

Daun Kingston had been selling magazine subscriptions with a traveling crew. She had knocked on the door of a large house and had been invited inside. The hostess offered her a cup of tea, and the last thing Daun remembered was drinking it. She explained that after knocking on doors for as long as she had, all houses looked alike and she had given her sales pitch automatically. At 23 years of age, she felt she had not made a mistake and was simply doing her job. She couldn't remember where the house had been but she did know the town had been Sioux Falls.

Pam Kennedy, 17 years old, Dana Warde, 19, and Margaret Olds, 15, all told stories similar to the others. They couldn't remember how long they had been incarcerated. Each, except Daun, had been picked up by the long, black limousine. Other than Judy, Rhonda, Coral, and Daun, all had been picked up on the streets of Sioux Falls.

"Who's been here the longest?" Judy asked.

"What difference does that make?" Daun asked. "One minute is just like the last and the next. There's no day or night. Nothing. Just the food. And I have no idea how much time elapses between meals. It could be an hour or it could be twenty-four hours. Who knows? I don't. I almost don't care anymore."

"I was here when all of the others were brought in," Dana said.

"You have no idea as to how long ago that was?" Judy asked.

"None. I will tell you this much. Every once in a while a girl will be missing after we've been gassed or whatever it is that happens when the hissing starts."

"What do you mean missing?"

"Well, when I first came in here, there were three other girls. I don't remember all of their names except one was Dianne. Don't you remember her, Pam?"

"Sort of," Pam said quietly. "I was too scared to even remember my own name at first. I guess I do remember some of the others."

"So what happens to them?" Rhonda asked.

"All I know is, the hissing starts, and you get dizzy and pass out. When you come to after a while, the place has been apparently cleaned, the smell of disinfectant is in the air, and you find a plate of food next to you. Because there isn't anything else to do, you eat it. And sometimes, somebody will be gone—missing. That's why we take roll call when we wake up, to make certain we're all here and that no one has been taken away."

"There's one other thing," Coral said, an air of dread threading its way through her voice.

When she didn't volunteer the information immediately, Rhonda and Judy patiently waited.

"I know what it is you're going to say, Coral," Daun said. "Go ahead. Tell them. They've got to know. It's better if they're prepared when it happens."

Coral waited again.

"For Chrissakes, tell us, will you?" Judy said loudly.

"Every once in a while—usually after we find someone has been taken away while we've been out—we'll hear screaming. Not very loud. But it's definitely screaming."

Before Rhonda and Judy could react, the girls, each one in her own cocoon of gloom, froze when the hissing sound began.

Tuesday, 6:04 a.m.

"Do you think they give us the meals at regular times?" Coral asked.

"What do you mean?" Judy asked, scooping up more oatmeal with her finger-tips. "Christ, what a mess! You'd think they'd give us a spoon."

"Think about it," Daun said. "A spoon could be converted into a weapon of some sort."

"And when would you use it? If they gas us every time they come in, you'd never have a chance to use a weapon," Judy said, slurping more of the gooey cereal from her fingers.

"So, do you think they do?" Coral asked again.

"You mean," Daun asked, "cereal in the morning and other types of food at noon and at night?"

"Uh-huh."

"Well, let's see," Judy said. "Rhon and I were picked up at night. Probably about nine-thirty or ten. Right, Rhon?"

"Right."

"This goop I'm eating now is going down like my breakfast would. In other words, I'm hungry but not starved. Follow?"

"Yeah," Coral said, "I understand. So we probably could go on the assumption that it's morning. What day were you picked up?"

"It was Monday," Rhonda said.

"Monday," Coral said the word softly, soothingly, as if she had found a long, lost friend, "And today is Tuesday. Jesus, that's the first point of reference I've had since I was brought in. Everybody keep track of your appetites. Maybe we can stay on top of time that way."

"Good idea," Dana said. "How come we didn't think of it before now?"

"Good question," Coral said, "but in the meantime, we can maybe keep our marbles in place by doing it."

The girls fell silent as they continued eating their meal.

4

Tuesday, 2:30 p.m.

"Your name?" the tall elegant woman asked before sitting down behind the desk.

"Linda Polchow." Linda shook her head, her brown curls wavering about her square face. Fixing her hazel eyes on the woman, she vowed to herself once more, that she would not be nervous. It was just a job interview. Lucky for her that she had found the classified advertising section of *The Argus-Leader* in the bus depot when she arrived the day before. She had not thought too much about working as a domestic in someone else's home but the experience of applying for the job would stand her in good stead when she went to an office to look for work.

"My name is Ida Chewell. I am a private and personal secretary. You will meet the woman for whom you will work at the house. Where are you from? Sioux Falls?"

"No, ma'am. Marion."

"Marion, South Dakota?"

Linda nodded.

"The reason I asked, Linda," the woman said, "is that there is a Marion, Iowa, as well as a Marion, Ohio, and quite a few others as well."

Linda smiled, admiring at the same time the woman's high-necked blouse. A brooch, punctuated with jewels, rested at her throat. "That's right. I just naturally assumed you'd think of Marion, South Dakota, ma'am."

"Sioux Falls is not my home. I had no idea there was such a place as Marion." Ida Chewell smiled warmly, fixing her eyes above and beyond Linda's head. "Tell me about yourself, Linda."

"Well, I graduated from high school this year, and I'm looking for a job. I'm eighteen years old, I can type fifty-five words a minute, and I take shorthand."

"Well," Ida said, "while this particular job doesn't require office work, I'm sure that someday you'll find something along those lines. Tell me about your family."

"My mom's widowed, and I have a brother who works in Sioux City. Mom runs a small dress shop in Marion."

"Have you helped her do any house-work?"

Linda smiled broadly, showing her

bright teeth. "For the last four years, I did all of the housework to help Mom out. I can do just about anything. Why?"

"The position I have to offer is one calling for regular housework in a rather large home, here in Sioux Falls."

"I . . . I really wanted to get into an office type job."

"The pay is rather substantial considering the job requires that you live in." The woman stopped.

Linda studied her. She appeared to be in her late thirties or early forties. Her lustrous black hair was pulled back in a bun that gave an almost severe look to her thin, pale face. If Linda had to catagorize her, she'd say she might have been a fashion model at one time because of her tall frame and the fact that there probably wasn't an extra ounce of fat on her. She held her upper body stiffly as if to deemphasize her breasts. "What would the pay be, ma'am?"

"You may call me Ida if you like. The salary is one hundred fifty per week. Of course, you'd live on the premises, and food of course would be no problem. In essence, the salary is money for you to do with as you'd like since all of your living expenses would be taken care of."

Linda thought for a moment. More than 600 a month? If she were working someplace else, she'd have to have another couple of hundred for a decent apartment, and food would probably amount to another hundred a month. She wasn't sure if she could find a job that would pay her almost a thousand a month to begin. "How large is the home, ma'am?"

Ida smiled. "It's a large Victorian mansion in an older part of town. Of course, you'd have help. There's a cook and two other girls. The work would not be that burdensome."

"Would I be working for you?"

"No. I'm merely Madame's social and business secretary. If you want the job, it is yours."

Linda looked around the office in which she sat. It seemed so barren, as if nothing ever happened there. She had called the telephone number in the ad and been given the address and time of the appointment. It seemed strange that there were no file cabinets and the desk behind which Ida sat didn't even have a telephone. Ida had answered the door when Linda had knocked.

Linda shrugged. "When do I start?"

"Tomorrow morning. Be on the northwest corner of Wayland and Eighth at ten o'clock this evening. I'll arrange for you to be picked up then."

Linda frowned. What a strange hour!

"You do want the job, don't you, Linda?" Ida peered intently at her.

Washing away any questions she might have had, Linda said, "Yes, of course I do."

Ida stood. "Be there, then." She

brusquely clipped the words. "A limousine will pick you up."

Linda got to her feet and thrust her hand out toward Ida.

Taken off guard, Ida mumbled something before accepting the proferred hand.

Linda turned, walking to the outer office and through it to the hallway door. She noted the outer office had no furniture either, other than a desk without chair or telephone. After stepping into the corridor, she shook her head. Why worry about such things? She had just gotten a job—a good job that paid considerably more than if she had looked for work in Marion. The best she could have done there was either work for her mother, become a waitress or work at the hotel. The options in Marion were not that plentiful.

Tuesday - 3:01 p.m.

Ida took the chair on which Linda had sat during the interview back into the reception office and placed it behind the desk. Retrieving her purse from the other room, she threw the key on the outer desk and fixed the lock to close automatically when she shut the door. Turning the lights out, she replaced the sign, "For Rent," back on the hook that allowed it to show through the frosted glass and left, closing the door behind her. The lock clicked loudly.

Tuesday · 5:15 p.m.

"Isn't that great, Mom?" Linda said, leaning against the wall. The pay phone had been kept busy for almost an hour by one of the other tenants in the hotel where she had planned to sleep that night.

"Oh, honey, that's wonderful. If you work hard, you won't have to worry about being laid off or anything. That could happen in an office, you know."

"I know, Mom. I plan on sending you some money every week."

"You don't have to do that, honey."

"I want to, Mom. It's my way of showing you how much I appreciate everything you've ever done for me."

"How will I reach you?"

Linda paused. She had no idea where the house was, its address, the telephone number or anything. All she could remember was the first name of the woman who had interviewed her—Ida. If she told her mother how little she knew, her mother would worry about it. She'd have to think fast.

"I . . . I don't know what the telephone number is at the house. As soon as I find out, I'll call you. Okay?"

"What about the address or the name of the people you'll be working for. Couldn't you look it up in the phone book right now and give it to me? I'd feel a lot better if I had it."

"It's all written down on a piece of paper that's in my room, Mom," Linda lied. "I'll call you tomorrow night if it's all right with the lady I'll be working for."

"Please look it up in the phone book, Linda."

"I can't. There isn't any phone book here at the pay phone," she said, playing with the book's cover.

"Well, I guess I can wait. By the way, don't call me after seven tomorrow night, honey."

"Why?"

"I've got choir practice. Remember?"

"Okay, Mom. I'll call you sometime during the day tomorrow. All right? I promise."

"That'll be fine, honey."

"Don't worry, Mom. I'll be fine. I really will."

"I know, Linda. It's just that now I'm all alone and I guess I'll be . . . Don't worry. I'll be fine. You'd better get off the phone now. Someone else might want to use it."

"Okay. I love you, Mom. Bye."

Linda hung up. She knew her mother was going to be somewhat lonesome, but when Linda had argued that she should stay in Marion, it had been her mother who had insisted that the small town had nothing to offer an 18 year-old girl. Besides, Linda would always be able to visit her mother on her days off. She wondered how many she'd get in a month's time.

Tuesday - 10:14 p.m.

Although the day had been hot, the cool
night air reminded Linda that summer had
not yet truly taken root. The street corner
on which she stood was deserted, and other
than an occasional car driving by, the only
sounds she could hear came from Highway
38, which lay to the south. She glanced at
her watch. It was already 10:15. The car was
late. Looking up at the street sign, she re-
affirmed that she was on the right corner.
Wayland and Eighth.

Could she have missed the car? There
hadn't been that many since 9:30 when she
first arrived. Hadn't Ida said something
about it being a limousine? Weren't limousines long and shiny? She hadn't seen any
such car go by the corner where she was
standing. She'd wait until 10:30—no, 11:00
o'clock. If the car hadn't arrived by then,
she'd go back to the hotel, get a room and
return to the office the next day. There must
have been something she didn't understand
about the arrangements. She hoped Ida
wouldn't be angry. It must cost a lot of
money to operate a big car like that. Maybe
there was even a chauffeur driving it. That
would cost even more.

Just then, she saw the lights of a car
coming down Wayland. Her heart leaped,
and she picked up her suitcase. The automobile slowly turned the corner but didn't

stop, continuing down Eighth Street, past the girl.

It was a long black car. It had to be a limousine, but had it been the right one? She set her suitcase back on the sidewalk. How many limousines could she expect to drive past here at this time of night? Linda decided she'd been either mistaken about the arrangements, or for some reason she couldn't quite understand, she'd been made to look like a fool.

She felt her eyes tear up. She'd bragged so much to her mother about the job and the money she'd make. Linda Polchow was a fool, no doubt of that. She probably would have broken things in the house of the lady for whom she'd been working anyway. There probably wasn't a house. The woman named Ida simply talked to young girls, built up their hopes and then made a fool of them.

But why? She wiped away the tears. Why should anyone do that? It made no sense to Linda. It had to have been that somehow she had misunderstood the woman. Her best chance of recouping something out of all this was simply to return to the hotel, get another room and go back to the office the next day.

Turning, she started along Wayland Street.

"Excuse me. Were you hired by Ida Chewell today?"

The voice came from behind Linda, and

she jumped at the sound.

"What?" she said turning around. The car sat along the curb, stretching seemingly down the full block.

"I said, were you hired by Ida Chewell today?" the man said, leaning over from behind the steering wheel.

"Yes, I was. Am I supposed to go with you?"

Without speaking, the driver got out and hurried around the front of the car. He took her suitcase, placing it in the trunk, before opening the side door to the passenger compartment. "Ma'am." He saluted when she bent down to enter.

Linda wanted to giggle, feeling quite giddy. It had to be wonderful to have enough money to hire someone to drive an elegant car like the one in which she sat.

Just as the car pulled away from the curb, she noticed that she could barely make out the outline of the driver through the heavily tinted glass separating them. She hadn't even looked at him. She wondered if he were young and handsome. Maybe she'd fall in love with him. Leaning back, she smiled, then frowned when she heard the hissing sound.

Tuesday - 10:30 p.m.

Ida Chewell paced back and forth in the huge drawing room. Antique furniture blended in with intricately carved woodwork

of a bygone era and 14-foot high ceilings.
Patting the bun at the back of her head, she
stopped walking when Aleigha Moraine
entered.

"Isn't he back yet?" Aleigha asked. Her
triangular face reflected her sense of
anticipation that edged her words as well.

"No, and I'm getting concerned. He
should have been here by now."

"What if he had an accident?"

"Don't be stupid."

"It could happen."

"It won't. It can't. She would never allow
it. *He* would never allow it."

"She can't control everything."

"No—but *he* can. You know that. It's
sufficient that she controls what she wants.
She controls you. She controls me. She controls her environment."

"That's true—and, of course, he
controls her, doesn't he? But what I'm
saying is simply this—suppose some
drunken fool ran through a traffic light or
past a stop sign and struck the limousine.
What then? What would happen?"

"Honestly, Aleigha, you can worry over
the most trivial things. I'm telling you that
it just will not happen."

Ida moved to the bay windows over-
looking the tree-studded front lawn and
shrubbery-lined drive. Half a block away,
traffic could barely be seen passing the
property. Where could Edward be? The fool!
All he had to do was drive downtown and

pick up the little slut. What could be taking so long?"

Aleigha moved up behind her. "Any sign of him?"

"None."

Both women turned to face the interior of the room. Ida watched Aleigha move cat-like toward the fireplace at the far end of the room. Only two lamps, one at the far end and one in the bay, lighted the 40-foot long room. Ida loved Aleigha but could not allow her to interfere with her duties or the wishes of their mistress. If their employer wanted Aleigha to perform her duties, Ida could not interfere.

Ida longed for Aleigha's body to be naked and lying next to her. She wanted to kiss the shorter woman's huge breasts and run her tongue down her smooth belly until she could intertwine it with the love hair growing on her vaginal mound. Aleigha would writhe beneath her expert touch and return the love she felt for Ida in much the same way. How Aleigha could be so loving and tender with Ida during those few precious moments they spent together and so vicious with the girls tethered in the sub-basement was something Ida could not fathom. Rather than question and perhaps ruin their relationship, Ida had accepted Aleigha's sadistic nature as part of her per-sonality.

Ida's function in the household was to furnish as much erotic pleasure for her mistress as she was able to produce. As long as the girls in the basement didn't cause problems, and as long as Aleigha dealt successfully with them, Ida's world was simple.

The sound of a motor approaching drew both women back to the bay window. Headlights stabbed the night, as the car drove up the drive and into the attached garage on the north side of the house, Ida and Aleigha hurried to the hall that would take them to the side entrance.

Just as they opened the door to the garage, the folding door dropped into place.

"Where have you been, Edward?"

The man stepped from the driver's seat and peered at them before closing the door. "There were several police cars in the vicinity, ma'am. I thought it prudent to drive around for a while as if going someplace else."

"Very well," Ida said curtly. "Take the little bitch to the dark room. Aleigha, are you in need of a fresh one?"

"Yes. I'll go along and select one."

Edward pulled the limp form from the back seat and effortlessly shifted the girl's weight to a comfortable carrying position. Ida stepped forward and closed the car door, while Aleigha opened the one leading into the house.

She followed Edward down the lighted stairway to the basement and to an arched doorway at the far end. She flicked a switch before opening the wooden door. Taking the lead, she started down a flight of steps that led another 15 feet below the level of the house's foundation. When they stood at the bottom, Aleigha reached out, turning a small valve next to another heavy door. After waiting for several minutes, the woman pulled open the heavy door. Swinging it wide, she flicked a switch, erasing the shadowy blackness in front of her.

The bodies of three young women lay in various positions on each side of the room along the limestone rock walls, held in tether by a wide leather belt around their abdomens. Securely tied to a ring, which was anchored to the wall, each girl lay on a platform-like area, the sides of which sloped down to a central drain. Two platforms and rings lay at the far end of the room. On one, a girl lay huddled next to the limestone. The remaining wall, the one with the door, held a ring on either side of the entrance. An eighth girl leaned against the wall, her eyes closed in drugged sleep.

Edward dumped Linda at one of the platforms next to the door and began undressing her. Pulling her blouse off, he jerked at her bra until it tore. When her breasts fell free, he roughly squeezed one.

"Don't take liberties with that one, Edward," Aleigha said, a threatening snarl to her voice. "You men are all alike."

Edward pulled off Linda's skirt and panties and looked at Aleigha who was checking Judy and Rhonda. Trimming off the excess leather rope with a sharp knife, he laid it on the shelf over Linda's head and crouched down.

"The two you brought in last night are very nice. It won't take too long before they'll be ready, Edward."

Edward stroked Linda's pubic area when Aleigha bent down to look more closely at Rhonda. Then he quickly stood upright. "I'm ready, Miss Aleigha."

Aleigha turned to face him. Dropping her attention back to the girls, she moved toward the doorway in a slow deliberate way. Stopping at the youngest, she smiled.

"This one will take a while, won't she, Edward?"

Edward nodded and licked his lips when Aleigha bent down to gently massage Sherry Blaine's small immature breasts.

For the next few minutes, while Edward picked up empty plates and hosed down the floor, running feces and bits of food droppings into a drain in the middle of the room, Aleigha went from girl to girl, pinching, teasing, massaging breasts and sex organs. When Edward finished spraying the disinfectant on the floor, she straightened up.

Stepping over the girls, she finally pointed with her foot at Dana Warde. "This one, Edward. Bring this one. She's as ready as she'll ever be."

Aleigha walked to the open door and

stopped, waiting for him to undo the rope from the wall ring. When the girl's body was freed, Edward picked her up, following the woman from the room, who extinguished the lights.

The door closed with a resounding thud, and the onyx blackness embraced the sleeping girls once more.

5

Hungary

October, 1614

Castle Csejthe clung to the low mountain top, outlined against the stygian horizon by the full moon. Clouds wended their way across the sky, at times obliterating the cool, yellow-white light over northwestern Hungary.

The high-pitched laughter had not yet begun, but the guards on duty at the main entrance knew the nightly, insane serenade would begin within minutes. The two men moved in closer to the fire for warmth against the chill night and the contrary brightness the flames would give to ward off the darkness.

Each held his breath, anticipating the mad rantings that would soon fill their watch.

Sandor Werböczi wiped up the gravy
from his plate with the last crust of dark
bread. Satisfied that none remained, he
thrust the dripping piece into his mouth,
chewed for a while and washed it down with
the last of his goat's milk. Standing up to
stretch, he burped loudly. His three children
looked up in awe at their father, stiffling
their giggles.

"Well? What is so funny, my little ones?"
Sandor bent down to the closest one and
hugged him.

"You make funny noises, Papa."

"Funny noises? Funny noises?" He
stood upright, pulling his shoulders back.
His flat stomach didn't need contracting.
Army duty had made certain that his body
was hard, firm and ready for action. "Funny
noises such as what?"

The three children looked at each other.

"Like the laughing from the castle," one
said, immediately casting her eyes downward to stare at the table. "I . . . I'm sorry,
Papa."

Sandor's wife, Trilka, bustled to the
table from the fireplace where she had been
finishing up her cooking duties for the day.
"Shame! Shame on your heads for compar-
ing your wonderful Papa to the beast. None
of you remember, do you?"

The children shook their heads.

"Your oldest sister, Maria, was taken by

that . . . that beast and was killed by her."
Trilka shook violently while her angry and
awful memories grew.

"Now, now, Trilka, you'll only get your-
self worked up and not sleep well tonight.
They are only children. What do they know?"
Sandor shrugged.

"For eleven years the people of this
village and all the countryside were as
children, allowing the countess to take our
young daughters and steal their blood for
what reason only that crazy woman and God
knew. Don't you miss our Maria? Don't you
mourn for our Maria?"

Sandor enveloped his wife in his large
arms, embracing her. "Of course I mourn
her and miss her, but will that bring her
back? Will that undo the awful things the
countess did? Take strength from the fact
that she is incarcerated for the rest of her
life, without the possibility of escape or the
opportunity to ever do again that which she
had done for so long a time."

"You go there every day, Sandor, yet
you never tell me anything. What is it like in
the Castle Csejthe? Tell, please?"

"You always ask. The one time I began
to tell you, you wept. I don't want that to
happen again." Sandor released her from
his bearlike hug.

"That was shortly after the trial and
executions. The terrible memory of Maria's
being taken that night was still very fresh in
my mind. Much time has elaspsed since.

Please tell me. Do you see her when you take
her food and water?''

"What of the children? Should they be
told as well?'' Sandor crinkled his eyes, their
brows forming a bushy ridge. Lowering
himself into a chair, he leaned back.

"Perhaps they should be told. At first,
when the countess laughed and screamed,
we were terrified, but like anything one is
exposed to for a long enough time, you
begin not to hear. It is best if they are told.
All of the children in the village and area
should know so that such a thing can never
happen again.''

"Perhaps we should ask Father Hunyadi. He would know if it is such a good idea
to fill young minds with tales of lust and
murder and madwomen.''

Turning to finish cleaning off the table,
Trilka said, "I already have. He thought at
first it might harm them, but then, to ward
off any such thing happening again in the
future, he said it would be good.''

"Very well, Trilka. Finish your work,
then I will tell you what I see when I go to the
castle.''

A particularly huge bank of clouds
slowly tumbled across the night sky, at first
threatening to miss the moon completely.
But a capricious fall wind exerted itself, and
in seconds the light that had glowed above
faded and a hellish darkness covered the
earth.

Five cloaked figures hurried through the scrub trees and boulders, up the hills surrounding the solid block of buildings at the crest. Darting from tree to boulder to shrub, the five shapes seemed more ethereal than solid. When a break in the giant cloud overhead spotlighted the hill-top, they stopped, instantly seeking cover. When the bright finger of light shifted and then disappeared, they continued their stealthy journey.

One of the guards stretched and moved in closer to the fire. The night was going to be cold, and he and his companion had to remain on duty until dawn, when they would be relieved. He wished he had the seniority that Werböczi had. All that man had to do was bring one meal per day to the walled-up madwoman, put it in the special drawer and take any refuse away from her chamber. Though he worked less than one hour per day, it wasn't the nicest duty when it came to emptying the chamber pot the woman presented to him. But everything in life carried a price of sorts. Werböczi's was to work little and smell the droppings of the mad noble woman.

The guard rubbed his hands together over the fire. Still, he'd rather do what Werböczi did than stand guard at the castle gate from dusk to dawn and listen to the ravings of the Countess Elisabeth Bathory Nadasdy. It wouldn't be long before the

screams and laughter would fill the night
again. And he knew his blood would run
cold at the sound.

Sandor huddled close to the fire, his
children hugging his legs, while Trilka sat
down in a chair next to the dancing flames.

"It won't be long now before she starts.
Won't she, my little ones?"

The children nodded but remained
silent.

"So you want to know what the inside of
the castle is like and what I see when I take
her food and carry away her slop?"

Trilka nodded while the children
screwed their faces up at the thought of
having to carry human manure.

Before Sandor could continue, the first
high-pitched, raving laugh filtered down to
the village from the mountain top. It was a
dreary and dull night despite the full moon
earlier. Overhead, clouds darkened the sky.
No night birds cried out. In most of the
houses of the village, the only sound, other
than occasional muted conversation, would
be the crackle of hearth fires and the
countess's insane laughing.

The guard coughed, clearing his throat
when the laughter began. Blessing himself
as he always did whenever she screamed
out into the night, he stepped even closer to
the flames. Nudging his companion who
had elected to nap for a while, the soldier

peered up at the tower wherein their
prisoner lived alone in constant Cimmerian
night.

When the laughter threaded its way
down the mountainside, the five figures
stopped, frozen in their tracks. The leader
threw back the hood from his head to better
hear the sound.

"What is. . . ?" He stopped. "Not—not
my lady?" He turned his head to the
darkened heavens and was about to unleash
a scream of his own when he thought of the
guards on duty. From where he stood, he
could see the fire and the two men huddled
around it. The animals. The filthy beasts.
What had they done to her? Why was she
screaming like that? Or—or was it laughing? Given time, he would be able to help
her, but he had to get to her.

The two men behind him rolled their
eyes while the women remained calm, quiet.

"Lord Thorko? Is that my lady crying
out to us for succor?" Ujuvary asked.

"I imagine it is. Come, we'll go the back
way. Our observance over the last months
have shown there are only two guards on
duty at any given time. We can enter
through the secret passage and no one will
ever be the wiser that we will have been
there and gone. Come."

The tall, white-haired man pulled up his
hood, covering the thin, almost cadaverous
face, before stepping out from behind the

rock where they had sought and found shelter for the moment. In a single file of shadows, the entourage continued up the hillside.

"Surely I have seen cleaner pig stys right here in our village than the first floor of our protectorate's castle," Sandor said. "Broken and overturned furniture everywhere is covered with dust as thick as my finger in places. Rats and other vermin run rampant. It is awful."

"Why is it so filthy?" Trilka asked.

"I can only guess it is because when she started on her bloody and murderous campaign, all else was forgotten. You heard how the lower levels of the castle were used to fatten up the young girls before bleeding them to death?"

Trilka sucked in her breath and nodded. A tear formed, careening down her fat cheek when she thought of her beautiful first born, Maria, being held in that horrible place, then being bled to death for the benefit of the countess.

"I looked around the top floor once," Sandor continued, "after I finished my appointed duties. The room wherein she was found—the one with the bathtub in which she bathed in girls' blood—was much cleaner. Of course, no one had touched it since the arrest and trial. I guess that was the only room kept in decent order, other than the kitchen, which was in pretty much the same condition as the bathing room."

"Did anyone ever find out why she did it? Have you ever heard her speak of it or have you ever asked her?" Trilka leaned forward, her own prurient nature aroused despite the heaviness in her heart for her dead daughter.

"There is speculation on the part of the guards that she wanted young girls' blood to stay young and beautiful herself."

"And . . . and she bathed in it to achieve this?" Trilka sat back, a sickly look crossing her round face.

"There's talk that she also . . . drank it as well."

Trilka slapped a hand over her mouth, controlling her heaving belly and fearful of vomiting up her evening meal. "Terrible," she finally managed. "Awful."

Sandor shrugged. "You wanted to know."

"I wanted to know what you saw and heard when you go to the castle."

Sandor nodded toward the open window. The maniacal laughter rose and fell on the breeze wafting down from the mountain. "That's about all I hear. That damnable laughter."

"I thought Prime Minister Rakoczy said she was to be walled-up alive. If she is, how can we hear her so well?"

"There are several openings through which fresh air can enter her apartment. There isn't much noise at night so the only sound you hear is her laughing."

"And you can neither see her nor speak to her when you are there?"

Sandor shook his head. "At first, she'd shout through the door that allows the food to be passed to her. She offered jewels she said she had with her to anyone who would knock down the walled-up doorway. She promised a rank in her personal guard to the person who helped her. She said . . ." He stopped.

After a moment, Trilka said, "Go on."

Sandor blushed and turned away.

Sensing his embarrassment, Trilka ordered the children to bed. Dutifully obeying, they stood, kissed their parents good-night and left to climb to the overhead loft.

When she and her husband were alone, Trilka said, "What else, husband?"

"She said she'd make her saviour a consort—her intimate consort."

"And you said?" Trilka leaned forward, waiting for her husband's answer.

"Nothing. I said nothing. She wasn't talking to me. Just raving. She's totally mad. She murdered our daughter. I wanted right then to break down the door—but only to choke her to death with my bare hands rather than set her free. But then suddenly I realized the wisdom of the prime minister's sentence. Dead, she would be free. Alive, she suffers every minute. Listen."

The man and woman turned to the open

window and listened intently to the cackling
of the madwoman.

Thorko led the four around to the rear of
the wall that enclosed the castle. Lightly
running his fingers over the wall, he
diligently searched for something. A
satisfied sigh escaped his thin lips, and
when he pressed the rock, a panel of the
wall popped out a few inches. Nodding to
the two men, he motioned for them to pull it
open. A wave of damp, musty air rolled out,
engulfing them. Thorko stepped inside and
struck a rock with a piece of flint until
sparks ignited the torches the two women
carried. Holding them high in front, they
started into the passageway.

"You know, Trilka, I have tried to
protect you from the knowledge I have
about the countess."

"I know, Sandor, I know. But you must
tell all of it."

"Why?"

"Because she killed our daughter."

"I don't know much more than what I
have already told."

"Have you learned anything from the
guards?"

"Not recently. At first, when she was
walled up, she'd rant and rave and carry
on."

"What did she say?"

"According to the guards, what she said

then at least made more sense than it does now. She called on someone named Thorko. Remember? The prime minister asked her where he was, and she wouldn't tell him. There were other names, but I don't recall them. She talked of bathing in blood and drinking blood and how delightful her evenings were when the girls were tortured and bled and they would scream. Naturally . . .'' Sandor stopped when he realized Trilka was weeping.

She leaned forward holding her head in her hands, shoulders jerking convulsively as she cried. For the first time since the trial, Trilka was able to mourn her daughter properly. For a long time, the tears of grief ran down her cheeks onto her hands only to drip slowly to the hearth. After a while, she sat up straight, wiping her eyes with the back of her hand. ''Go on, husband, with what you were saying. Naturally what?''

Sandor reached out to stroke her black hair. She leaned her plump cheek onto his hand and managed to smile. For the first time since Maria had been taken, she felt cleansed of her grief.

''Naturally she spoke of revenge,'' he continued, ''and what she would do to other girls when she was freed from her prison.''

A silence, punctuated with the laughing, closed in on Sandor and Trilka. Neither spoke, offering each other a quiet

strength that words could never communi-
cate.

The laughter turned to high-pitched
screams that seemed to be filled with terror
and horror.

Sandor leaped to his feet, peering into
the darkness in the general direction of
Castle Csejthe. What was happening?

Trilka hurried to his side. "What is it?"

"I don't know. I've never heard her do
that before."

"Nor have I."

The man and woman stared into the
darkness, trepidation overriding any sense
of complacency or well-being they might
have enjoyed a few moments earlier. They
instinctively knew something unusual and
horrible was taking place in Castle Csejthe.

The guards stared up at the tower that
held their prisoner. Screams pierced the
night, penetrating farther than her insane
mirth had ever done—rising, falling, mixing
with her wild laughter. The men turned to
stare at each other. What was going on? Was
this a new penance they and the countryside would have to endure? Was this a new
facet in the ever deteriorating mind of their
former protectorate?

The horror-filled screams and laughter
rang through the blackness. Then the
sounds stopped, and an awful silence
poured into the valley below from the

castle. The only sound the guards could
hear was the firewood snapping and
crackling as it burned and their own hearts
beating furiously.

6

Tuesday, 10:50 p.m.

Edward carried Dana's body as though it were weightless, making his way up the steps to the first floor. When he reached the door, he opened it, stepping through. Aleigha, right behind him, closed the heavy oak door.

Their footsteps barely sounded as they walked, as though some vacuum sucked away the very noise of heel and sole striking the clay tiled floor. Passing along a corridor, lined with doors every few feet, Edward stopped, moving to one side.

Aleigha stepped around Edward, opening the door second from the end, before reaching in to turn on a light switch. White walls dully reflected the soft, subdued

lighting, lending an indefinite aspect to the
room's depth and width. Racks along one
wall held whips, chains, leather thongs,
clamps, screws, weights of various sizes
and other paraphernalia. On the opposite
wall, a small white cabinet with glass doors
held vials, hypodermic needles, tubing and
small valves. A table with a trough built into
it, one end tipped several inches higher
than the other, was centered in the middle
of the room. Overhead, several large hooks
protruded from the ceiling, spaced evenly,
one from the other.

Edward unceremoniously dumped
Dana's limp body onto the table and walked
to the racks. Selecting a long leather thong,
he returned and tied the girls wrists
together, binding them tightly. He threw the
free one over one of the hooks and pulled,
hoisting Dana's trussed up hands toward
the ceiling. Her shoulders lifted, her head
lolling backward. When her buttocks
cleared the stainless steel tabletop, she slid
along it until her feet cleared, and she
swung back and forth as she was lifted
toward the ceilng. Her head hung forward,
her drugged eyes closed while she sailed to
and fro in an ever decreasing arc, not unlike
a grotesque pendulum.

"Thank you, Edward. That'll be all. You
may go. Tell Mistress Ida that I am ready."

"Very good, ma'am." Edward bowed his
head and backed toward the door.

After it closed quietly, the silence in the

room deepened until Aleigha chuckled.
Striding across the room to Dana, she ran
her hand down the unconscious girl's bare
belly. She leaned forward, kissing the girl's
pubic hair.

"You little sluts have no idea what your
role in life is, do you? No one else wants you
or cares about you. You run away from
reality and look for love and romance and
fame and fortune. When you come near us,
destiny is set and molded for all time. You
will serve our mistress." Grinning, the
woman stepped back, slowly unbuttoning
her blouse. She slipped out of it, exposing
her large breasts. After releasing the zipper
at her side, she stepped from her slacks
after they fell to the floor. Wiggling from her
tiny bikini panties, she murmured. "I am
almost ready for you, my sweet."

When the door opened, she turned to
greet Ida who stepped in, closing it behind
her. The tall woman stopped, drinking in the
scene. One nude young woman hung from
the ceiling, tied up not unlike an animal
ready to be slaughtered. The second stood
before her naked, her eyes half-closed, her
lust smouldering.

Without speaking, Ida hurried to
Aleigha, embracing the younger woman
when she reached her.

Separating, Ida looked at Dana. "She's
lovely, isn't she? And very healthy looking.
She should last for a while—at least several
days, don't you think?"

"It depends how quickly we take it from her. I'm sure we'll not rush it too fast. We have learned, haven't we, how to keep a steady supply without being obvious?"

Ida smiled, reaching out for Aleigha. Grabbing the shorter woman by the neck, she pulled her close, crushing her bare breasts against her own, smaller ones. Kissing her on the mouth, Ida ran her tongue into the familiar cavern, touching the teeth, the tongue, the insides of the cheeks. "I do love you, Aleigha," she said softly when they broke.

"And I, you, Ida. It has been such for a long time before and will be forever."

"Shhh, don't speak so of the past. We have now and forever, the future before us until . . ."

Dana moaned, and the two women reacted instantly. Turning, they examined her without moving closer.

"We have time, don't we?" Ida asked.

"It usually takes a short while for their eyes to adjust to light once more. It's as if they're blind at first. That's why I have insisted that the lighting in here be controlled on a rheostat. This one has been downstairs for almost thirteen weeks, and it'll take the full time to have her see. She'll come around nicely."

Aleigha stepped closer, running an appraising hand along the girl's thigh. "There are two more down there who've

been here almost as long and will probably
be next."

To while away the time before Dana recovered full consciousness, Aleigha went to
the cabinet to get her necessary equipment.

After some time had passed, Ida
stepped closer and stroked Aleigha's back.
"I think it's awful that you wait until they're
fully awake before tapping into them." Ida
folded her arms, hugging herself in a tight
embrace as if to protect herself from the
acts she was about to witness.

"Why? Why awful? I gain pleasure from
hearing them scream. It . . ."

Dana moaned again, and Aleigha went
to her, recognizing the recovering sound in
the girl's voice.

"Where . . . ? What . . . ?"

"You're perfectly safe, dear," Aleigha
said quietly.

Dana blinked her eyes. "I . . . I can't see.
Is there light? I can't see. My God, I'm
blind!" Dana cried out loudly, half-
screaming, half-sobbing.

Aleigha stepped closer until she could
stroke the girl's shoulder and back. "There,
there, child, you'll be all right. You've been
in the dark for a long time. This is the first
light you've seen in weeks. It'll take a few
hours but your eyesight will be perfectly
normal."

"Where am I? What happened? What was
that place I was in? Am I safe now?

Who . . . ?"

"Shh," Aleigha whispered. "A little at a time. First, you are as safe now as you will ever be in your life. As to where you are, you are here—with me. What could be more important?"

"But who are you?"

"My name is not that important, Dana."

"You know my name. Why can't I know yours?"

"In time, in time."

"What was that dark place I was in? Who were the others in there with me?"

"The others are unimportant to you at this time. As to where you were, let's just say it was a sort of preparatory room. You were wanting for nothing, isn't that so?"

"I didn't like being tied up and literally kept in the dark about everything. It's not too nice down there."

"But why worry about that now, Dana? You're up here—with me." Aleigha's voice stroked the atmosphere in a relaxing, sensual way.

"And where is that?"

"Why, here in my lab." She gestured with open arms.

"Lab? Are you a doctor of some kind? Am I all right?" Dana squinted her eyes, trying to view the woman standing close to her. Little by little, as her body responded to her awakening, she realized she couldn't move. "Hey, what's going on? Why can't I move?" Dana wiggled. "Jesus, I'm tied up!

What the hell's going on? Who are you, lady?
Why am I tied up like this? Christ, it hurts.
At first I couldn't feel anything. Now I think
my shoulders are going to tear right out."

"You're perfectly safe, my dear. I won't
hurt you, and I won't allow anyone else to
hurt you either. All I need is—some of your
blood."

The expression on Dana's face told
Aleigha and Ida both that the girl was about
to scream. When she did, they made no
move to stop her. Her cries rose and fell,
shrieking for help. When she stopped to
catch her breath, the two women stepped
forward.

"You can't be heard, you know. Let me
tell you about the house you're in and what
it is like. First," Ida began, "the exterior
walls are twelve inches thick, filled with
insulation and are of heavy cement block
construction. On the inside, the walls also
are lined with twelve inches of sound insulation. If you ever had the opportunity to see
any room other than this, you'd notice a certain smallness about each. Of course the
windows are triple insulated, not unlike a
sound studio. So, my dear, no one, other
than Aleigha and I, can hear you. Now be a
good child and don't scream anymore."

Ida stepped back, allowing the nude
Aleigha to come forward, closer to Dana.

Dana wept. "What are you going to do to
me?"

Aleigha picked up a syringe from the

table, walking slowly toward the swinging
girl. "This is nothing other than a
tranquilizer, Dana. It will relax you and
prevent you from fighting what is about to
take place." She smiled, her eyes half-
closed. "There is also a reaction retardent
that I have developed over the years. It will
slow your nervous system down until the
knowledge of pain takes all of several
minutes to reach your brain and have it
react."

Dana struggled as best she could, suspended from the ceiling, but could not
avoid the women coming closer with each
step. Her eyes bulged when a stream of the
drug shot into the air. Gritting her teeth,
she wriggled as much as she could to no
avail and cried out when the needle jabbed
her. She felt a coolness at first at the site of
the injection, but it quickly turned warm,
then hot and then simply wasn't there anymore. Her head swam for a few moments,
and as much as she could make out of her
surroundings seemed to be spinning about.
She felt her stomach heave when Aleigha
turned to face her once more; she held a
tube in one hand and a broad, flat object in
the other. It looked like a shiny needle,
greatly exaggerated. Dana threw her head
back and managed one final scream before
the drug struck home and she sensed everything about her body, her mind and her
being slowing, until her cry of terror dissipated from her hearing.

Aleigha smiled and, rearing back, slapped Dana as hard as she could across the face. The impact of the blow spun the girl's head to her right but no reaction followed. Nothing. Then, several minutes later, tears formed, and she whimpered as if in slow motion.

Turning, Aleigha picked up the wide needle and, after locating the femoral artery, inserted it. Blood spewed forth in a spurting jet, splashing onto Aleigha's nakedness. Fumbling with a short length of tubing and a valve on the table, she quickly fixed it to the needle and turned off the flow. Licking blood from her fingers, she turned to face Ida.

"It's not like in the past," she said. "These gadgets make for a much neater job, and a girl lasts much longer than when all I did was pierce an artery someplace and let the blood run freely. I rather enjoyed that part. The most beautiful patterns formed against their white skin while the blood coursed downward into a tub." She chuckled.

Ida nodded but could not contain shuddering at her lover's sadistic pleasures. "I'll take some up to her now if the girl is ready."

"She's ready." Aleigha opened the valve and held a beaker beneath the dangling bit of plastic tubing. It quickly filled as the blood spurted into the glass container. "Here."

Ida took the glass.

"Will you be with her tonight?"

Ida nodded. "Yes. I'd best hurry. I'll see you in the morning." She moved closer, and the two kissed, their tongues bidding one another farewell for the night.

When Ida was gone, Aleigha turned back to Dana who had passed out when the shock of the flat needle piercing her skin reached her brain. Aleigha reached up, stroking Dana's full breasts. Drawing concentric circles with one long-nailed finger, she drew in closer to the brown aureole on the girl's right breast. When she reached it, Aleigha tweaked it before pushing in hard with her nail, until a trickle of blood ran down the creamy flesh.

Standing on her tiptoes, Aleigha licked the droplets and smiled. "It won't be long, my darling, and you'll be all mine to do with as I want." She turned, hurrying to the rack and searched out a pair of ankle chains. Crouching before the girl's feet, she encircled first one leg with an iron, then the other, just above the foot. When they were secure, she fastened the end links of the short chain to a snap lock anchored to the floor. There was no sense in taking the risk of the girl kicking her while Aleigha performed her duties for her mistress or later when she indulged herself in the enjoyment that would come once the girl had served her primary purpose.

With Dana strung between ceiling and

floor, Aleigha stepped closer, running her tongue up one leg almost to the buttocks. Retracing her route, she stopped midway in the thigh and opened her mouth. She bit down hard as she could without breaking the skin. That would come in time.

Spinning on her heel, she picked up her clothing after slipping into a white coat. Checking the room once more, she turned the lights down even lower and left.

Several minutes later, Dana's eyes opened when the pain of the savage bite registered in her drugged brain. They widened, and as the reaction set in, her mouth opened lethargically. Her screams began more as a gurgle, slowly growing in volume and pitch until it tore through the silence like the cry of the damned.

Tuesday - 11:59 p.m.

Ida closed the door to the lab behind her and made her way through the kitchen toward the hallway. She passed the different oil paintings, dark with age, which hung at the foot of the stairs and on the walls lining the casement that led to the second floor. She hurried up the wide steps to the landing where she turned to the left.

Without lingering, she rushed up the stairs, moving as a shadow toward the dim hallway of the second level and the south wing. She stopped at a huge oak door and patted her high-collared blouse, making certain that she would look proper. She did not want to offend. She never had in all her time in service. Still, she would not take a chance.

Reaching out, she gently knocked. She waited for several minutes. Then the answer came, soft and delicate through the heavy door.

"Yes?"

"It is I, Ida."

"Yes, Ida?"

"I have something for you—something nice and warm, to help you sleep better."

"Come in, Ida."

Ida opened the door and entered, closing it behind her with a definitive click.

7

Hungary, 1614

Shadows of the north wall and buildings of Castle Csejthe sprawled along the ground concealing dense undergrowth and rock, trees and brush. Beyond, some 70 feet, the countryside lay swathed in bright moonlight. Padded footsteps sounded through the night, spewing out from the mouth of the passageway opened by Thorko and his men. When the party of hooded figures, which had increased by one, reached the entrance, they stopped.

"Curse the moon!" Thorko said, choking on the words. "Why couldn't it have stayed cloudy?"

"Can you do something, my Lord Thorko?" Ujvary asked.

"I thought alchemists could control the elements."

"Those on the earth, my Lord."

"Show us your mighty power, Thorko," Darvula cackled from behind him.

Whirling, he glared at her, his eyes virtually glowing in the darkness. "And you, witch, why don't you conjure up a spell to blacken the moon?"

"The liquids of earth and animals and the powders I concoct are powerful, but I hold no sway over the heavenly lights." Her laughter cackled again, ringing through the night.

"Then it is my task?" Without waiting for an answer, he stepped forward and outside the secret entrance. He reached into his cloak and brought his hand out, clenched in a fist. Pointing to the north, he mumbled an incantation and threw dust he had taken from within his wrap in that direction. He stepped back, waiting.

"How long, my lord?" Ujuvary asked.

"It will not be long, not long at all." He smiled, his white teeth flashing in the semi-darkness of the moon-induced shadows.

The northern horizon seemed to come to life, writhing, undulating and twisting. Clouds quickly grew in size, tumbling upward into the heavens, heap upon heap of gigantic tenebrous piles. The mountainous banks moved swiftly through the night, eerily devoid of wind or sound. Swelling until the skies overhead were filled, they continued moving southward, obliterating the faint starlight and blocking the bright moon.

When the blackness covered the countryside, Thorko turned to his companions. "Come." He stepped into the night, and the others followed. Ujuvary, the alchemist, followed Thorko, and Darvula swept through the darkness behind him. The two henchmen held up the figure of the Countess Elisabeth Bathory Nadasdy.

As if able to see in the stygian night, Thorko unerringly led them northward, away from the castle, avoiding any rocks or boulders that might otherwise block their passage. In minutes, the shadows swallowed them as the small entourage entered the forest fringing the hills.

After several hours, the party made their way deep into the forest. It was only after the clouds had dissipated that the sorcerer called a halt to their flight. Motioning for them to rest in the clearing, he stepped apart from them, peering to the west, lost in deep thought.

Darvula approached him, coughing as if to announce her presence. "My Lord, Thorko?"

At first he didn't answer, appearing to complete the thoughts on which he had been concentrating. When he turned, he stared down at the woman. She wore a bandana around her head, concealing all but a few wisps of hair, while lines in her face belied her age.

"What is it?"

"What are we to do now?" she asked.

"We must bring back to normalcy our mistress, the Countess Bathory Nadasdy. Then we must assure the fact that this will never happen again."

"How are we to do that, my lord?"

"Do what? I grow impatient with your stupid questions, woman."

"Bring her back to normalcy?"

"It is simple."

"But how? She acts as one who is mad. She stares into the night, seeing yet not seeing. We speak to her, and she hears yet does not hear. She speaks but not to us. She speaks to beings and entities we cannot see. What . . . ?"

"And you call yourself a witch?" Thorko threw his head back, laughing but making no sound.

Darvula dropped her head in shame. "I only wished to make you aware of our lady's condition."

Thorko glared at her, his eyes eating through the wrinkled grin. "Yes, but I already know of her condition. I know they have made her like a village idiot, but it is within my power to restore her to her previous state. That is of no consequence. The task is simple."

"When will you perform this . . . this simple task, my lord?" Darvula dropped her

head, concealing the sardonic grin cracking
her face.

"When I wish. right now, I have older,
more important things on my mind."

"What could be more important than
restoring our lady?"

Thorko chuckled, this time in such a
way that the sound unnerved the woman
who fell back several paces.

Noticing the exchange, Ujuvary stepped
forward. "What is it, my lord, that bothers
you?"

"This old hag bothers me. She
questions my strength as a sorcerer. She
nags at me, wondering of my power. She
eats at me like a maggot, asking my plans."

"What is it you wish, My Lord Thorko?"
Ujuvary, slightly bowing her head, stepped
back a pace, showing her respect for Thorko
and at the same time her willingness to be
subject to his every whim and command.
Ujuvary knew well the way of diplomacy. She
felt she could be, in time, an equal to the
sorcerer, but now she had to be as crafty as
he was magically powerful.

"Before I restore the countess to her
former state, it is vital that the coterie be
whole once more. When that is accomplish-
ed, she will have no trouble in accepting her
freedom and her status as a noble woman
once again."

"But restore the coterie, my lord? I do
not understand your words."

"Restore the coterie. Bring back Ilona Joo. Bring back Szentes."

"They are dead, My Lord Thorko. One beheaded. One burned until there was nothing but ashes. I witnessed it myself, concealed in the crowd." Ujuvary kept her eyes diverted from his.

Thorko reached out, grabbing Ujuvary around the throat. With one hand, he lifted the woman above him, shaking her as if she were a piece of cloth. "Dare you question my powers, too? Fool!" He threw her across the clearing.

Ujuvary landed on her back, the breath knocked out of her. Gasping, she clambered to her feet after a few seconds.

Thorko raised both arms in the center of the clearing, spotlighted by the moon that rode at its zenith. "I am Thorko, master of all, master of the earth, master of the universe. Thorko can do anything he wishes. Remember that, you fools!"

The two men assisting the countess swallowed, their mouths and throats dry. For the few coins they had agreed upon to accompany the strange man, they suddenly found themselves wishing they had either demanded more money or had not complied with the request in the first place. Still, they obediently held the noble woman's arms to contain her movements.

Countess Bathory Nadasdy stared at the tall man standing some distance from her. She suddenly cried out, "Thorko! Thorko!

Thorko, my love. You have rescued me. Thorko! Thorko! Thorko!" She repeated his name over and over in a singsong fashion that sent tremors down the backs of the two men on either side.

Ujuvary warily approached Thorko once more. "You misunderstand me, my lord. I do not question your power nor anything about you. I merely wished to know the meaning of your words. That is all."

Thorko laughed. "I will bring Ilona Joo and Szentes back. I know full well that Ilona Joo was beheaded and that Szentes was burned to death. I sat on the roof of the church, watching. I sat with the pigeons as one of them."

Ujuvary bowed her head in awe of the man's statement and obvious abilities, knowing he could do such things without much effort. It would not be beyond his ability to bring back the two who loved Elisabeth Bathory Nadasdy so much. Ujuvary had been a fool to speak in the manner in which she had.

"How, my Lord Thorko, will you accomplish this? Will you need from me? Will you need from Darvula?"

Picking up a stone, he enfolded it in one hand and blew on it. Unfolding his fingers, a brilliant diamond shone brightly in the moonlight. "I have been in knowledge and ability where you are at now. I have been where the old hag, Darvula, is in power and capacity. She is stagnant in her development. You are younger and show more promise. But I need nothing from either of you. I shall render this miracle myself."

"Where, my lord?"

"Where?" He gestured around the clearing. "Here."

"Here? In the woods? You will work your magic in the woods?"

"I work magic wherever and whenever I want."

Ujuvary fell silent.

"You and Darvula take charge of the countess." Raising his voice so they could hear him, he called to the two men. "Build a fire in the center of the clearing."

Ujuvary hastened to do his bidding, taking Darvula with her to the spot where the countess sat, leaning against the bole of a tree. The two men, in turn, walked into the forest, picking up windfallen branches. When they had erected a pile of wood some three or four feet high, they fell back when Thorko waved them away.

Staring first at the cloudless sky, then at the earth beneath his feet, he pointed at the pile of firewood. It burst instantly into flames.

Holding his head in a rigid position, he stared into the dancing fire. His lips barely moved as he spoke words that only he could hear and whose meaning he alone understood.

Shadows clung to his hollow cheeks and sunken eyes, lending an even more skeletal appearance to his thin face. His eyes smouldered like the coals of the fire before him, calling all attention to them and away from his other features. Throwing back his hood, his white hair flowing like a mane, Thorko shook a fist at the heavens, then returned his attention to the fire and the ground beneath his feet.

Flicking his hand, a rod appeared in it, and Thorko touched the ground with it, turning slowly in a circle.

"I am Thorko, who brought himself into being within the belly of his whore mother. Those who are with me know not of me. Behold, I gather together the charm from every place where it is and from every man with whom it is, swifter than the hounds of hell and quicker than light. Grant me the charm that created the forms of being from the mother and which both creates the gods and makes them to be silent and which gives the heat of fire and life unto the gods. Behold, the charm will be given to me from wherever it is and from him with whom it is, swifter than the hounds of hell and quicker than light and faster than a shadow."

The circle complete, he scribbled into the earthern floor of the clearing different characters and words and names of netherworld beings to protect and help him. When he finished, the rod in his hand disappeared, and the sorcerer stood as still as if he had been rendered into a statue.

Throwing his head back, he chanted

loudly. "Ofano. Oblamo. Ospergo. Hola Noa
Massa. Beff. Cletemati. Adonai. Cleona.
Florit. Pax sax sarax. Afa Afca Nostra.
Cerum. Heaium. Lada Frium."

He repeated the chant a second time.
Then for a third time the words were
uttered, floating away on the wind in a
quiet, deliberate way. The two men and the
women holding the countess watched spell-
bound from the shadows of the trees surrounding the small clearing.

Spreading his arms, Thorko seemed to
be calling for silence in the dead calm
holding the forest in its tight grip. Peering
downward at the earth, he continued
chanting. "Cerberus. Hecate. Chaos.
Mercury. Charon. Persephone. Demogor-
gon. Pluto. Earth. Styx. Elysium. Fates.
Furies."

He repeated the strange chain of words
twice before moving to the next ritualistic
prayer, ending with the words, "Venite—
venite—venite!"

When he repeated it the second time
and then a third, one of the men turned to
his companion. "He calls for someone to
come—come—come. Who is it he calls?"

His friend shrugged.

Ujuvary kicked out with her foot,
catching the one who had spoken in the
groin. He yelped from the pain coursing
through his lower body.

"Be quiet, you fool, or you'll call the sorcerer's doom down on all of us."

In his trancelike state, Thorko didn't hear the commotion at the edge of the clearing and continued his invocation.

"I, Thorko, son of Thalda, whose god is Lucifer, call on the powers of evil. Take from the bodies of those deceased the shroud of death. Remove from them the sleep of eternity. Make them whole once more. Tear from them the death given by those who were not empowered to give death. May the groaning of their flesh and their spirits be consumed by thee and breathed full of life in return. May the degradation of their muscles be removed for all time. May the poisons that eat upon their bodies be wiped away. May the maggots of corruption be taken from them forever. Tear from them the ban of life and breathing. Gather together the parts and parcels that comprise them, making them whole once more."

A silence gripped the forest and the clearing, gagging even the night birds whose songs should have been ringing out through the dark.

"Os," Thorko intoned in his deep voice. "Nos. Inos. Tinos. Notinos. Chnotinos. Ochnotinos. Ri. Iri. Riri. Briri. Shabriri." The wind caught the words, carrying them southward over the trees and rocks and trails, southward toward Castle Csejthe.

The guards, still in awe that the laughter and screaming had stopped abruptly several hours before, voiced their thanksgiving that the sky had cleared of the sudden clouds that had risen shortly after the countess had stopped her nightly serenade.

Then a wind, not uncommon for October, rose, moaning and groaning around the castle's towers and buildings.

"It almost sounds like a person speaking in whispers, doesn't it?" one guard remarked absently to his partner.

He listened carefully for a full minute. "It sounds almost as if it's saying something. Listen."

Both men strained their hearing, almost but not quite able to distinguish the words being carried on the wind.

By the time the words floated by the third time, the first guard said, "I tell you, Bela, there are words in the wind this night."

Bela threw back his head and laughed heartily. "You fool. Next you'll be saying that it's the countess and she wants us to come up to dine! You fool. It is the wind and nothing more, I tell you."

The first man fell silent under his compatriot's tongue lashing, but the wind continued, wafting its way down the hillside toward the sleeping village below. Winding its way through the narrow streets, it skirted houses, leaving its magical sounds lingering for a moment before slipping away to another place.

*   *   *

Sandor Werböczi opened his eyes. What was that sound? He nudged Trilka, snoring blissfully next to him.

Startled, she sat up in bed. "What is it? What's wrong? Sandor, why did you wake me up?"

"Listen."

She stared into the darkness, intently listening as she had been ordered.

"What do you hear, Trilka?"

"Nothing."

"The wind. Listen to it."

"Of course I hear the wind. What else?"

"Listen to the wind. It sounds somehow different."

Throwing back the covers, she got out of bed and walked to the window. Opening the shutters, she leaned out. Sandor got up and followed her.

The wind whipped through the streets, moaning its message of necromancy, winding its way around the corners of each building.

"So?" Trilka said, straightening up and glaring at her husband in the pale light of the moon. "So what is different about the wind this night?"

"It sounds different—like a person whispering something. Don't you hear it?"

"I hear the wind, you foolish man." She spun around and went back to bed.

"I wonder what it is saying," Sandor said wistfully from the window. "Look how the dust dances along the street. I can just see it. Look, Trilka, look."

His only answer was a hearty snore.

Yawning, Sandor pulled the shutters closed and returned to bed.

Outside, the dust in the streets and on the rooftops moved, gathering speed as it was carried along by the wind. The gale continued through the village, past the edge of town and centering on the grave-yard next to the small Catholic church. The fieldstone wall surrounding the mounds of earth, marking the final resting places of those who had gone to meet their maker, seemed all the more formidable by the single mound on the outside, along the far wall away from the church. The wind sailed through the cemetery, leaping the wall, forming a funnel of dirt, dust, leaves and small sticks. It seemed to bore into the isolated grave itself.

The earth moved, heaving a bit, then as it erupted, a hand, flesh falling from the bones, thrust up into the night. More con-strictions and seizures loosened most of the ground covering the damned soul's body, which had lain there for four years. Another hand, as skeletal as the first, poked through, free of its mud prison, digging away to allow escape for the rest of the rotting cadaver. When the headless body stood upright, it dumbly froze in position, as if trying to calculate its bearings. The words that were carried on the wind

wrapped about the dead thing, giving it life
and motion, emotion and motivation. It
slowly took one step, then another and
another. Making its way along the stone
wall, it came to the corner and turned. The
wind quickly filled the empty grave. The
rotting body walked until a small pile of
earth blocked its way. Falling to its knees,
the thing began digging, and when it had
cleared a bushel of dirt away, the top of a
head lay exposed. Reaching down, the bony
hands picked it up and set the head in
place. Lying back on the damp grass, the
cadaver waited while the wind continued its
curative moaning, the words crystal clear to
one who would listen. The earth tumbled
back into the smaller hole, filling it.

Little by little the flesh grew, giving
shape and figure to the rotting meat. The
face renewed itself quickly, and the thin,
sharp features of Ilona Joo became recog-
nizable. Once the flesh had been totally
restored, she stood and walked along the
wall toward the town.

The wind hurried on ahead, back toward
the sleeping village, carrying with it certain
dust that had lain about the countryside for
four years, wafting it aloft along the road.
The particles of gray dust gathered together, building a thick, opaque cloud,
which the wind carried toward the village
square.

Wailing louder than before, the wind
rose and fell as it sang its unholy song. One

by one, candles were lighted in homes or shutters thrown open allowing the towns-people to see what sort of storm was blowing through their village. Gusts tore at the shutters, and those windows that had glass and had been opened instantly vomited their curtains in furling salute to the gale.

The people looking out screamed in accompaniment to the whistling tempest. They had never before seen a wind blow along the ground yet not have trees move. A few clouds overhead hung motionless, and the people blessed themselves, praying to the Almighty to spare them from whatever demon was loosed on their town.

Those villagers who lived near the stream that passed on one side of the settle-ment winced when they saw globs of mud sucked from the bed of the small river. The mud and muck flew through the air, straight at the houses, only to swerve at the last minute and career around a corner.

The whirlwind enfolded the entire town, searching and sweeping up every particle of dirt in the area, sifting and sorting it before bringing the gray dust to the center of the settlement where it gathered on the ground. When a rectangular shape had been attained, the gray dust lay several inches deep and a bit over five feet in length. The width, no more than 18 inches, held firm as the gale continued.

Lashing about the shape of dust, the

wind pushed and heaved, formed and
reformed the miniscule pieces of gray ash
together, molding a form and shape of a
large breasted woman. When the shape lay
complete, the wind, the words still there,
wound its way through the gray shape. The
dust darkened in color, turning black, then
dark brown, then a lighter shade of brown
until it took on the color of flesh. Hair, long
turned to carbon, settled to sprout from the
changing head, and the breasts that had
exploded in the fire of death some four
years prior completely reshaped themselves. When the nude body of Szentes had
lain still for a long moment, the eyelids
fluttered and opened.

When she raised her head, Szentes
could see a naked figure walking into the
square, directly toward her. She waited.

In minutes, Ilona Joo stood over her,
smiling. The naked woman reached down,
offering her hand to Szentes, who stood.
They embraced and lustily kissed each
other.

Turning, they made their way through
the narrow, winding street and stopped at a
house where they found women's clothing
drying in the night air, hanging across the
fence. They dressed quickly and started
down the road that would take them past
the mountainous trail that led to Castle
Csejthe and the woodland to the north.

When the wind died down and stopped

blowing altogether, those villagers brave enough to look outside once more saw nothing. Even the leaves seemed to be in the very place they had been the previous day. Candles were extinguished and people returned to bed, wondering how the wind could have blown the way it had and not have disturbed anything, not even the branches on the trees.

Sandor turned over and fell asleep, comforted by Trilka's snoring.

8

Tuesday - 11:59 p.m.

Elizabeth Browne Nargella gazed lanquidly into the dressing table mirror, admiring her oval face. A tiny, curved smile danced on her full mouth. How absolutely lucky for her to enjoy circumstances that allowed her to live beyond anyone's wildest expectations. She had had help, of course, but it had been her discovery that led to the events that marked her life. Holding one hand out, she turned it slowly, catching the light from the lamps on the table. Beautiful! Over the years she had learned that one of the first places a woman, or a man for that matter, began showing signs of aging was the hands. Red spots, wrinkles, loosening skin and yellowing nails all showed that the person's body was beginning to falter and soon the trip through life would be over.

Her discovery, yes, but without the help of Thorko, and Darvula, the long-dead forest witch, and Ujuvary, the ancient alchemist, Elizabeth Browne Nargella would have long since disappeared from the face of the earth. Darvula had died many years before, not too long after Thorko and the others had managed her successful escape. The miracle wrought by Thorko, the mightiest of sorcerers, when he resurrected Ilona Joo and Szentes had completed the events that brought about her own continuation of life.

A light tapping at the door broke her reverie.

"Yes?"

"It is I, Ida."

"Yes, Ida?"

"I have something for you, something nice and warm, to help you sleep better."

"Come in, Ida."

She heard the latch turn and sensed more than heard the door open. It closed with a quiet yet definite click. Turning on the bench she watched Ida cross the room. The woman was tall, well-formed but lean to the point that she resembled a high fashion model. Ida moved not unlike a cat on the prowl for prey, quietly with every muscle keen to the movement of her body. Her small breasts barely jutted out through the high-necked blouse she wore.

"My lady," Ida said when she stood next to Elizabeth and handed her the cup.

"A new one?"

"Yes, my lady."

"How many are in process now?"

"Twelve and another eight in the lower level."

Elizabeth raised the cup to her lips and sipped. Her icy, blue eyes sparkled when the coppery taste exploded in her mouth. Smiling, she looked up at Ida and said, "Very good. You always think of me, don't you, Ida?"

Ida lowered her head at the unexpected compliment. "Of course, my lady."

"Do you love me, Ida?"

"You know I do, my lady."

"And do you love Aleigha as well?"

Ida blushed and nodded.

"That's fine. I wouldn't want you to feel jealousy whenever Thorko comes to visit."

"I worship you, my lady, and I love Aleigha. There is nothing I wouldn't do for you. I believe you know that."

"Of course. I find it reassuring to have you state your allegiance to me on occasion." Elizabeth raised the cup again, gulping down the blood, only to have it spill over her lip and onto the lap of her gown. When she had drained every drop, she set the cup on the saucer and examined the sanguine blot on her thigh. Rubbing it, she worked the blood through the material onto

her leg beneath. "When will there be enough
for me to bathe?"

Ida pursed her lips. "I would think in a
few days or so. Surely by the weekend. Is
that soon enough?"

"It will have to do, won't it? In the meantime, I imagine I will have to shower with
ordinary water." She stood, opening her
gown at the same time. Letting it slip from
her shoulders, she walked, nude, to the
bathroom that adjoined her bedroom and
dressing room.

Ida hurried ahead of her, turning on the
water. Shower heads in the ceiling and on
each of three walls spewed out steaming hot
water. Adjusting the temperature, she
stepped aside, making way for Elizabeth.

The countess stepped in, throwing her
head back to allow the water to run over her
face. Cascading down her front, back and
sides, she revelled in the relaxing spray.
Rivulets tumbled over and around her
breasts, dripping from her nipples, blazing
new trails as the water writhed its way to the
tile floor.

Ida's hand appeared through the partially open doorway, handing her a bar of
perfumed soap.

"Thank you, Ida." Her voice rose above
the pounding water in a musical way, con-
tradicting the bestial desires and tastes
coursing through her brain and body.

She soaped her well-proportioned
limbs, spreading the frothy lather to her

breasts, abdomen and genitals, rubbing
and massaging the scented cleanser into
her skin. It felt good but was as nothing
when compared to her own special baths. A
smile spread across her soapy face, her eyes
sparkling. Countess Elisabeth Bathory
Nadasdy, who had adopted the more common name of Elizabeth Browne Nargella,
was happy.

After almost an hour had passed, she
stepped from the shower room, accepting
the bath sheet held by Ida. Ida diligently
helped her mistress towel her body dry,
making certain that she touched each
private part several times in the process.

"Would my lady desire a massage
before retiring?"

"That would be most lovely, Ida. You do
such wonderful things with your hands."
She passed through her dressing room into
the large bedroom. Sliding onto the
canopied bed, she lay belly down, resting
her head on one arm.

Ida quickly undressed and opened a
bottle of oil on the dressing table in the
adjoining room. Returning to the bed, she
climbed on, straddling the countess' feet.

"A woman, my lady, is like unto a fruit
which will not yield its sweetness until it is
rubbed between hands," Ida said, lightly
massaging the Achilles tendons above the
heels.

"You have said that so many times over
the years, Ida. I believe it. I also believe that

only another woman can release that sweetness. As much as I adore Thorko, it is you
who brings out my deepest feminine
feelings."

"Thank you, my lady." Ida fell silent,
and the countess closed her eyes as the
woman's fingers continued their magical
spell. She touched the right places, stoking
Elizabeth's desire to a fevered pitch. Little
innuendoes she had learned over the centuries would be brought to the fore, tiny
subtleties that would relax inhibitions even
in the most frigid person.

Ida stroked her fingertips up Elizabeth's
legs on the inside of the calves, stopping at
the knees, only to return to the ankles along
the outer extremeties of her lower legs.
Each time she reached the back of the knee,
her fingertips lingered, stroking and
rubbing ever so gently, sending micro-
scopic charges of desire racing through the
countess' body. Over and over, Ida repeated
the strokes, never varying the rhythm or the
motion.

After a while, she moved up the legs,
straddling them before reaching for the
bottle of oil. Pouring a small amount in the
cup of her hand, she applied it to Elizabeth's
buttocks and small of the back. She spread
the liquid in broad, circular sweeping
motions without applying too much
pressure. Years of experience had taught
her the right amount of force to use in
massaging. Concentrating on the firm

cheeks, she traced a line on the inside of
each thigh with her thumbs, lightly trailing
the tips of her fingers along the back to the
legs. Firm but gentle pressure rippled her
taut skin, and Elizabeth moaned from the
pleasure of Ida's fingers. When the tall
woman's fingertips reached the small of the
back, she separated her hands, one to either
side, lightly passing over the hip bones and
returning to the base of the buttocks. Her
thumbs   tenderly   brushed   Elizabeth's
genitals but didn't linger.

Instead, Ida moved up to straddle the
lower back and worked her hands up toward
the neck and shoulders, bringing her fingertips back along the ribcage, her stroke light
and feathery, never varying the pattern for
fear of distracting the countess. When she
finished with the back, Ida moved up even
higher until she could reach the blond hair
falling to one side, away from Elizabeth's
relaxed face. Handling the hair as if
shampooing it, she rubbed it, stroked it and
brushed it between her hands. She continued the gentle oscillations for several
minutes and then, without speaking, moved
off the body of her mistress.

Elizabeth turned, knowing full well the
massage was but half completed. When she
lay on her back, Ida continued her erotic
massage, constantly keeping one hand at
all times in contact with her lady's body.
Finishing with the hair, once her mistress
was on her back, Ida leaned forward, taking

first the right ear into her fingers. She
delicately massaged it, rubbing the lobe
and upper ear. Leaning even closer she ran
her tongue over it, quickly jabbing it inside
several times before blowing gently into it.
Then she repeated the ritual with the other
ear.

Pouring more oil into her hand, she
dribbled it onto Elizabeth's breasts, gently
sliding her hands over them. Moving her
own body down the length of her mistress',
she slid her hands downward, over the flat
stomach, toward the navel and pubic bone
where the fingers turned outward to return
with delicate circular movements to the
breasts, exerting light pressure all the way.
When she passed over the navel, she
pressed more, creating a flow of blood to
the genitals. Reaching the pubic bone, she
increased the pressure each time she
passed over it. The last time, she allowed
her hand to remain over the bone, pressing,
releasing, pressing open the blood vessels
to the pubic area.

Slipping from the straddling position,
Ida moved to one side of Elizabeth and in
turn massaged first the hands, then the
feet. Returning her attention to the hands,
she ran a finger from the back of one then
the other to the elbows before reaching
down to touch the same place with her
tongue, moving it along the same route,
creating the same pattern her finger had
made.

Restraddling Elizabeth's body, she
stroked the woman's breasts with grazing
touches to the sides and up and over the
smooth mounds. Each time she came closer
to the aureoles, she changed her touch to
the most delicate of contacts and brought
the nipples up to an erect, taut position.

Elizabeth shuddered. She was ready.

Ida lay down beside her and took her
mistress' head in her arm. Reaching over,
she kissed her full on the mouth, their
tongues touching.

When their lips parted, Elizabeth
pushed Ida away.

"When is Thorko coming back?"

"I have no idea, my lady." Ida did all she
could to refrain from snapping at Elizabeth.
She had not worked so hard to bring her to
the state of readiness only to have the
image of Thorko, the sorcerer, rear up
between them.

Elizabeth caught the tremor in Ida's
voice. "I'm sorry, Ida. I shouldn't have
mentioned him now."

"It . . . it's nothing, my lady." Ida felt
she had triumphed. Hardly ever did the
countess apologize to anyone. Still, she had
to do so under the circumstances, for if Ida
left, the countess would spend a miserable
night without anyone to pay her physical
homage.

Elizabeth propped herself up on one
elbow. "I do long for him but you are every
bit as good, when he is not around. How can

a dead thing like you have such feelings and be able to arouse the fire of passion so hotly within me?"

Ida looked away. She hated when the countess reminded her that she and Aleigha were not as their mistress. Darvula had died long ago. Ujuvary had balked at Thorko's offer of extended life because she felt her ability as an alchemist could achieve the same. It hadn't, and Ujuvary appeared as the most ancient of people. They had no money problems because of Ujuvary's power to turn worthless baubles into gems.

On the other hand, Thorko had not changed in over a millenium, he claimed. But she thought it cruel to be reminded that Aleigha and she had been executed and brought back to a form of life from which there was no escape, as long as Thorko willed it.

Ida's hand moved to her throat, the fingers lightly touching the long since whitened scar circumventing her neck where the executioneer's axe had severed her head from her body.

"I . . . I am happy to be of service to you, my lady."

Elizabeth leaned down, kissing Ida on the mouth again, her hand inching its way along the thin body.

Wednesday - 12:09 a.m.

Aleigha stepped to the next door after

closing the one on Dana. Opening it, she turned on the lights and checked the girl hanging from the ceiling. Assured that all was well there, she went to the next cell and then the next. Each was equipped in the same manner. Each had the tools for draining blood and torture. Each held a young woman, hanging from the ceiling.

At the last of 12 such doors, she turned on the light. A smirk crossed her pouty mouth. She remembered this one—long black hair that hung to her waist, large breasts and a certain paleness to her skin that made her most attractive and appealing to Aleigha.

Stepping inside, she turned up the lights a bit, and after a few moments, the girl's eyelids fluttered. The girl was weak enough that the nerve retardent drug was no longer necessary.

"Who's there?" she managed in a hoarse whisper.

"Aleigha, my sweet." She laid her clothes on a small table and donned a white coat.

"What do you want? Why don't you just kill me and get it over with?"

"I couldn't do that. I could not deprive the countess of your blood and me of my pleasure."

"You get pleasure from doing this?"

"Of course. I love to watch beautiful girls slowly give their lives for my mistress."

"Who is she?"

"No one you would know. Rest assured

though that it is a privilege to be where you are. She would never consider a girl who was not young and beautiful or healthy and vibrant the way you are."

"You mean were, lady. I feel about as strong as a kitten."

Aleigha moved closer. The girl fascinated her. The large breasts. The smooth alabaster skin. The long flowing black hair. She loved the girl. She loved all the girls. She loved the pain she could inflict on them as well as the pleasure she experienced from it.

When she stood next to the girl, she encircled the tiny waist with her arms, hugging the helpless form.

"Stop. Please stop."

Aleigha ignored the plaintive request, kissing the girl on the breasts, biting savagely at the dark nipples.

The girl cried out.

Aleigha ran her hands down the full length of the body, pressing in with her nails, breaking the skin, noticing the infinitesimal amount of blood she drew. The girl would not live much longer. She had been drained each day, a little at a time, giving her blood for the benefit of one mightier then the street girl could ever imagine.

She continued fondling the fair-skinned body. The girl, although weak, still knew what was happening and reacted violently, gagging at the thought of the woman touching her with such intimacy. Her stomach, empty for days, heaved drily.

"Stop that!" Aleigha cried. "Stop that this instant. Do you hear me?"

The girl paid no mind to the unreasonable demand.

Angry and frustrated at the show of disobedience, Aleigha stomped to the rack along the wall. Tearing off her white coat, she threw it on the floor and picked up a club.

"I'll show you, you bitch!"

The girl's eyes widened, horrified at the expression on the woman's face. Struggling in vain, she sobbed, "No! No! Don't hurt me! I'm sorry for whatever it is I've done. Don't hurt me!"

Aleigha felt the familiar rage building within her. An uncontrollable passion rose within her to the point of boiling over, and Aleigha leaped on the girl, tearing at her with her nails and teeth. Biting, scratching, chewing, beating with her fists, she attacked the helpless girl. Her savagery unabated, she tore away chunks of flesh with her teeth, spitting them out only to attack another new, unaffected area.

The girl's screams grew weaker and weaker until she made no sounds of any sort, and Aleigha, realizing she had triumphed, fell back, blood running down her front, dripping from her lower pouty lip. She panted, catching her breath. She wanted Ida. She wanted Ida desperately, and Ida was with the countess. What could

Aleigha do? Grabbing her genitals, she masturbated savagely, waves of passion flowing through her body—the body that had been burned to ashes at one time, only to be reformed by the wizardry of Thorko.

When she climaxed, Aleigha fell to the floor in an exhausted heap, sobbing uncontrollably.

Wednesday · 1:45 a.m.

Rhonda jerked awake. What was that? Someone was crying. No, wailing was a better description. "Who . . . who's here?" she asked, when she recalled where she was and what had happened to her and the others.

There was no answer, but the crying continued, even more wildly than before she had called out. Whoever it was, and Rhonda felt certain it would be a girl, cried and panted, sobbed and moaned, all at one time.

"Hey," Rhonda said firmly, "don't cry. It won't help. Talk to me."

"What's the matter, Rhon?" Judy asked as she awakened.

"Someone's really crying up a heap. We didn't do that, did we?"

"Hey, we had each other. Remember?" Judy listened for a moment. "Boy, you're not kidding that she's crying. Hey, kid, come on. Knock it off. Tell us who you are. Talk to us. It'll help. I'm Judy. Jude to my

closest friends. The other gal talking is
Rhonda or Rhon, whichever. What's your
name? Who are you?"

The crying diminished until the only
sound coming out of the blackness was
sobbing. Then, between deep gasps for air,
she said, "Lin . . . Linda. Where am I? What
is this place? How . . . how'd I get here? Who
are you two? What are you doing here? And
why am I tied up like this? Who took my
clothing? Tell me, please. In the name of
God, tell me what's going on."

One by one the other girls recovered
from the gassing, and each took turns ver-
bally comforting the new arrival and
answering to the best of their ability the
myriad questions she had—the same ones
that each of them still held within their own
minds.

It took a long time to quiet Linda, and
when she seemed to be subdued, Coral said,
"Let's take roll call. We were either put to
sleep so they could bring Linda in, or they
brought her in and took someone out. I'll
start. Everybody just say your name. Coral."

"Judy."

"Rhonda."

As each name was intoned, the girls
began feeling a bit more secure with the
knowledge that more than likely none had
been taken. After Sherry, Daun, Pam and
Margaret had added theirs, they waited.

"Hey, Linda, speak up or we'll think you
took off and left all of us here," Judy said,

forcing a laugh.

"Lin . . . Linda. Linda Polchow."

They waited. Someone was missing after all.

"Do it again," Coral ordered after several minutes. "Coral."

Judy answered next, and one by one the names were repeated.

"Dana's gone," Coral said quietly as if announcing the fact the girl had died or been in a fatal accident.

An ear-splitting silence fell over the girls, its intensity matching the blackness enfolding them.

"Hey?" Rhonda whispered.

"What?" Judy answered.

"Did you hear something just then?"

No one spoke. Each girl held her breath.

"I don't hear anything," Coral said.

"No. Listen. I swear I heard something," Rhonda said.

They listened again.

After a few more minutes passed, Coral said, "What'd it sound like?"

Rhonda didn't answer immediately. She coughed. "It sounded like—like someone screaming."

"I didn't hear anything. Did anybody else?" Judy asked.

One by one the girls said they hadn't heard anything other than their own voices, heartbeats or breathing.

"Try again. Listen very carefully," Judy

said. "Hold your breath if you have to. No sound at all. All right?"

They sat perfectly still, holding their breaths. Then they heard just a tiny, miniscule sound not unlike a scream, miles away, feeding down to them from some-place overhead. It wasn't loud. It could barely be heard. But each girl reacted in her own way to the thought that someone else outside their room actually existed and was in trouble like they were.

Each girl held her breath, listening. Each prayed that such would not be their fate.

After a while the screaming died out, and they relaxed for a moment.

"Listen," Judy ordered.

They strained every fiber but weren't certain if the cries had begun again.

"I swear I heard someone screaming again," Judy said.

"Shh," one of the other girls ad-monished. "Everybody listen."

The tiny, pitiful sounds filtered to them again.

"I hear it now," Linda said. "I didn't before, but I do now. What is it?"

"We're not certain," Coral said. "We usually hear them right after somebody's been taken from us."

"You mean that might be Dana?"

No one answered, and the silence raged at them.

"Hey," Rhonda said brightly.

"What is it?" Judy asked.

"I think I've found a loose thread in my belt."

"The one around your middle?" Coral asked.

"Yeah. It's unraveling. I pull and it comes out. Maybe it'll fall apart if I pull all of it out."

"Let me feel mine once," Coral said. "Everybody else do the same. Maybe we can get loose."

Each girl ran her fingers over the wide belt with which they were tethered to the wall.

"I can't get mine," one cried.

"I think I've got a loose one," another said brightly.

For the first time since any of them had been kidnapped, a glimmer of hope shone through.

Rhonda continued pulling hers out until there was no more. "Hurry, you guys, I think I'm going to be free in a minute."

Wednesday - 2:30 a.m.

Rose Gordon stared into the blackness of their bedroom. Swinging her legs over the edge of the bed, she turned on the night-stand light. Her husband, Ray, sat up in bed.

"What's the matter, Rose? Can't sleep?"

"I'm worried sick. We should have heard from the girls by now. I'll bet Bob and Clare

are both going nuts. I think something happened to them."

"I think you're panicking over nothing. They left the day before yesterday. Monday. They were supposed to get to Rapid City Tuesday. Today's Wednesday, and it's too early for them to call."

"But damnit, Ray, they had explicit instructions to call home the minute they got there. Why didn't they?"

"You know kids, Rose. Christ! It's the first time away from home for both Rhonda and Judy. They're excited and aren't thinking about explicit instructions their folks gave 'em."

"Something's happened to them. I just know it. You don't give a damn."

"You don't know something's happened for certain."

"You don't know that it hasn't, Ray."

"And I do give a damn, Rose. Jesus Christ, Rhonda's my daughter. I'd kill any sonofabitch who laid a hand on her in the wrong way. You know that. I think you're upset because they haven't gone along with your 'explicit' instructions—yours and Clare's. I'm sure Bob's thinking along the same lines as me."

"Call the police. Please, Ray? Call the police."

"I want you to think for a minute and put yourself in Rhonda's place, Rose. How would you feel if your folks allowed you to go to a resort center like Rapid City to work for the summer? You'd feel pretty darn grown-up, wouldn't you?"

Rose didn't respond.

"Now, let's say, you get all carried away with the excitement of being there with your best friend, and you're meeting new people and being trained for your new job, and you totally forget about calling home to tell Mommy and Daddy that you got there all right, that the bus wasn't hijacked and driven to Cuba or that the driver took a wrong turn and got totally lost."

Rose couldn't help but smile at Ray's explanation. "You might be right, Ray, but damnit, it just isn't like Rhonda not to call. Or Judy for that matter."

"At best it's barely twenty-four hours since they would be missing if something did happen, but I don't think it did. I tell you what, honey. If we don't hear from them by tomorrow night, we'll call the police. Is that fair enough?"

"Do we have to wait that long?"

"Do you want to embarrass the crap out of your only child by having the police walk up to her in front of other people and say, 'If you're Rhonda Gordon, you're supposed to call home to your mother.' She'd shit green, I tell you."

Rose pursed her lips. "I guess you might have a point. Clare said Bob said something pretty similar, now that I think about it. At the time, I guess I wasn't thinking too clearly. All right, Ray. If we don't hear by five o'clock tomorrow night, we call the police."

"Six o'clock."

"Why?"

"Rapid City is an hour behind us. Maybe she'll call when she gets home from work. Do you have the number of the boarding house where she and Judy are staying?"

"Yes."

"Why didn't you call it?"

"I . . . I guess I didn't want to embarrass her either."

"See? We'll call there first. Why bring the cops into it if we don't have to?"

"I guess you're right, Ray."

"Of course I'm right. Now get in bed, turn out the light and go to sleep. I've got a big day ahead of me tomorrow."

Rose reached out, pulling the chain on the lamp. The darkness spilled in on her, and she slipped between the sheets. Lying on her back, she stared into the darkness, thinking of Rhonda.

Next to her, Ray turned over, staring into the black corner of the room, wishing Rhonda were in her room down the hall.

9

Wednesday - 10:00 a.m.

"To stay young, send $39.95 for a one month's supply of *Sta-Yung,* or dial 1-800-STA-YUNG. That's 1-800-STA-YUNG, and we'll rush you a one month's supply of *Sta-Yung*. That's 1-800-STA-YUNG. Offer may be withdrawn without notice. Hurry. Do it now."

Aleigha smiled at the television set. "Such fools," she muttered. Her mistress, the countess, had the secret to eternal youth. This stuff advertised on television had to be something phony. She refocused her attention on the small set beneath the upper kitchen cabinets when the morning news continued.

"Union negotiators have announced that agreement on a new contract for the local carpenters has been reached. Union members are expected to ratify the agreement this morning at 9:00 a.m. at the Union Hall. Workers then can report to their jobs." The announcer shuffled papers and continued. "With the seven month labor strike over, the carpenters and the other unions, which refused to cross the picket lines during the shutdown, will be able to complete many of the jobs that were left in various stages of completion. The new office building on Phillips Avenue, for instance, will be finished within six months. Plans to pour concrete are being made for tomorrow morning, according to Bo Stewart, superintendent of construction for Richard's Construction." A heavyset man suddenly filled the screen, virtually repeating word for word what the announcer had just said.

Aleigha whirled around when Ida entered the kitchen.

"Good morning, Aleigha," she said, her voice carrying a musical lilt.

Aleigha pouted. She hated those mornings when Ida came down after spending a night with the countess. Aleigha much preferred Ida spending her nighttime hours with her. She frowned. Was she jealous? Of course, she was. Over the years, her frequency of being summoned to the countess' bedroom had grown less and less until at best it had become almost non-existent. The only consolation she could draw from the situation was Ida's anger whenever Thorko arrived unexpectedly and the countess paid him, her full attention, virtually ignoring Ida. Then Aleigha became deliriously happy. Ida was all hers, and she enjoyed every second, every kiss, every touch and caress.

But this morning Aleigha felt concerned for what she had done the previous night. She hadn't meant to kill the girl. She had simply gotten carried away, biting and scratching. It was all Ida's fault, wasn't it? She should pay more attention to Aleigha, then Aleigha wouldn't do such things. She wondered if Ida would detect her uneasiness. A chill ran down her spine, and she knew the woman was intensely watching her. Wheeling about, she found Ida glaring at her.

"What's wrong, Ida?"

"Indeed? What *is* wrong, Aleigha? You tell me. You have done something you shouldn't have. What?"

Aleigha looked away, knowing full well guilt had to be showing on her face as surely as if the word had been printed on her forehead. "Nothing. I've done nothing."

"You lie. Tell me."

"I've done nothing out of the ordinary." That was no lie, and she smiled confidently. Perhaps this one time she could bluff her way through the situation.

"So what have you done within the

framework of the ordinary? Tell me,
Aleigha. You know I'll find out sooner or
later."

Aleigha fell silent and looked away.

"What did you do last night after I went
to the countess?"

Aleigha smiled. "I checked out the
rooms to make certain that all was well."

Ida hesitated. "And?"

"Everything was fine."

"Was fine? How is everything *now*,
Aleigha?"

"I suppose things are much the same as
I left them last night. I haven't checked this
morning." She directed her attention to the
coffee pot.

Her hesitant manner told Ida that something was amiss someplace, and it was her
duty to discover what it might be. "What is
wrong, Aleigha? Why can't you look me in
the eye?"

"Nothing is wrong."

"There *is* something wrong. I know you,
Aleigha, and I know when you are lying. And
you're lying to me now. What is wrong?"

Aleigha's heart pounded, not that she
was in any danger from either Ida or the
countess. Her main concern simply lay in
the disposal of a body when they hadn't yet
planned on having to do so. The only thing
she felt anxious about at that moment was
Ida's air of superiority when she would learn
that one of the girl's had died pre-
maturely—and how she had died. Aleigha

couldn't help her wild, uncontrollable
passions for girls' bodies and the maddening desire to bite them before, during or
after having touched them and made love
with them. Ida had always felt safe with
Aleigha because of her age. She had been 15
years older than Aleigha when they were
executed. Nor was it that Ida was unat-
tractive. Ida was radiantly beautiful as was
the countess. Aleigha envied them their
stature. Despite her shortness, she had a
sensual body, one that not only aroused Ida
and the countess at times but herself as
well. She loved her body; touching it and
caressing it made her feel warm and good
all over. She looked up to find Ida
scrutinizing her. She might as well tell her
and get it over.

"One of the girl's died last night."

"Is that all?" Ida appeared relieved.

Aleigha nodded, failing to conceal the
expression of physical gratification she had
experienced while biting the girl to death
and the magnificent climax she had attained immediately thereafter.

Ida half-closed her eyes. "How did she
die?"

"I imagine it was from loss of blood and
the accompanying shock."

"You're certain that's all?"

Aleigha shrugged.

"Where is she? Which room? Show me!"

Aleigha looked up, startled. Ida loved
eroticism but had never developed

Aleigha's taste for the bizarre thrills that accompanied dealing out pain and torture to their victims. She had seen Ida on rare instances stroke a breast or fondle a girl's genitals. Still, as soon as Aleigha brought out the instruments for drawing blood or the other tools with which she had become so adept, Ida would quickly close her eyes or leave the room. Aleigha swallowed and took a tentative step toward the hallway lined with the heavy doors.

"You normally dislike things like this, Ida. Why do you want—?"

"Because," she said, interrupting, "I don't believe she simply died. Was she finished giving her blood for the countess?"

"She had some yet—not much, I assure you."

"Show me, Aleigha."

"Very well." The shorter woman hurried across the room to the door leading to the hallway off the kitchen. "I hope the sight of her makes you ill."

"That's not very nice of you, Aleigha."

"You spend all night with the countess and then come down here accusing me of all sorts of things after I had to spend practically the whole night alone. It's not fair of you, Ida."

Ida stopped in the center of the room, "Perhaps you're right. Maybe I am being unreasonable with you. You're probably frustrated. Am I right, darling?"

Aleigha turned, keeping her hand on

the knob. She nodded and opened the door.
"Maybe the two of us could take a nap this
afternoon. Would that be possible?"

"Perhaps. I think I won't look at the
girl."

"Oh, no. That you are going to do. You'll
see. She hasn't died any differently than
most of the others. Come on. Ida. Follow
me!"

"But . . ."

Aleigha realized she had the upper hand
now and pressed in for the victory she could
realize by making Ida look at the dead girl
hanging from the ceiling. "Come, Ida, you
wanted to see this."

Ida followed, half-heartedly protesting.
"But I said it wasn't necessary for me to see
it."

Whirling about, Aleigha glared angrily
at her, in full control. "Come here, Ida," she
ordered, opening the door to her right. She
stepped back, gesturing with a sweep of her
arm for the taller woman to enter.

Eyes cast down, Ida entered the chilly
room. Aleigha followed her and turned on
the lights, spinning the rheostat to its
highest reading. Brightness flooded the
room as Ida looked up.

"*Aleigha!*" The word escaped from her
like a gas. "What have you done? This is
worse than I've ever seen."

The girl's chalky skin stood out in sharp
contrast to the dark streaks of gore that had
dried on her body during the night. Bite

marks covered her arms, legs and body. One breast had been torn open, and her nose had been bitten off, down to the bone.

Feeling her stomach heave, Ida spun around to block out the sight. Aleigha stood behind her, rubbing her crotch and fondling her large breasts.

"Let's get out of here, Aleigha," she said, stepping around the smiling woman.

Reluctantly, Aleigha turned, darkened the room and closed the door behind her. "What do you want, Ida?"

"We'll have to make plans for disposing of the remains."

"You're so blasted proper at times, I could puke," Aleigha growled.

"Perhaps my propriety is the thing that attracts the countess to me more than you. I appreciate your lovemaking, but I do not understand the vicarious pleasures you receive when you torture these young girls. Do you have any idea what we should do with the body? The lime pit has not been enlarged, and we can't allow the body to hang longer than today. We'll have to think of something else."

Both women frowned for a moment before Aleigha brightened. "I have an idea. I just heard on television that the office building on Phillips Avenue, the one that's been under construction for a long time, is going to have concrete poured tomorrow morning. Perhaps Edward could bury the body where they're going to pour concrete and then no one would ever find it."

Ida smiled. "That's an excellent idea. I'll have Edward take the body tonight. It's the middle of the week, and there shouldn't be too many people out after midnight."

Aleigha stepped into the kitchen behind Ida. "Something else we could do in the event the construction site doesn't work is use the garbage disposal unit. I've done that in the past."

Ida shuddered. "I imagine you enjoyed it?"

Aleigha nodded. "I'd rather enjoy you sometime today."

"Perhaps. The countess asked about taking a bath. How long will it be before there is enough blood?"

"By Friday or Saturday. We'll put a fresh one in the place where the one died last week, but I won't rush the draining. The slower we take it, the longer they last."

"What'll you tell the countess if she wants to look at the rooms today?"

An expression of fear crossed Aleigha's face, her dark eyes narrowing, her lip pouting. "I don't know. Do you think she'd tell Thorko when he comes back?"

Ida shrugged. "Who knows when Thorko will be back? I don't think it would make much difference to her one way or the other if the girl is dead by reason of loss of blood or that she succumbed the way she did.

Where's Edward?"

"I don't know. I haven't seen him yet. I suppose he's still in his room if he isn't washing the car."

"Go find him and tell him that he'll be busy this evening. Don't tell him what it is he'll be doing. He'll find out soon enough. It's a miracle that he doesn't become squeamish over the work he does in picking up the girls."

"As long as you give him his daily ration of heroin, he'll behave. The day he doesn't I'd like to have him in one of the rooms for a few hours to work out some ideas I've developed." Aleigha ran her tongue over her lips and left the kitchen. She hurried through the hallway bordering the dining room and turned to make her way through the long corridor that passed by the living room, parlor, library and sewing room. At the end, after passing through French doors that separated the servants quarters from the rest of the household, she stopped at the last door on her left. Knocking softly, she waited for a moment before knocking again, louder than the first time. The door, standing ajar, swung in a bit. She saw Edward sprawled on his single bed, head back. Noting the syringe on the bedside table, she shook her head. He'd be out for several hours yet, and by dark he'd be ready to perform the task she had made necessary with her frenzied attack the previous night.

10

Marion, South Dakota

Wednesday - 5:01 p.m.

Ann Polchow locked the door to her shop. An unnatural sense of panic tore at her heart. Why hadn't Linda called? Was her daughter so busy that she couldn't find the time to call her mother and give her the telephone number where she could be reached? It wasn't like Linda. She had always been reliable and dependable. If she said she'd do something, her mother could always rest assured that the task would be performed. But now this feeling of longing to hear her daughter's voice virtually overwhelmed her.

Stepping from the curb, she crossed the street, walking toward the hotel. When she reached the west side, she continued south hurrying toward her home. It had been so lonely the first day that Linda had been gone but everything seemed to brighten considerably when she had called from the hotel where she had gotten a room.

Ann quickened her step. She had to get home. She wanted to call that hotel in Sioux Falls. Perhaps Linda was still there and for some reason the new job hadn't worked out. Maybe her daughter was ashamed of that and had planned on not calling until she had found another job. That had to be it.

She turned into the walkway that led to her front porch. The house had been built sometime in the 1920s, and she and her husband had worked hard to pay it off. Now she lived in it alone. Her husband had died, her son lived in Sioux City, and her daughter had left to conquer the world.

Ann fought back the tears she felt forming. Silly fool! She was thinking only of herself. She had to keep Linda's well-being uppermost in her mind, and that called for her to check on her daughter's where-abouts.

Once inside the house she made a pot of coffee and went to the telephone. Opening the phone book, she found the number of the hotel she had jotted down when Linda had given it to her. She picked up the receiver and dialed the number.

"Minnehaha Hotel," a nasal voice said.

Ann winced at the sound. "Yes. I'd like to speak to Linda Polchow. Is she in?"

"Just a minute."

Ann nervously twisted the phone cord while she waited.

"Ain't got nobody here by that name, lady."

"What? You must be mistaken. She called me from there Tuesday. She had a room there."

"Just a minute."

After what seemed an eternity, during which Ann mumbled a prayer under her breath, the man came back.

"Yeah. She checked in on Monday and out on Tuesday. She didn't leave no forwardin' address."

"Are you absolutely positive?"

" 'Course I am. I been in the hotel business for thirty-four years and know how to keep records. She checked in Monday—"

"I know that. That's when she called me the first time and gave the hotel's number."

"—and out on Tuesday."

"That's when she called me and said she had a job. You're sure she didn't leave a forwarding address or telephone number?"

"Nope. Nothin'."

Ann bit her lip. Something was wrong. She sensed it. She knew it. But what? What could she do from Marion? A tear formed, and she jumped at the sound of the man's voice.

"Hey? Is that it?"

"What? Oh, yes, thank you." She hung up.

She had to do something, but what? For a long minute, Ann stared at the telephone and then went into the kitchen, her shoulders slumped.

Wednesday - 6:11 p.m.

"Is this O'Malley's Boarding House?" Ray Gordon asked.

"Yes. This is Joan O'Malley."

"My name is Ray Gordon. I believe my daughter is staying at your place this summer. Could I speak to her? She's working at a motel there in Rapid City."

"What's her name? We have lots of people staying here for the summer."

Ray grinned foolishly. "That's right. It's Rhonda Gordon. I suppose it would help if I gave you her name." He laughed a bit to cover his own embarrassment.

"Rhonda Gordon? Rhonda Gordon." The woman repeated the name several times, as if trying to place it. "You're certain she was supposed to stay here at O'Malley's Boarding House?"

"Yes. The employment agency said that you people had a setup with several places that employ high school and college kids during the summer. Is that right?"

"Yes, we do have such an arrangement, but I've met no one named Rhonda Gordon. Where was she supposed to work? Which motel?"

Ray put his hand over the mouthpiece

and turned to his wife, who anxiously waited in the doorway of the kitchen. "What was the name of the motel where she was supposed to work? I can't think of it."

"Collins Motor Inn," she said, her voice cracking.

Ray repeated the name of the motel.

"Yes, that's right. We have several people staying here who work there. When was she supposed to be here?"

"She and Judy Merton left Sioux Falls Monday. They were supposed to be at the motel on Tuesday afternoon for work assignments and one thing and another. You're absolutely certain you don't have Rhonda Gordon? What about Judy? Is she there? Can I speak to her?" Ray's voice raised several decibels as it usually did whenever he became upset or angry.

"I'm sorry, Mr. Gordon. Your daughter isn't here. I'd suggest you call the motel. Perhaps they sent her someplace else to live during her stay here. That could be it."

"Do you have the number of the motel?" He sensed the panic rising within him.

"I've got it, Ray," Rose said, handing him a damp piece of paper she had been holding in her hand.

"Never mind," he said quickly. "I've got it right here. Thanks for your help. Goodbye." He hung up before the woman could say anything else.

"I knew something was wrong," Rose said, turning away from her husband while he dialed the number. "Oh God, where's my daughter? Where is she?"

Ray waited while the relays clicked into place. They had called Bob and Clare Merton shortly before 6:00 o'clock. Judy's parents were just as upset because they too hadn't heard from their daughter. At least they weren't being cavalier when it came to knowing of her whereabouts.

"Collins Motor Inn," the man said, his voice crashing into Ray's thoughts.

"Yes. I'm calling from Sioux Falls. Do you have a Rhonda Gordon working there?"

"I'll give you the personnel office. I believe there's still someone there."

Ray drummed his fingers on the table, impatient with the delay.

"Personnel, Sally Rambeau speaking."

"I'm calling from Sioux Falls. Do you have a Rhonda Gordon working there?"

"One moment. Let me check. The name seems to be familiar."

Ray smiled reassuringly at his wife. Thank God! The woman knew Rhonda's name. That meant Rhonda was working there if the name seemed familiar.

"Yes. Now I know why the name was familiar. She and a Judy Merton were supposed to report for orientation yesterday at one o'clock."

"What do you mean 'were supposed to'? Did they or didn't they?"

"They didn't. Of course that happens a lot of the time, and we don't pay too much attention to such things. You see, a lot of people will apply for work here in the Hills and then find something better, closer to home, or they decide they don't want to spend the summer away from their families and don't bother to call us or the employment agency through whom they were hired in the first place. It's rather irksome at times, but we—"

Ray hung up without saying anything.

Rose looked at him, knowing full well what he had been told. Her throat constricted.

"I'd better call Bob and Clare. See what they want to do. Neither Rhonda or Judy showed up yesterday."

"Oh, my God," Rose moaned.

Wednesday - 6:29 p.m.

"Jesus Christ!" Bob Merton yelped when Ray finished telling him what he had learned. "Call the fucking police. Right now!"

Ray wanted to tell him to simmer down while condemning himself for his own attitude the previous night. They should have done something right then, but he had insisted to Rose that everything was fine.

"You'd better call them yourself, Bob. They'll ask questions Rose and I can't answer. They'll probably want a picture, too. I think you should call about Judy, and I'll call them about Rhonda. All right?"

"Yeah, I guess I wasn't thinking. I'll do that. Call me right away if you hear from your girl. D'y'hear?"

"Yeah, Bob, I hear you. You call us if you hear from Judy." He hung up and turned to his wife. "I think we'd better go to the police station rather than call. Get Rhonda's picture. Hurry up, Rose."

Wednesday - 6:30 p.m.

"Sonofabitch!" Coral snarled.

"Now what's the matter?" Pamela asked.

"Nothing. I'm just generally pissed off. Goddamn belts!"

Rhonda cleared her throat. "Hey, I'm sorry. I thought I was onto something. How was I supposed to know the stitching was just that and not part of how it was put together?"

"Nobody's blaming you," Coral said. "It's just that I thought we might be able to get the hell outta here. You know what I mean? I've been down here for one helluva long time. So's Pam and a couple of others—even longer'n me. I'm just pissed— not at you but at the assholes keeping us down here. Thinking we might be able to free ourselves and find a way out, only to be still tied up, sort of renews the hatred I had for them at the beginning."

"Yeah, it's strange all right," Daun said quietly. "I almost was to the point of feeling sorta comfortable here in the dark."

"Comfortable?" Judy snapped. "How the fuck could you feel like that, knowing someone's controlling your life, keeping you prisoner with God-knows-what in mind for your future? Where's Dana? What happened to her? Will we ever see her again? Shit! That's funny. Have any of us ever *seen* her? We haven't seen each other, have we? Sure, we hear one another but we've never touched or laid our eyeballs on each other. I know what Rhonda looks like, and she knows what I look like. Beyond that— nothing."

"The only decent thing they do is clean us and feed us. The food was good today, wasn't it?" Margaret asked.

"Yeah, kid, it was good," Coral said.

A silence fell over the blackness and Coral sniffled. "Sonofabitch!"

Wednesday - 10:30 p.m.

Police Captain Michael Lord looked up when the door to his office opened and two scruffy men walked in.

"Did you want to see us, Captain?" Gus Weaver asked.

"Yes, I do. Sit down, Weaver. Hewlett." He indicated the chairs opposite his desk.

Jerry Hewlett sat down and pulled out a cigarette. Lighting it, he blew a cloud of bluish smoke into the air.

Gus coughed and glared at his partner.

"When are you going to quit?"

"When I'm ready."

"Enough of that," Lord said. "I'm re-assigning you two to juvenile. That'll mean I want you in suits and ties—and shave every day. We got a couple more missing-kid reports tonight."

"How many does that make now, Captain?" Gus asked, running a hand over his four day growth of beard.

"Since the middle of May, five. Oh, there have been others but these five seem to be somehow related."

"I was going to say it was sort of different to be pulled off the streets to go looking for five kids. Haven't there been quite a few?" Gus wrinkled his nose at the smoke.

"There's the usual number of runaways and kids taking off for a couple of days because they got in trouble at home. But these five, I think, are different."

"Similar M.O.?" Jerry asked, blowing a smoke ring.

"Yes and no." Lord stood and threw five folders across the desk at the two men. "Five girls between twelve and seventeen. They're all from good homes. They're all good students. All good citizens. Their parents are good parents. The girls missing have never been in trouble of any kind. They're not the sort to just run away."

"It's happened before. Kids like that can

commit suicide and no one ever knows why." Gus coughed.

"True. But I just don't think five girls from middle class homes—oh, one or two are from working class homes—but you know what I mean. Five girls from good homes and good records just don't disappear."

"You think it might be more than simple runaways?" Jerry asked, picking up one of the folders. A picture of a 12 year-old girl fell to the floor. Written on the back was: Sherry Blaine, age 12.

Lord shrugged. "It could be."

"What are you thinking, Captain?" Gus asked.

"Okay. We could be facing a sex maniac of some sort who is really smooth. There's been no report of any bodies being found or any reports of any of the girls being sighted by anyone. No matter who or what sort of person or persons we might be looking for, we're going to have our hands full. They're good."

"What about a serial killer?" Jerry asked, laying the folder back on the desk and picking up another.

"That's another option. It could be five unrelated incidents as well, although if that were the case we'd have something on some of the earlier cases by now. I'm sure of that."

Jerry put out the cigarette and smiled

when Gus's face reflected his relief. "When did the last one come in?"

"Tonight. Two of them." He told the detectives of the Gordons' and the Mertons' reports and how the two girls had been together.

Gus rifled through the folders and found the most recent additions. "We'll probably start here with these, since they're the freshest. Anything else, Captain?"

"We've got at least one other that might be somehow related. She's not from Sioux Falls, nor is she a teenager, but she was last seen here in the city." He laid a sixth folder on the desk. "She was with one of the traveling sales crews canvassing the city, selling magazine subscriptions."

"Fly-by-night," Jerry said. "Probably just took off."

Lord shrugged. "I don't know. Again, she seemed to be a reliable sort of person. She was making decent money doing what she was doing and simply didn't show up where she was supposed to. They backtracked some but moved on without waiting. They did call in and give us her description and the other information. There's a photo in the folder."

Gus picked up the folder and perused the contents: Daun Kingston. Age 23. Five foot seven. About 120 pounds. Auburn-reddish hair. Green eyes. Last seen wearing slacks, blue; blouse, white; and sandals. Carrying briefcase containing order book, brochures and sample magazine covers. Home town: Allentown, Pennsylvania. College graduate.

Gus glanced at the captain. "A college graduate selling magazines? You've gotta be kidding."

"She had just graduated this spring and was waiting for a job opening with the state of Pennsylvania. She wasn't going to start until August. It's all in there. Again, from what the crew chief told me when he reported her missing, she was reliable and had an excellent work record. This was the fifth summer she'd worked for the same company, and she always made good money."

Gus frowned and picked up the other folders. "Where's the employer located?"

"Dallas, Texas. It's in the folder if you want to contact them for more information."

"Is this more or less the normal number of reported missing girls, Captain?" Jerry stood, sensing that Gus was about ready to leave.

"As I said before, the usual runaways and what have you have been pretty consistent with this time of year, but the girls, because of these five or six, upset the picture."

"Hellsfire," Gus said, standing, "kids take off all the time. They get in trouble at home with their folks or at school. Of course, school's out now, but there's always kids getting strung out on dope and crap."

He purposely looked at Jerry before continuing. "Sometimes kids get so dependent
on each other—girl-boy things—that if they
have a fight or breakup it's the end of the
world for them, and they take off. Sometimes they're just plain ornery. Who knows
what prompts them to run away? There's
more now than ever."

"That's right, Gus," Lord said. "Still,
once you get digging into those files, you'll
find, like I did, that there seems to be something solid about them. And that seems to
be the connecting link."

"Have any of them ever been involved in
the drug scene at school?" Jerry asked.

Lord shook his head. "If you were going
to pick a teenager showing good qualities,
these five would be the finalists. Your job,
gentlemen, is to find them. Find out where
they're at, why they did what they did. Just
find them. I've got a creepy feeling about
them and the fact they're missing."

As Jerry and Gus turned to leave, the
phone rang.

"Captain Lord speaking. Yes—Yes—
Right—Just a moment, please, ma'am." He
cupped his hand over the mouthpiece.
"Come on back, fellas. I think we got
another one." Then into the mouthpiece, he
said, "Go ahead, Mrs. Polchow."

Thursday - 1:02 a.m.

The stretch limousine glided out of the

driveway and turned south on North Duluth Avenue. The construction site wasn't that far away, and Aleigha, who rode with Edward in the front seat, silently chortled at the fact that they'd be burying the girl's body so close to the mansion.

She glanced at the driver. Edward's eyes seemed clear in the dim light of the dashboard. She hoped so. It would be awful if they were involved in an accident of some sort with the dead body in the trunk. Still, for some reason she couldn't understand, Edward could be in a heroin induced state most of the day, yet at night his head cleared and he functioned in an absolutely normal fashion.

He turned to look at her for a moment when he realized she was watching him. "Is something wrong?"

"No, nothing's wrong. Everything's fine with the world. Right, Edward?"

He smiled. "You and I should get to know each other better, Aleigha. I think we could make some good music together."

"Not likely," she said, turning away. The last thing she wanted was a man's cock jammed into her body. She'd had enough of that when she was young—before the Countess Elisabeth Bathory Nadasdy had picked her up in the black coach one night. For some reason, the countess had taken a liking to her and not had her killed. Instead, when the noble lady discovered that Aleigha or as she was called then, Szentes, had a vicious nature, she put her in charge of bleeding the victims that were picked up across the countryside at night.

During that span of 11 years, the countess had been responsible for the deaths of over 600 young women, but it had been Aleigha who had murdered most of them. It had been then that she learned the thrilling pleasure involved in biting a person to death. When they were weakened from loss of blood it was a relatively simple thing to do, and she reveled in the feeling of human flesh in her mouth—living human flesh. She ran her tongue over her full lips, shuddering when she relived the sensation of tearing that same living flesh from a body.

"Well?" Edward asked, an edge to the single word.

"Well what?"

"Weren't you listening?"

"Not really. I was lost in my thoughts for a moment. What did you say?"

"I asked you what the big deal was in our going out to dinner in some nice restaurant some night. We could go dancing or do something else afterward."

"That's stupid. You realize that, don't you, Edward? Think for a moment. At night you work for the countess, driving the streets and picking up girls, who are put to death after a while. And you want a date? You're crazy. You really are."

"When I drive around in the daytime,

I'm free at night. Why couldn't we go for it then?"

"Watch my lips, Edward. I don't like you. I don't like men in general. I like my work. I'm not going to run the risk of losing it. Are you?"

Edward stared through the windshield but didn't respond.

"Let me put it to you this way, Edward, old boy. Fuck up on the job and you lose your daily supply of heroin."

"I'd spill my guts to the cops."

"Who'd believe a junky like you?"

Again he fell silent and turned the corner onto Phillips Avenue. Driving around to the back of the construction site, which was walled in with a solid board fence, he stopped and got out to remove the barrier. He turned into the drive that led to the excavated basement. Turning off the headlights, he got out and went around to the trunk.

Aleigha followed him.

He pulled out a spade and jabbed it into the ground, looking for a soft place to dig. When he found it, he began digging a shallow grave, stopping when he reached a one-foot level, and took off his black jacket. Handing it to Aleigha, he picked up the shovel and continued.

When the hole was sufficiently deep, he dropped the spade and went to the trunk. He picked up the girl's body, which had been wrapped in plastic, and unceremoniously dumped it into the grave. The dirt flew into the hole more quickly than he had removed it, and in minutes he tamped down the earth to flatten the top of the grave. Spreading the excess dirt around, he examined his handiwork and looked expectantly at Aleigha.

"Is that good enough?"

"It should be. If they get going on the job tomorrow, she'll be buried forever."

They got into the car, and Edward drove out of the basement with only the parking lights showing the way. Once the barrier was set back in place he returned to the car, and they drove out of the alley and toward the mansion.

Thursday - 1:30 a.m.

Spider Chanely watched, his eyes popping from his skull. What the hell were those two up to? Why was the guy digging behind that long car? When the digger stopped and went to the trunk where he picked up something that looked like a body, Spider bit his tongue to keep from crying out. Instead, he pulled out his bottle of wine and tipped it to his mouth. The muscatel dribbled down his numb throat. He needed that. Now he'd be in better control.

Sure enough, they had buried a body there. He was positive. And he wasn't so drunk that he didn't remember this was the

last night he'd be able to spend at the construction site now that the strike had been
settled. Tomorrow night he'd be sleeping
someplace else, because they were pouring
the floor tomorrow. He'd heard that someplace. Where? Maybe he read it. He couldn't
remember details like that very well anymore. All he knew was he had to find a
better place to sleep.

When the limousine pulled out of the
area, he waited a few minutes before
crawling out of the box in which he had
been resting. Walking across the dirt to the
spot where the car had been, he hiccupped
and staggered a couple of times. He hadn't
planned on walking anymore tonight. He
kicked at the soft earth with his worn shoe
and frowned. What should he do? If he
stayed here and the cops came and found
the body, they might think he'd done it.
That wouldn't be too smart on his part. The
best thing he could do was get the hell out
of the construction site and find a new place
to sleep. He had to do that anyway so it
might as well be tonight.

He hurried up the inclined plane to the
alley and stumbled along the dark passageway to the street. When he reached it, he
turned to his right and hobbled along the
walk. He didn't see the brick laying in the
middle of the sidewalk and stubbed his toes
against it.

Screaming out with pain, he jumped
around on his one good foot and instantly

lost his balance, falling to the side and striking his head against a lamppost. The last thing he saw was the headlights driving toward him. As he sank into unconsciousness, he heard two voices.

"Just a drunk, Nick."

"Right. Radio for an ambulance. This dude's bleeding from his head. Probably loaded, couldn't walk and fell down."

"This is Car Four. Send an ambulance to . . ."

Spider heard no more as the soft caress of unconsciousness firmly gripped him.

11

Thursday - 9:00 a.m.

Gus Weaver stood up to stretch. His back hurt and his eyes burned. He and his partner had been studying the folders, containing the cases of the missing girls, ever since they had arrived at the station house. He yawned.

"Why the hell don't you get more sleep at night?" Jerry said, looking up.

"Funny. Very funny. I must have had all of two, maybe three hours last night." Gus sat down heavily and threw the folder he'd been perusing across his desk to Jerry's. Captain Lord had taken them off under-cover street duty and assigned them to work specifically on the missing girls. Gus wished he was back on the street.

Jerry looked up. "Other than the backgrounds of the girls being similar, I don't see any connection. Do you?"

"Well, all we've got to go on is the captain's instinct, and in a way, I sort of agree with him. I sense there might be a tie-in, only in the fact that the same person or persons might be responsible."

Jerry shook his head, picking up the folder Gus had thrown on his desk. "Anything special about this one?"

"It seems to be the only one where we'll find any sort of lead. Daun Kingston was selling magazine subscriptions on North Duluth. That much we know. We also know the approximate blocks on that street. Her employer, Leisureading, Incorporated, was thoughtful enough to provide us with her itinerary as well as those of the other sales personnel."

"Think we should start with her?"

Gus nodded. The Rapid City police had already been alerted about the Merton and Gordon girls.

Jerry held up the five by seven photo of Daun Kingston and whistled softly. "She was pretty darn attractive."

Gus smiled. Ever since Jerry had gotten married the year before, Gus had watched his partner, three years his junior, go from the ordinary womanizer that most of the un-married men on the force pretended to be, if in fact they weren't, to a happily married, very much in love, husband.

"Is that the best you can do?" Gus asked.

Jerry looked up. "If you settled down and stopped cattin' around on your off hours, you'd appreciate that this young lady is beautiful and probably has every guy who sees her hoping and praying she's a nymphomaniac."

"That's the Jerry I used to know." Gus chuckled but sobered up immediately. "Actually, she's the only one we can start with. We can retrace her steps and hopefully find the path she walked the day she disappeared. We might even determine the last house she called on. Then, at least, we'll know where she disappeared from. Right?"

"Makes sense to me. Did you notice that she'd done some modeling while going to college?"

Gus nodded.

"Just out of curiosity, how old would you say she is?" Jerry asked, handing the photo to Gus.

Gus studied it for a minute. "She's twenty-three, right?"

"According to her file she is," Jerry said, nodding.

"Hell, at most I'd say she looks like she's—what?—eighteen or nineteen?" Gus snapped his fingers. "I see what you're driving at. She looks like she's a teenager but is really twenty-three. Right?"

Jerry nodded. "That's why Captain Lord said she was maybe tied in somehow—the only one who wasn't a teenager but sure could pass for one."

"Well, I guess we should go to North

Duluth Avenue and start hoofing it. Right? Have you got the addresses she was supposed to have called on?"

"Yeah. Too bad we don't have some samples. Maybe we could pick up a buck or two on the side." Jerry grinned.

"Boy, married life sure has changed you. Now you're looking for ways to moonlight *on* the job. Shame on you."

Jerry stood and followed his partner from the office.

"Hey!" The call came from behind them as they entered the hall.

Gus and Jerry stopped and turned to see Nick Jarking, the duty sergeant, coming down the hall toward them. "I'm glad I caught you two. I want you to go to McKennon. There's a drunk there who might have something for you."

"Come on, Sergeant," Gus said, "we're up to our necks in missing girls. Can't somebody else take it?"

"That's just it. The drunk said something about seeing somebody burying a body. Since you two are the only ones investigating anything that might be remotely connected, I thought you should be the ones to go."

Gus glanced at Jerry. "All right—but if it's not connected in anyway, you get it back. Okay?"

"Fine with me. We've got all sorts of young, eager and ambitious cops running around here who'd like to make a name for themselves." Jarking winked and turned.

What Jarking said made sense to Gus and Jerry. There might be a connection. Maybe they'd get a break right away and it wouldn't take any time at all to clear it up.

While driving to the hospital, Jerry braked the car to a stop for a traffic light and turned to Gus. "What sort of person would go around snatching teenagers?"

"Guys like you and me. Healthy, normal, horny guys." Gus laughed sardonically. "Christ, I don't know. I'm not a fucking psychiatrist."

"If we don't hit something real soon, I suggest we call on one. Maybe he could give us a personality profile of some sort."

"As I said, I'm no psychiatrist, but I'm willing to bet my first-born that the best he could do with what we've got is tell us the perpetrator's likes in girls and not a helluva lot more."

Jerry pulled away from the stop and said, "You're probably right. He hasn't left a clue of any sort, has he?"

"Not that we know of. Then, too, you chauvinist, we're not a hundred percent sure it is a 'he,' either, are we?"

"What? You think a woman might be doing this?"

Gus laughed. "I wish you were a woman. That way, I'd have finally gotten one over."

"I don't understand."

"Well, you automatically said 'he,' right? Most of the time, if there's a woman

around, she'll climb all over a guy's frame if
he suggests something is male or uses a
male term to describe something, like
'chairman of the board.' She'll quick as
anything butt in, correct him and say 'chair-
person.' You know?"

"Then you don't really think it could be
a woman?"

"Hell, no. Nor do I think it's a Martian. It
could be either or it could be both. It could
also be a man, and that's where the smart
money will be bet."

Jerry parked in a no parking zone near
the front entrance of the hospital, and both
men got out. After getting the room number
from the information desk, they went to the
ward where they found Spider Chanley, his
head swathed in bandages.

After showing him their identification,
the two men separated to either side of the
bed.

"Tell me, Mr. Chanely," Gus began, "what
it was you saw and where it took place."

"Call me Spider, will ya, fellas? Ain't
nobody ever calls me mister. It sorta
bothers me. Ya know what I mean?"

He sighed heavily, and Gus caught the
full brunt of his foul breath. "Right, Spider.
So tell us. What did you see?"

"Dis big car . . ." Spider began, looking
first to the bed to his right, which was
empty, and then to the wall on his left.
". . . real big. Christ, it musta been two cars
long if it was a foot, I'll betcha."

"Okay. So it was a big car. Was it a

limousine?"

Spider looked up dumbly.

"Were there lots of windows along the side? Two, maybe three doors on one side?"

Spider rubbed his grizzled chin. "Cheez, I didn't count no doors. Don't know how many it had. Don't know how many windows dere was, either. But it was long. Oh yeah, it was long, all right."

"Where'd you see the car, Spider?" Jerry asked from the far side of the bed.

Spider jerked his head toward him. "Over on . . . at . . . oh, you know where I mean, don'tcha?"

"We weren't there, Spider, remember?" Gus asked. "Think real hard. Where'd you see the car?"

Spider rubbed his chin again. "Well, dere was all sorts of stuff around. See, I been sleepin' in dis big box. Dere was a couple o' more just like 'em around dis place. And barrels and lumber and steel rods and beams all around the hole where dis box where I been sleepin' in was. Ya know the place, don'tcha?"

Jerry looked up at Gus. "It sounds like a construction site or something, doesn't it?"

Gus nodded. "Where'd the slip say he was picked up?"

Jerry pulled the note out. "Phillips Avenue, 600 block."

"There's a new building going up a couple of blocks from there," Gus said, turning his attention back to Spider. "Was it a construction site, Spider?"

"Yeah, dat's it. I 'member now. Sure. I 'member telling myself dat I had to find me a new place to sleep. See?"

"Why'd you tell yourself that?" Gus asked.

"The strike was settled," Jerry said. "The carpenters and all of the other trade unions were going back to work this morning."

"Listen to me, Spider. This is important. What did you see?" Gus stared down at the small man.

"When?"

"Last night. Did somebody hit you and knock you out? Is that why you're in the hospital?"

"Naw, nobody hit me. Leastwise, I don't think nobody did. See, I was finishing off my bottle of 'scatel when I heard dis crunching sound. Turned out to be a car what drove down into the place where I been sleeping most of the last couple o' weeks. I kept real quiet, 'cause I figured it might be da big boss or somethin' 'cause da car was so big. Did I tell you about da car? Cheez, it was big. Real big."

"You told us, Spider. Get on with what you saw."

"Well, two of 'em got outta da car and one went around to da back. He pulls out a shovel and starts ta diggin'. Right away I knowed somethin' was wrong someplace. You know what I mean?"

Gus and Jerry nodded.

"After a while, dey pulled dis long thing all wrapped up in plastic outta da trunk. It coulda been a rug or a body. I tink it was a body."

"What makes you say that, Spider?" Jerry leaned down closer until he caught a scent of the derelict's breath and straightened up.

"Who in der right mind would go 'round buryin' a rug? In da middle a' da night? Dat don't make no sense ta me, no sir. I say 'twas a body. You fellas better go down dere 'n' dig it up. Then go arrest the guys what done it."

"We'd better swing by there—just to check out his story," Gus said, turning to leave.

Jerry stepped around the foot of the bed. "How'd you get several blocks away from the construction site, Spider?"

Gus stopped at the door.

Spider wrinkled his face and grinned sheepishly. "I ran."

"Ran? Why?"

"I figured if'n da cops came by, they're gonna tink I done it. So I run. Musta fell down or somethin'. Don't know what happened. I sure gotta get outta here."

"Why do you say that?" Gus asked, stepping closer to the foot of the bed.

"Dis bed's too goddamned soft. I gotta find a new place to sleep, anyways."

"You aren't going back to the construction site when you get out of here?"

"Can't. Too much goin' on."

"I don't follow you, Spider."

"Der pourin' cement today. Heard dat on TV in a store—or was it a bar? Don't 'member. 'Member 'bout da cement. Yes sir! Said dey was goin' ta pour it in da cellar. Dat's where I been snoozin' at night and now I gotta find another—"

"You're sure about the cement being poured?" Jerry asked, excitement topping his voice.

Spider nodded.

Gus said, "We can radio headquarters and ask them to check on it."

"You mean you believe everything he told you?"

"S'long, Spider," Gus said, waving and turned to leave.

"Take it easy, Spider," Jerry said, before catching up to his partner.

"Of course we've got to check it out. He might have seen something, but I'm not betting my first-born on it," Gus said, striding down the hall.

Thursday - 10:22 a.m.

Before they reached the construction site, Gus and Jerry had their answer. Sergeant Jarking had called the owner of the construction site, who agreed to hold up the work until Weaver and Hewlett arrived.

"What'd he say, Sarge?" Gus asked.

"He said one more delay was all he

needed. Don't drag your feet, fellas,"
Jarking said.

"We won't," Gus said.

The car leaped forward when Jerry
floored the accelerator.

Hanging the mike on the dash, Gus
said, "You'd better hit the button, Jerry.
We've got to get over there pronto."

A few minutes later, Gus and Jerry had
told everything to the foreman at the construction site.

"All you have to do is ask that cement
truck to wait while we make a quick investigation of the ground down there," Gus said,
glaring at him.

"How long?"

"If your men help us, it won't take more
than . . . say half an hour."

"You realize, don't you, that the strike
was just settled and that this building has
been waiting since March to be put up? Now
you want to hold up pouring while you go
down there and poke around?"

"You got any kids?" Gus asked.

The man nodded.

"Suppose one of them was missing?
Suppose the possibility existed that the
missing child was buried someplace down
there." He jerked his thumb over his
shoulder. "Wouldn't you insist on holding
up the cement truck?"

The foreman looked away, frowning, but
the expression told Gus that he had
managed to drive his point home.

"As long as the owner says it okay. I'll get the men. What're you looking for?"

Gus shrugged. "I imagine a soft spot in the ground. Since there hasn't been any work done around here for some time, I think a soft spot would be pretty easy to find, don't you?"

He nodded. "Get some lengths of reinforcement rod, Mike," the foreman called to a short, stocky man who stood nearby. "Do what this guys tells you."

After only 15 minutes, they found the grave. When the workmen's shovels exposed plastic wrapping, Gus and Jerry called a halt to the work and radioed in the finding and requested help. Once the forensics team was on the job, they left, ready to begin their canvassing of North Duluth Avenue.

Thursday - 11:33 a.m.

"I suppose it would be quicker to have each one of us cover a different side of the street but we'd best follow our team instincts," Jerry said, setting the emergency brake.

"Team instincts?" Gus said, half-laughing.

Jerry smiled shyly. "Don't make shit out of me, Gus. You know as well as I do that if one of us forgets to ask something, the other usually remembers."

"And you call that team instinct?"

"Besides, we've only got one folder," Jerry said hurriedly.

Gus opened the door. "That makes more sense."

The two men walked up to the house on the corner and knocked. At each house, wherever they found someone home, the same questions were asked. Did they remember being approached by a young woman, they'd ask, showing the photo, who was selling magazine subscriptions for Leisureading? They found the reactions interesting in that most who had not purchased subscriptions were thanking the gods for telling them that the scheme was crooked. Those who had ordered believed the police were investigating a scam of some type.

Walking up to a one story bungalow, Gus reached out and tapped on the screen door. They heard someone coming to the door and stepped back. Looking up, they saw a pleasant looking woman who appeared to be in her seventies open the inside door.

"Yes?"

"We're from the Sioux Falls Police Department, ma'am. We'd like to ask you a few questions if we could." Jerry and Gus both showed their shields. "I'm Detective Jerry Hewlett and this is Detective Gus Weaver."

The woman lowered her head, peering through thick-lensed glasses at the shiny

badges. Without a word, she unlatched the
screen door and pushed it open. "I'm Kate
French. We can sit here on the porch or in
the living room if you'd like." She stepped
into the living room, making the decision
without waiting for the two men to choose.
"How may I help you?"

"We would like to know if you remember
seeing this young lady," Jerry said, handing
the woman the photo of Daun Kingston.

"Where could I have seen her?" Mrs.
French took the proferred photo and
studied it closely. She turned and walked to
an easy chair at the end of the living room
and sat down. Turning on a light, she moved
a small magnifying glass into position and
held the picture under it. "My, she's a pretty
girl. Now that you mention it, she *does* look
familiar."

Gus shot a quick glance at Jerry, then
turned his attention to Mrs. French. "Tell us,
Mrs. French, if you remember her coming to
your door, selling magazine subscriptions.
It would have been within the last month or
so."

"Of course," Mrs. French said, her face
lighting up. "I remember. She looked so
nice, dressed conservatively if I remember
right. I invited her in and we chatted, but
when she got around to talking about
magazines, I told her I don't even take *The
Argus-Leader* anymore. My eyesight isn't
what it once was." The woman stopped. "Oh

my, she hasn't gotten into trouble, has she? She was so friendly."

"We don't believe she's in any trouble with the law, ma'am," Gus said. "She's missing, and we've been following the route she took the last day she was seen."

"Well, I don't think I can be of any help. I did talk with her, but that was some time ago and I haven't seen her since."

The policeman stood to leave. "Thank you for your time, Mrs. French," Jerry said, smiling broadly.

Gus said good-bye, and they left.

"She reminds me of my great-aunt Catherine," Jerry said, when they stood on the sidewalk in front.

Gus said nothing, striking out toward the house next door. They continued their door-to-door canvassing, slowly acknowledging that being an undercover street cop and a detective investigating missing girls posed many differences.

An hour later, they stood on the south side of St. Joseph's Cathedral. The nondescript house facing them seemed hardly the type of place a salesperson would approach. From the exterior appearance, they decided if the occupants could read, it would be a miracle, and more than likely, unheard of that they would order a subscription.

"Well, we've got to check out every house," Gus said, starting up the broken sidewalk with Jerry following. When Gus knocked on the door, it rattled loudly.

"Yes? Who's there? If that's you kids again, I'll paddle your behinds good."

They heard footsteps stomping from the back of the house, and both men grinned inwardly when they saw the diminutive blonde confronting them.

"Oh, I'm sorry, gentlemen. I thought it was my kids banging on the door again."

"I'm Gus Weaver, and this is my partner, Jerry Hewlett," Gus said, holding up his badge. "We'd like to ask you a few questions, Miss . . . ?"

"Darcey Blake, and it's Mrs. About what?"

Gus held up the photo and repeated the same questions he and Jerry had been asking since they got out of their car the first time some four or five blocks back.

Just as she was about to speak, four children, the youngest of which couldn't have been much over two years of age, came running into the living room and out through the front door.

"Kids!" she screamed, and both policemen stepped back, amazed at the volume of the small woman's voice.

"Yours?" Gus asked, nodding toward the open door and the children running around in the yard.

Darcey nodded. "I remember the girl. I told her she couldn't come in, that she'd be wasting her time and mine. I'm on ADC and haven't got an extra penny for anything like that."

"Well, thank you, ma'am. You're at least candid about it." Gus put the photo away and continued talking with her for a moment while Jerry stepped back.

He had caught sight of a child peeking around the corner and walked over. There he found a small boy spying on them.

"Hi, what's your name?" the man asked, crouching down to the boy's height.

"Mickey."

"Mickey what?"

"Mickey Blake."

"What have you got there, Mickey?" Jerry asked, pointing to the black object the child held behind his back.

"That's my business stuff."

Jerry smiled. "What kind of business are you in?"

"Su'sc'iptions."

"What? What do you know about them?"

"Mommy and that man over there are talking about them, ain't they?"

"Do you know what they are?"

The dirty faced boy shook his head.

"May I see your 'business'?"

Nodding, the boy handed Jerry a small valise. A paper label that had covered most of the center of the black bag had been torn off. Red letters "es" remained on the right side above the letter "r." The next line showed "er" and the one below it displayed "Inc." He wished it would have read Leisureading, Inc. At least they'd have a tangible clue in their hands and might be a bit closer to learning what happened to Daun Kingston.

"Is this the name of your company?" Jerry asked, handing the bag back and pointing to the letters.

The boy nodded again, taking the valise.

"What's it mean?" Jerry asked.

"I dunno."

"You ready?" Gus asked from the front step.

"Yeah." Jerry stood up straight and tousled the boy's hair. "I'm coming. Well, son," he said, holding out his hand, "I hope business goes well. By the way where did you get your bag?"

The boy looked away.

"What's the matter, Mickey?" the boy's mother asked, raising her voice.

The boy ran to his mother and hugged her legs.

"Did he do something he wasn't supposed to?" Darcey asked, glaring at Jerry, then at Mickey.

"No, ma'am. I merely asked where he got his little valise, that's all. He doesn't have to tell me."

"Where'd you get that thing, Mickey? Tell me."

"You'll spank me."

"Where'd you get it from?"

"Ma! Don't make me tell you. You'll spank me."

The woman raised her hand, and Gus reached out, grabbing her wrist. "Ma'am, if it's all the same to you, why not punish Mickey there in the house, after Detective Hewlett and I are gone? We wouldn't want to have to arrest you for child abuse."

Jerry grinned, knowing full well that Gus would not carry through on the threat.

Darcey paled, her nostrils flaring. "Oh, my God, I forgot you were here. I'm sorry. I seldom punish my children by spanking, but I do believe in the old-fashioned ways." Crouching down, she said, "Tell me where you got that, Mickey."

"I found it in a trash barrel." He looked away from his mother.

Before Mickey could say another word, she stood up, grabbing him by the ear, and pulled him inside the house. "We may not have everything, but by God, no kid of mine is going to go rooting through other's junk piles for toys. No sir. You go to your room, young man. I'll tend to you later. Glancing back at the two policemen, she shook her head. "Boys!"

The next block offered older houses that had been built before the turn of the century or shortly thereafter. Jerry stopped and looked at the first one, an elegant Queen Anne style mansion.

"Do you suppose people who lived in

these houses subscribed to magazines?"

"Why wouldn't they?" Gus asked. "Besides, we've found that Daun stopped at the last house across the street." He head motioned behind him to the previous block.

"Well, let's go." Jerry half-turned away.

Before either could take a step, Jerry's walkie-talkie burst to life. Stopping, he pulled it from his coat pocket.

"Yeah? Hewlett here."

"You and Weaver get back to the station on the double. We've got some information on the body they found on Phillips Avenue."

Jerry looked at Gus before both spun on their heels and hurried to their car, parked in the next block.

Behind them in the Queen Anne mansion, the curtains of a second floor window dropped back into place.

12

Thursday - 4:00 p.m.

Jerry shook his head while reading the coroner's report concerning the body found in the grave at the construction site. The autopsy had been performed while he and Gus tracked the route Daun Kingston had taken on North Duluth Avenue.

He looked up when Gus walked in, carrying two cups of coffee. "Read this and give me your first impression," he said, taking one of the cups and handing the report to his partner.

Gus set his cup on Jerry's desk. His experienced eye flicked across the pages, picking up the essential information. "Janet Mulrooney?" he asked, looking down at Jerry.

"Right. We got a hit on fingerprints. Go

ahead and read it first. Then, we'll talk,"
Jerry said, sipping his coffee.

Gus returned his attention to the papers
he held. *Janet Mulrooney—18 years old at
the time missing persons report filed in
1987—subject is 1.68 meters long—weight
at time of disappearance about 46.27 kilograms—weight of body at death, 53.5 kilograms—death may have been caused by
what appears to be numerous bite marks.*

Gus looked up to find Jerry watching
him. "Bite marks?"

"Read on, Gus. It gets better—or worse,
depending on one's tastes in such matters."

Gus slowly refocused on the papers he
held. What in hell did Jerry mean by that?
He continued reading. . . . *death may have
been caused by what appears to be numerous bite marks—size, shape and depth of
indentations seem to indicate a human
bite—all wounds remarkably free of blood.*

Gus looked up again but said nothing,
feeling the hair on the nape of his neck
moving of its own accord when he saw his
partner's grim face. *One breast completely
torn off—remaining breast mutilated and
attached to chest by a few shreds of
skin—numerous bites heavily concentrated
on throat, breast area, lower abdomen and
genital area—difficult to tell if bites actually
caused death or loss of blood might be
cause—condition of the body makes
questionable at best the idea of loss of blood
causing death since the body was virtually*

*free of blood stains as was the plastic in
which the body was wrapped—less than five
deciliters of blood, which would account for
the gray pallor of the body—death probably
occurred within 24 to 36 hours of the body's
discovery—peculiar bruised area inside of
right thigh, anterior inner part around what
appears to be an incision-like cut into
femoral artery—never tended or bandaged
from all indications—on a speculative basis
only—because of low blood content, subject
probably succumbed when attacked as
indicated by teeth marks.*

"I don't get any of this, Jerry. What the
hell's Doc trying to say?"

Jerry leaned back in his chair and
sipped his coffee. "I'm not certain. To say
the least, it's weird."

"That's putting it mildly." Gus picked
up his cup and sat down at his desk. "Jesus,
what sort of freak are we looking for? He
bites his victims to death after bleeding
them? What?"

"You said victims. Why?"

"We *are* looking for more than one
missing girl. How come this one wasn't on
our list?"

Jerry drained his cup. "I think it's because she didn't fit the family background
like the others."

Gus screwed up his face.

"You know," Jerry explained, "good
family, good student, never in trouble, no
drugs—all that sort of thing."

"What did this one do to break the pattern?"

"We have her prints on file. She was picked up for prostitution when she was sixteen but was released to her mother's custody."

"How come she was printed?"

"There were a bunch of girls arrested, and because of her age, she was sent to Juvenile at the last minute."

"Her family still around?"

Jerry nodded. "Did you notice anything out of the ordinary in that report?"

Gus scanned the pages again before looking up at his partner. Whatever Jerry was referring to escaped him at the moment. "What?"

"Look at the weights—at the time she was reported missing and when the coroner weighed the body."

Gus found the figures—a little more than 46 kilograms a year ago and more than 53 at death. He looked up. "So? I was never any good at converting things. What's it mean other than the fact she gained weight in a year?"

"She weighed about a hundred pounds a year ago. Let's assume she was on the street or hiding out from her family. Would that mean she would be eating real good?"

"Not necessarily. What are you driving at?"

"Most kids who run away from home suffer physically. They're in their formative years for the most part. They need good food to maintain their health and growth. At least that's been the general idea, right?"

Gus nodded.

"The girl weighed one hundred and eighteen when she died. That's about a fifteen percent increase in a year. Did you notice the report on the blood?"

"Just that there wasn't much. How much is a deciliter?"

"Not very much. Five equals less than a quart."

Gus whistled softly.

"But that blood was heavy in iron. Real healthy blood."

Gus squinted at him. "So?"

"What happened to her blood? It wasn't in the body. The wounds were free of blood. It wasn't in or on the plastic shroud."

"I hope you're not going to say we've got a vampire on our hands."

Jerry grinned. "No—although the thought jumped in for a split second. I think we're dealing with some sort of cult if there's more than one or a really sicko if there is only one. He'd have to be strong as hell to lug around dead bodies and keep them secured."

"Whoa! Wait a minute. You're sort of going off half-cocked here, Jerry. First of all, the bum in the hospital said he saw two people at the time the girl's body was buried."

"Assuming he wasn't seeing double."

"He said nothing about two bodies being buried, so let's assume his eyesight was all right. Since two people were reported at the scene, I think we should forget the idea that there's only one really sick sonofabitch out there doing this sort of thing."

"What do you suggest we do first?"

Gus stood up, finishing his coffee at the same time and throwing the cup in the waste basket. "Let's go visit the girl's family. Got the address?"

"Yeah. One of the first things I checked after I got the report."

Jerry followed Gus into the hall where they met Captain Lord.

"You men going off duty?" he asked.

"Not yet, Captain. We've got a stop to make before we call it quits."

"How's the investigation of those missing girls going? You have started on it, haven't you?"

"Yes, sir," Jerry said. "We've got a couple of more leads but nothing concrete yet. Did you hear about the Mulrooney girl?"

"Yes. There's a coroner's report on my desk. I only had time to glance at it, but it looks terrible. Does it fit?"

"We don't know, Captain," Gus said. "This girl didn't fit the mold of the others. She had an arrest record for prostitution."

Lord furrowed his brow. "It's probably not related to the others."

"We'll find out," Gus said, stepping around Lord.

"Keep me posted," he called after the departing detectives.

Thursday - 4:45 p.m.

Jerry tapped at the trailer door and stepped back.

"Who the fuck's out there?" a woman's voice demanded.

"Police, ma'am. We'd like to ask you a few questions."

"Go away. I'm busy."

"Are you Lucille Mulrooney?" Gus asked.

"What if I am?" the voice said, muffled by the closed door.

"If you are, we'd like to ask you some questions concerning your daughter, Janet Mulrooney."

"Don't waste my time with her. That little ingrate of a bitch don't live here no more."

"Nevertheless, we have to ask you some questions."

The only answer was the turning of a key and the door opening. A woman in her late thirties appeared in the doorway, her robe hanging half-open, exposing most of her breasts and stomach. From the bleary-eyed expression on her naturally pretty face, both men concluded she'd been drinking quite heavily.

"Did you find her?"

"We may have."

"What do you two want then?"

"We'd like to ask you a few questions."

She pushed open the screen door and stepped aside to allow the men entry.

"Where is she? Is she all right?" She turned to face them.

"When was the last time you saw your daughter, Mrs. Mulrooney?" Gus asked, doing his best to ignore the sour smells filling the hot trailer.

Lucy puckered her full mouth into a provocative pout. "When she disappeared. When I turned in the information on the little scum-bucket."

Gus winced and glanced at Jerry.

"Do you have any idea where she might have gone at the time?" Jerry said, taking over for Gus.

"Naw, the fuckin' li'l hosebag just ran away—and after all I done for her."

"She had a record for soliciting men for the purposes of prostitution. You were given charge of her at the time instead of sending her to a halfway house. How did she behave when you brought her home?"

"Like always. Is she in trouble again?"

Ignoring the woman's question, Gus stepped forward, doing all he could to stop himself from grabbing her and shaking her as hard as he could. Instead, he asked, "Was

Janet a healthy girl? Robust? Did she have a weight problem?"

"Her? Shit, no. She had a nice figure like me." Lucy threw her shoulders back, almost completely exposing her breasts.

"What did she weigh when you last saw her?" Gus asked.

Again Lucy puckered her lips and narrowed her eyes, while she studied Gus. "I dunno. Maybe a hundred. Hundred five or so. Why?"

"Did she ever have fits of eating and gaining weight and then dieting to lose the weight?"

"Her? Naw, she barely ate. Always thought of her figure—just like her old lady." Lucy smiled and snorted a little at the same time.

"We've found a body. We believe it's your daughter, Janet. The fingerprints taken at the time she was arrested match those of the girl we found. However, the dead girl weighed a hundred eighteen. We thought you might have seen her since the missing report was filed or could tell us if she had a fluctuating weight problem."

"How . . . how'd she die?" Lucy asked, sitting down on the edge of a worn couch. She dropped her head into her hands.

"We're not at liberty to say, ma'am. The coroner's not finished with his report yet." Jerry glanced at Gus. It was better not to get her hysterical by telling of bite marks and missing blood. In fact, it would be better for everyone concerned if they didn't further question Mrs. Mulrooney at this time.

"If you'd like to identify your daughter, Mrs. Mulrooney," Jerry said, "you may, but its not necessary cause of the positive fingerprints we have."

"Someone from the department will be in touch with you," Gus said, turning to leave, "when the body's ready for burial."

Lucy Mulrooney stared at them, wide-eyed, unable to shed a tear for the daughter she had lost to the streets.

Thursday - 5:26 p.m.

Gus slowed the car, braking to a stop outside of the apartment house where Jerry and his wife lived. "Take care, partner. I'll see you in the morning. Say hello to your bride for me."

"I'll do that. Want to come up for a beer?"

"Naw, I'm pretty beat. Get a good night's sleep, and we'll hit North Duluth again tomorrow morning."

"Right. You going to pick me up?" Jerry asked, closing the door and bending down to peer in at Gus.

"Don't I always?"

Jerry straightened up and Gus pulled away.

Gus drove slowly. He was angry. How could that woman think of her daughter,

her own flesh and blood, in the way she had
when he and Jerry had questioned her? Was
it any wonder kids got into so much trouble
and suffered so much? It wasn't their fault,
not that Gus could see. For the most part
the blame could be traced right back to the
home—to the kid's parents. It seemed to
Gus that people wanted the privilege of
legalized fucking but didn't want to assume
the responsibility for the end result—
children.

Braking to a stop for a traffic light, Gus
shook his head. That blonde with the kids
running wild was another example. Why
couldn't she control them better? Sure, she
was trying to raise them alone. But who said
she had to go to bed with losers, who'd take
off and not stay with her to help raise the
offspring their lust fostered? It irked the
hell out of Gus when he thought of the fact
that some of his tax dollars were going to
help raise those kids.

He didn't blame the children. It was the
goddamned adults who were at fault. It was
always the goddamned adults, but no one
seemed to want to tackle the problem.

And to think that his friend, his partner,
the man with whom he entrusted his life to
everyday of the week, wanted him to get
married. That would be the day.

Thursday - 9:00 p.m.

"What's everybody doing?" Judy asked.

"Nothing," came from one direction out of the dark.

"Reading a fucking book," Coral snapped.

"Hey, don't get testy," Judy said.

"I haven't heard it in a long time," Rhonda said softly.

"Heard? Heard what?" Judy asked.

"The screaming. It's been an awfully long time since we heard it."

"Yeah," Coral said. "It seems like hours. Maybe it's been days for all we know."

"I don't think it's been days," Judy said.

"What makes you say that?" Rhonda asked.

"We haven't been gassed, and there's no food left for us. Plus the fact that somebody took a healthy crap a while ago and I can still smell it."

"Hey, it goes with the territory," Coral said.

"Are you sure you've thought of every possibility to get out of here?" Judy said.

"Everything. Every angle. Every idea. The last one—the one Rhonda came up with, pulling the stitching out of the belts—was the last new idea. And you know how successful that was. I'll say this much. You gotta give the bastards credit. They've thought of everything."

"Where do you suppose we are?" Rhonda asked.

"Who the fuck knows?" Coral snapped. "We could be anyplace. It's got to be a pretty elaborate setup though, you know."

"Elaborate? How do you mean?" Linda Polchow asked, her voice still tremulous.

"Well, the gas for one thing. That had to be installed. Who did it? What reason was given to whoever installed it? The room itself. The floor. From the way everyone describes where she is, it sounds like the place I'm sitting on. Sloped for runoff on both sides, which probably leads to a drain in the floor. Who did the cement work? Who was the plumber? Why didn't they ask questions like 'Why are these things being put in?' and so on."

"I see what you mean," Linda said softly. Her mother had to be going crazy since Linda hadn't called. What would her mother think? Would she call the police? Could the police rescue her? Had these other girls wondered the same things? If for no reason other than taking up time and learning something more about her fellow captives, Linda opened her mouth to speak at the same time the hissing started.

"Hold your breath," Judy yelped.

"Yeah, hold your breath as long as you can," Rhonda said.

"Forget it," Coral said, "it's time for nighty-night. The gas runs a lot longer than your lungs can hold air. Believe me. I've tried it, and it doesn't work. The only thing that happens is you recover more quickly than if you breathe it all in."

"Well, do it anyway, and we won't be un-

conscious so long," Judy said, sucking in a
huge breath of air and holding it. She'd hold
it as long as possible. She'd hold it until she
passed out from lack of oxygen or the gas,
but she'd fight it as long as she could.

Judy could hear one or two falling back,
a soft, gentle thudding sound that sent
shivers up her back. How long could she
hold out? One by one, she counted four
more passing out, hearing their bodies lay
back against the wall or flooring. There were
eight of them. She and one other had been
able to hold their breaths longer. Then she
heard the seventh one slide to a reclining
position and she felt light-headed. She was
losing it. She didn't think she had inhaled
any gas yet. Was she simply going to faint?
Her head reeled as she slumped forward and
then on to her side.

The hissing stopped a few seconds
later, and the door opened. Dim light
flooded the room. The eight naked girls lay
in varying positions, tethered to the walls, a
wide leather belt around each waist.

Aleigha stepped in, carrying a tray with
three plates of food. Edward followed her
carrying a tray with four plates. After
placing the trays on a shelf inside the door
next to the knife Edward had laid there,
Aleigha nodded to him and he picked up a
hose, flushing the floor with water.

The woman stepped through the
bodies, eyeing each one, appraising their

health and physical condition. The last one they had brought in was far from ready, but one girl caught her attention—the one who had stopped by the house in an attempt to sell magazine subscriptions. Once Ida learned the girl was far from home and with an itinerant group of sales people, Ida had offered her a cup of tea, laced with a drug to render her unconscious.

Aleigha stooped down next to Daun while Edward placed the plates of food near the other girls. Reaching out, she stroked the unconscious woman's breasts and belly. "This one, Edward. We'll take this one up to the empty lab."

Before she straigthened up, something caught Aleigha's attention, something laying next to Daun's body. Thread. Picking it up, she ran her free hand over the belt around Daun's waist. She smiled. The stitching served no purpose in the belt's utility. Looking about, she found more and quickly gathered up all of it.

Aleigha stood back, allowing Edward to finish picking up the empty food plates. Once they were stacked on the trays, he handed them to Aleigha and returned to Daun. Bending down, he scooped her up in his arms and carried her into the outer chamber.

Taking one last look at the girls, Aleigha stepped out, following Edward.

Judy's eyes fluttered and opened just as

the door closed. For a split second before the darkness returned, she saw the room bathed in brilliant light.

Thursday - 10:45 p.m.

Judy sat up. Had she dreamt it? Had she had a dream wherein she saw a room of stone walls with girls tied to the . . . ? No! She *had* seen it. She had actually seen the room wherein she and the others were being held captive. She must have held her breath long enough to avoid too much of the gas and had recovered before the person or persons, whoever was responsible for their incarceration, had turned out the lights. The light had been brilliant. She thought for a moment. Perhaps it had been brilliant to her because she had been exposed to nothing but darkness for—how long? How long had she and Rhonda been here? Only a few days. The others had lost track of time. Coral had been able to tell them that she had been here for some three months, only because she and Rhonda had told her that it had been June when they had been picked up along the interstate.

"Hey?" she called quietly. "Wake up! Come on. Rise and shine. I've got great news. I really do. Open those peepers. Come on."

While she waited for the others to regain consciousness, Judy replayed in her mind the quick view she had had of their cell.

There had been the girls, naturally, but her head had been turned toward the direction of the door—something that led to someplace other than here.

The door! She envisioned it and suddenly opened her eyes wide in the dark. There was a shelf next to the door, a shelf right over the head of one of the girls, a blonde with pretty long hair. She'd have to make a mental note. Wait! There was something on the shelf, something sticking out over the edge. It had looked like—no, it couldn't have been a knife handle. Still, as she replayed the second's worth of memory over and over in her mind, she felt it had indeed been a knife. Was it really a knife? Her heart palpitated at the thought. If it were, would it be sharp enough to cut their bonds? Could they even get it?

Someone moaned.

"Come on, wake up," Judy urged. "Who is it? Who's waking up?"

"Huh? Oh, it's me, Linda."

"I can hardly wait to tell you," Judy began.

After she finished telling Linda, the other girls began waking up one at a time, and Judy excitedly told each one. When they were all awake, she said, "How many blondes are there in here?"

"I'm blonde," Coral said.

"So am I," Linda said, coughing.

"The one who I saw was under the shelf had long blonde hair—almost white."

A quiet followed for a second before Linda spoke up. "That'd be me, I guess. I've got hair like that."

"Reach up and over your head."

"Okay."

"But do it slowly. You don't want to knock the knife, if that's what it is, out of reach or off the shelf."

Judy pictured the girl stretching her arm up. "Can you find it?"

"Yeah, I got the edge of the shelf. Just barely though, my fingers are just clearing it."

A sigh collectively sliced through the blackness.

"Be careful now. The thing you don't want to do is knock the knife out of reach or off the shelf," Judy said, repeating her admonition. "We might never find it in the dark."

"Okay," Linda said quietly, a strained effort in the single word. "I've got it. Now what?"

"Bring it down," Judy said excitedly. "Boy, I can't believe that anyone who is this clever could get careless like this and leave a knife laying around. It is a knife, isn't it?"

"Yeah," Linda said. "Now what'll we do?"

"I've been thinking and I've got a plan," Judy said. "Listen carefully."

Thursday - 11:29 p.m.

Aleigha gazed at the body of Daun Kingston hanging from the ceiling and anchored to the floor to prevent her from kicking. If one of the girls could kick with their legs, they might jar the needle from its position in the femoral artery, resulting in the girl bleeding to death unattended. The blood would be lost, and that must never happen. Aleigha enjoyed her role of blood-letter almost too much. She enjoyed even more the reward of doing with the girls whatever she wished as long as she didn't interfere with the gathering of blood.

Daun Kingston was beautiful, and Aleigha appreciated feminine beauty. Her breasts, although not large, jutted out, firm globules of flesh. Aleigha had kissed them and fondled them after Edward had set the girl in place. Shortly after injecting the drug to slow her reactions and inserting the needle and valve, she had set up the flow to run into a quart-sized cannister on the floor.

Daun's well-muscled body held Aleigha's attention. This one had to be the most beautiful of all the girls they had had in many years. Perhaps Aleigha would con-tain her own emotions and refrain from harming her too much right away. She could keep one like this for an awfully long time if she set her mind to it. Hadn't the girl she had just killed been around for months, giving her blood a little at a time for the countess?

Aleigha wondered if the Countess would ever grow tired of having just Ida for a lover. Over the years Aleigha had tended the countess on an almost equal basis with Ida, and Ida and Aleigha had made love thousands of times over the centuries. But lately, Ida had been the only one summoned.

Crossing the room, Aleigha stood before the unconscious Daun. She reached out, touching the pubic hair that had been trimmed neatly to allow the briefest of swimsuits to be worn. Aleigha drew a line along the lighter brown that had been hidden by the string bikini Daun had worn and then stepped closer. She ran her tongue into the girl's navel, wiggling it about. A few seconds later, Daun reacted to the sensual feeling.

Laughing under her breath, Aleigha bent down, slowly drawing a damp line with her tongue on Daun's clitoris. Working it enthusiastically, Aleigha had climaxed by the time Daun began reacting to the stimulation.

Grinning broadly, Aleigha stepped back, watching the woman climax without anyone touching her. Daun's body jerked, reacting to the oral stimulation her torturer had applied.

Aleigha turned, striding to the door. Checking the room before she turned down the lights, she smiled and stepped into the hallway. Just as she closed the door, the front bell sounded.

Who would be at the door at this time of night? She hurried to the front of the house, hoping whoever the intruder might be would refrain from ringing the bell again. When she reached the front hallway, she raced past the steps leading to the second floor. A sudden pounding on the front door reverberated through the high-ceilinged downstairs, echoing its way up the broad staircase. Surely, if the countess or Ida hadn't heard the bell, the pounding would awaken anyone—even the dead.

When she reached the door, she threw it open, unafraid of who might be on the other side. "Yes? Who is it?" she demanded.

Falling back as she recognized the tall, gaunt man standing there, she managed one word.

"Thorko."

13

Friday - 12:02 a.m.

Aleigha fell back, her eyes widening as she stared at the tall, gaunt man standing on the wide porch.

Clearing her throat, she managed, "Come in, Lord Thorko. Come in!"

Without speaking, he swept by her and into the entry hall. While she closed and locked the door, she could feel his stare burning into her back. Slowly turning to face him, she lowered her eyes.

"Where is your mistress?" he asked, his deep voice hollow, threatening.

"Up . . . upstairs."

"Look at me, woman. Look at me, when I speak to you."

Aleigha raised her head until her gaze rested on the grim visage before her. His dark piercing eyes glared at her, unblinking. She felt he might be able to see into her immortal soul, if she had one, but the mere thought that he might be able to read her mind sent tremors through her. The one thing that always bothered her was the fact that when Thorko spoke, he barely moved his mouth. The high cheek bones seemed impervious to movement, while his thin lips, which were almost white, stretched over his yellow teeth in a grimacing grin. His pallid complexion appeared even whiter against the teeth and eyes, emphasizing the shock of white hair that lay combed straight back from his forehead where it came together in a widow's peak. His ears, narrow and pointed, balanced his thin long face that ended at the bottom with an enlarged, angular jaw.

She jumped when he brought his thin, bony hand up to unfasten his long, black cloak. Peering up at the tall man, she realized her own short stature even more. She stepped forward when he swirled the cloak around, offering it to her.

Bowing her head, she took it and hurried to the closet off the main entry. When she returned, she stopped a respectful distance from him.

"How may I be of service to you, My Lord Thorko?"

"Where is the countess?"

"Upstairs, my lord. Sleeping, I assume."

"And Ida?"

"I believe Ida is with my lady."

Thorko turned, hurrying into the front drawing room. "Close the drapes," he ordered, rubbing his hands together. "It is chilly in here."

Pointing to the fireplace where three logs lay, he peered intently at it for a moment before they burst into flame. He moved closer, thrusting his hands toward the flames to warm himself.

"Fetch them." His sepulchral voice echoed through the high-ceilinged room for an instant.

"Yes, my lord," Aleigha said, turning on the overhead lights.

Thorko jumped at the sudden brightness, spinning about to glare at her.

"I . . . I'm sorry, Lord Thorko."

"It's all right," he said magnanimously. "Electricity is the one thing I have been unable to control. The lights were unexpected."

"It is?" Aleigha could hardly believe what he had just said. He was able to control everything, or so she thought.

"No one knows what it is—not even me. If I am to control anything, I must know it completely. Oh, man has managed to harness it but within certain restrictions. If it was known what electricity actually was, then I could control it without effort."

Aleigha turned down the lights, forcing a smile at Thorko.

"Fetch them—now!"

Aleigha backed from the room bowing

subserviently until she stood in the entry hall. Turning, she hurried toward the wide staircase.

Friday - 12:02 a.m.

"Put the knife back up on the shelf again, Linda," Judy ordered.

"Do I have to? I'm tired."

"If you want to get out of here, it's vital that you can put that damned thing back on the shelf in a couple of second's worth of time. Got it?"

"Yeah," Linda sighed.

"Do it once more. Then we'll talk about my plan."

"I can hardly wait," Coral said sarcastically.

"Hey, I think it's a good one and it could work. We'll need everyone's cooperation."

"This had better be good, Judy," Coral said.

"Okay. The knife is back on the shelf. Now what?" Linda asked.

"Here's my plan. We start cutting ourselves loose. Then—"

"No," Coral said, interrupting Judy.

"What? I don't believe you. Why not?"

"Suppose they come back?"

"I don't follow you."

"Suppose they come back and find half of us free and the other half cutting themselves loose. What are they going to do?"

"I don't believe this. Do you like the situation we're all in?"

"Of course not."

"Are you willing to just sit around and wait for them to come and take you away to God-only-knows-what?"

Coral didn't answer immediately. "I . . . I guess not. I'm sorry, Judy. Go ahead. I'll listen."

"Maybe I'm getting ahead of myself. Since Linda can get the knife back onto the shelf without any problem, we've got to practice passing the knife between us, so that each one of us can cut herself loose. From what I saw, we should be able to pass it around."

"But Judy," Rhonda said, "suppose they *do* come back and half of us are loose and the other half isn't, like Coral said. Then what?"

Judy fell silent before answering. "Okay, we cut most of the way through the belt, far enough so that a good pull will break it the rest of the way. We'll weaken the belt. Then—and this is the critical part—if the gas comes on before we're all finished, be sure to lie down in such a way that the cut you've made is under you. Got that?"

Agreement mumbled out of the dark at Judy.

"Another thing that's going to be important is practicing to hold your breath. I don't know how much longer the gas continued in here after I went out, but I was the first one who came to afterward, so I think it's vital that none of us take a full load. Understand?"

Again words of agreement sounded.

"Now, the instant we hear the gas or someone coming, we get the knife back to Linda and she puts it on the shelf."

"Hey, I got a question."

"Who are you?" Judy asked, not recognizing the voice right away.

"It's Pam Kennedy. Will we have enough warning to do all that?"

"The first thing we hear is the gas, right? If we all hold our breaths, we should have enough time to pass the knife back to Linda. We'll start at the girl who is farthest from Linda. That way, each time one is almost freed, the distance back to the shelf will be less."

"That makes sense," Pam said.

"Yeah," Coral said, a note of brightness in her voice. "I guess I was getting too used to our captivity to think clearly before. Sorry, Judy."

"Hey, no problem."

"One thing's for certain," Margaret Olds said. "We can't sit around here waiting for something to happen."

"Does this mean we're going to get out of here?" Sherry Blaine asked, a whimpering sniffle following her question.

"That's right, honey," Judy said comfortingly to the 12 year-old.

"Hey, I just thought of something," Coral said.

"What's that?" someone asked.

"With all the excitement of Judy's plan, we forgot to take roll call after we came to. Coral."

"Right you are, Coral. Judy, here," she said brightly.

"Rhonda."

"Sherry."

"Pam."

"Margaret."

"Linda."

They waited, then took roll call again when they realized that only seven girls had responded. The second time around they knew Daun was no longer in the room.

Friday - 12:45 a.m.

Hair carefully set in place, Elizabeth descended the stairs in regal fashion. Ida followed, and Aleigha, a smug look of revengeful satisfaction on her face, brought up the rear. Apparently, Thorko was going to be angry with them but not with Aleigha. For that she was thankful. If Ida was to be punished, Aleigha might have more of a chance to tend the countess in her quarters. Still, she hoped Ida would not be punished severely.

The small entourage entered the room where Thorko waited.

He spun on his heel, eyes blazing when they came in.

For a long minute he didn't speak and then said, "The body that was found at the construction site—did it come from here?"

Perplexed, the countess looked up at Ida who returned as blank an expression.

"Body?" Elizabeth asked.

"Yes. Body! I investigated and discovered that the cadaver had little blood and that the cause of death was not only loss of blood, but the girl in question had been bitten to death." He half-turned to include Aleigha in his sweeping, accusatory glare.

Elizabeth and Ida turned to stare at Aleigha, a genuine look of displeasure on the countess' face and a forced look of horror on Ida's.

Aleigha's spirits plummeted. She had thought if anyone would be chastised it would be Ida for something or other, and now she was being accused of being careless with a dead body. Still, Ida had known, but Aleigha knew the woman well enough not to expect her to leap to anyone's defense if it meant jeopardizing her own safety or position. Yet knowing she'd have to say something, Aleigha thought it might as well be the truth. That way Ida would be implicated as well.

Elizabeth stood. Crossing the room toward Thorko, she said, "I knew nothing of a dead body being disposed of in any way other than that which you prescribed years ago."

Thorko looked down at her, an almost kindly expression on his thin face. "I know." Looking past the countess, Thorko said, "Szentes, tell me what you did."

"Call me Aleigha. It is my name now. I haven't been called Szentes since you brought me back to life. Call me Aleigha, or I won't speak to you."

"Would you prefer I find out my own way and then punish you doubly—once for transgressing and once for disobedience?"

Aleigha looked away from the sorcerer. "I just did what I ordinarily do. Nothing more. Ida knew of it. Ask her."

Thorko turned, fixing his attention on the taller woman. "Well?"

"She speaks the truth. I did know, but it is as she said. Nothing out of the ordinary transpired."

"Nothing out of the ordinary?" Thorko shouted. "The girl's body has been found. This could lead to trouble. You all may have to leave this place and move to another city. Tell me exactly what you did after the girl died."

Aleigha stepped forward, stopping when Thorko turned to face her. She went into detail about the morning when she and Ida decided to dispose of the body at the construction site.

"And why hadn't you simply placed her in the lime pit?"

"The lime pit, my lord, must be en-larged, and that has not been done yet," Aleigha explained.

"Where is the man?" Thorko looked from woman to woman, waiting for an answer.

"In his room, I imagine."

"Why hasn't he done his work?"

"I believe it was his intention to begin today, my lord."

"The police will be determined to find the person responsible for the strange condition of the girl's body. Of that I'm cer-tain." Thorko stroked his chin thoughtfully.

"If you had controlled yourself, we wouldn't have this problem right now," Ida said, folding her arms and tapping her foot while she stared at Aleigha.

"If you didn't spend every night with the countess, I wouldn't be so tempted to do what I did."

"You're a savage, sick pervert," Ida ex-claimed, turning away.

"You're a whore," Aleigha shot back.

"Please, ladies," Elizabeth said, "don't argue in front of Lord Thorko and me."

"It's your fault as much as Ida's," Aleigha snarled at the countess.

"Well, I . . ."

Thorko clapped his hands, and all three women fell silent. The fire in the fireplace held fast, the flames not moving.

"Listen to me, and listen to me well, you three. For almost four centuries, we have

lived and done whatever we have wanted.
Now, because of jealousy, you are ready to
throw it all away. Could I but change your
natures, I would, but not unlike electricity,
no one understands woman and her moods
or her different natures."

He crossed the room, moving first to
Aleigha, whom he examined carefully
without touching. He moved to Ida and did
the same before stopping at the countess.
Their skin fascinated him, and though he
ran a finger over it without touching, he was
able to experience the sensation of touch.
Their skin had not been affected over the
years the way his had been. Of course,
Aleigha and Ida both had been restored
from death to life, thus their bodies were in
a state of suspension that allowed no
change. The countess on the other hand
had the treatment of young blood to care
for her skin—and it was lovely, soft, pliable,
exquisite to the most rough touch.

Thorko looked at his own hand,
marveling at the solidity of the tiny lines
that covered it. The network ran together
until, by the very number of age lines, they
seemed obliterated. From a short distance,
his face, arms, hands, and body all
appeared to be those of a man no older than
50 or 60, rather than a being who had
existed since the time of Christ.

Reclaiming his spot near the fireplace,
he said, "While I am here, I will care for and
service the countess. Do you understand?"

He smiled when he recognized the understanding in the eyes of the three women, who remained motionless under his spell.

Friday - 1:45 a.m.

"Okay, I'm just about through my belt," Rhonda said.

"Good," Judy said. "When you're finished there'll only be three more to do. While I'm doing this, keep practicing holding your breath. That part is going to be more important than anything else."

"Why?" Sherry asked.

"Because," Rhonda said, "if we can't hold our breaths and keep from being knocked out when the gas goes on, nothing else will matter."

"Oh," the girl said quietly.

"Hurry with the knife, Rhonda," Coral said. "I'm next."

"Yeah, yeah." Rhonda continued sawing the knife through the tough leather, the back of the blade rubbing against her bare stomach.

Friday - 1:50 a.m.

Thorko clapped his hands.

Instantly reacting, the three women showed their regret with sorrowful expressions. Each in turn, beginning with the countess, approached the sorcerer, grasping his long, thin hands and begging him for forgiveness.

Thorko smiled at the noble woman. "You are well, Countess?"

"Yes, I feel very well, as if I'm thirty or thirty-five. Certainly not over forty as I was when you rescued me." She smiled, her teeth gleaming in the firelight. Her eyes twinkled, and to anyone other than the three with her in the room, she would have appeared as someone in her early thirties—not someone in excess of 400 years.

When Ida approached him, he took her proferred hand. "You feel well, Ida? Or should I call you Ilona?"

"Ida is better, since I always am called that now. That way there is no chance of error."

Thorko smiled and accepted Aleigha's apology when she approached him. "Tell me of Ujuvary."

Ida stepped closer. "Ujuvary stays in her rooms. As long as she provides us with wealth, we let her be. She is getting very old and at times unreasonable."

"Very well, I will see her later," he said. "Now that we are all friends again and safe from harm, perhaps you'd like to show me the girls you hold now."

Aleigha stepped forward, an expression of eagerness playing on her round face. She'd take full advantage of showing off her domain to Thorko. "Where would you like to begin, Lord Thorko?"

"At the lowest level in the dungeon. That way I can work my way up to your laboratories." He bowed to the countess. "I'm certain you'd like to accompany us, my lady."

She placed her hand on his when he held it out to her.

Aleigha, content with the way in which the crisis had dissipated, led them out of the drawing room into the hall.

Friday - 1:54 a.m.

"Just remember," Judy said after Rhonda had passed the knife to Coral," that when you hear the sound of the gas, you quickly take a deep breath and hold it as long as you can. Be sure that when you lie down, the cut in your belt is under you. Linda? I hope you can hold your breath long enough to get the knife on the shelf."

"I'll be all right, Judy," Linda said.

"Don't forget to make that cooing sound when the gas comes on, so whoever's got the knife can start passing it to you at once. Got that, everybody?"

Everyone acknowledged Judy's careful instructions.

"Just don't hurry. We'll have a full minute or so before the gas gets to you."

Judy had just stopped speaking when the hiss of gas began.

Linda started her cooing sound, and Coral handed the knife into the dark.

"Where's the knife?" Pam asked, waving her arms around in the dark.

"Here." Coral said, then held her breath.

"Are you moving it, Coral?" Pam asked, gasping as little as possible."

"Yeah."

"Don't. I'll be able to find it better." Pam continued waving her hands back and forth, searching for the knife and finally closing her hand on the handle. She turned, holding the weapon out in front of her to her right. "Linda?"

"Hold it still. I'll get it in a minute," Linda said and at the same time found the knife. Stretching her arms overhead, she found the shelf and laid the knife in the approximate position it had been in earlier.

Judy could hear someone lying down. "Everybody down. Make sure your cut belt is under you." Her head swam as she slipped into unconsciousness.

A few seconds after the last girl passed out, the lights went on.

14

Friday - 2:30 a.m.

Linda opened her eyes. How long had she
been out? Stretching, she called out in a
tiny voice. "Is anyone else awake?"

There was no answer other than a soft
moaning, then someone spoke. "Who's
that? I'm Pam."

"It's Linda," she said, turning to her
left. "Are you all right?"

"Yes, I think so. Is anyone else awake?"

"I am," Judy said, yawning. "I wonder
how long we were out this time?"

"Who knows?" Coral said, coughing.

"Hey, my belt is still cut," Judy said
brightly.

"What made you think it wouldn't be?"

"The gas went on, we went out, and they
didn't see it. Right? That means we're a step
closer to getting out of here."

"I see what you mean," Coral said.

Murmurs of understanding came from the other girls.

"Okay, now," Judy said, raising her voice a bit, "who hasn't cut through their belt yet?"

"I'm almost through mine, but I don't have the knife," Coral said.

"Linda, get the knife and pass it to Coral. Who else hasn't cut their belt?"

"I haven't," Pam said.

"Nor have I," Linda said. "Here, Pam, take the knife."

"I wonder if they'll be back," Margaret muttered.

"I'm sure they will," Judy said.

"I mean sooner than we might expect."

"Who knows? How much time elapses between their visits? This last time was sooner than the others, I think."

"How do you know that, Judy?" Rhonda asked.

"Are you hungry?"

"No."

"The food that was brought—the time we found that Daun was gone—is still in our bellies. At least it is in mine."

"I see where you're coming from. But if that's the way it is, why did they come back so soon?" Rhonda asked.

"The roll call," Margaret said. "We didn't take the roll call."

The girls quickly said their names and

relaxed, knowing that no one had been taken this time.

"Goddamnit!" Coral growled.

"What's the matter?" Judy asked.

"This fucking knife is getting dull."

"Take your time. It'll do the job."

"That's the question. How much time do we have?" Coral said, mumbling as she struggled to free herself.

"Hurry, Coral," Pam urged. "I want to get my belt cut. Hurry!"

"I'm hurrying, I'm hurrying."

"I still wonder why they came back," Linda said.

"How you coming, Coral?" Judy asked.

"I'm just about through."

"Can you tear it apart and free yourself?"

"Yeah, I think so."

"Then do it," Judy said. "Everybody who's cut their belt, pull them apart. Coral, pass the knife on to the next one."

The girls' grunts filled the blackness as they struggled to tear the last little bit of leather holding them prisoner.

When gas hissed loudly, the girls gasped, surprised in the midst of what they were doing. The sound of the knife clattering to the floor rattled in their ears. They quickly succumbed to the noxious fumes and fell unconscious.

Friday - 2:35 a.m.

Aleigha closed and locked the door to the room wherein Daun Kingston hung, her blood dripping through a tube into an enclosed vat at her feet. She smiled, reflecting on the compliments with which Thorko had lauded her. "Excellent work." "Well maintained laboratories." "The girls in the dungeon are healthy appearing and should give the countess much sustenance and pleasure."

The four made their way back toward the front of the house, Ida leading, with Thorko and the countess walking arm in arm behind her. Aleigha brought up the rear. When they reached the front entryway, Thorko stopped.

"The three of you," he said calmly, "can exist forever with my help. You know that, of course. As long as I am, you are. I am more powerful now than at any time in my long life. That makes me the most powerful man on earth. My sorcery could stop an atomic bomb in mid-explosion." He smiled, pulling his thin lips over yellowed teeth.

Ida and Aleigha glanced at each other. They knew full well the power of Thorko. Hadn't he brought them back to life after they had been dead four years?

The countess merely nodded, acknowledging the man's ability and power. She had wanted eternal life with beauty and youth, and she had it. What more could she want?

"You, Ida or Ilona," Thorko said. "You are happy? You enjoy tending the erotic pleasures of your lady?"

"Yes, my Lord Thorko," Ida said quietly, bowing her head at the same time. "You have been most generous to me by extending my life beyond all reasonable length."

"Your life?" he cried. "Your life? You have no life. You have intelligence and a body that appears normal. But life? No. Your very existence depends on my existence. If something happens to me, you are forfeit. Aleigha! Szentes! You are forfeit, too, should anything happen to me. Fear not. There is no man or woman on the face of the earth who even approaches being my equal. Charlatans—all of them—they who say they have knowledge. I alone—I, Thorko—am master of this planet. In time, I shall make my move and conquer all beings on it."

"Could you not do that right now, my lord?" Elizabeth asked.

"Of course, but I need a bit more time. I need the perfect plan to have my power span the globe."

"Are we included in your plans?" Ida bowed as she spoke, showing her gratitude.

"Of course. Since the time they crucified the Man of Galilee, I have been preparing. I came out of the desert from the monastery where I first encountered my god, my leader, my power—Lucifer. I have recruited souls for him the world over for countless centuries. When his plan for world-wide domination was formulated and made known to me, I approached you, my lady, to be my partner. You have outlived your children by hundreds of years. It was your dead husband who first brought to your attention the black arts that made my introduction to your court possible."

Elizabeth, Ida and Aleigha all listened intently. Never had Thorko told them any of this. They knew they had been granted a special existence on earth and that their own debauchery could not be the sole reason for it. Now they were learning the full purpose for the resurrection of Ilona Joo and Szentes from the grave. They were learning everything.

"You, my Lady Elizabeth, shall reign at my side for all time. Lucifer has stated it and made these things possible through me. Enjoy your baths of blood and your drinks of blood."

She blushed, nodding her head.

"The two of you shall be at her side for all time," he said, turning to Ida and Aleigha, "answering her every beck and call. Now, tell me, what of Ujuvary? How does the alchemist fare?"

"Ujuvary is getting so very old, my Lord Thorko," Elizabeth said.

Thorko shook his head. "Why Darvula and Ujuvary did not believe in my powers is one thing I will never understand. Did I not offer them eternal life and youth, just as I did you three?"

The women nodded.

"Why then did they turn their backs on me?"

"Jealousy, my lord?" Ida ventured the suggestion but kept her eyes lowered.

"Yes, you are probably right," he said, shaking his head. "Somehow Ujuvary has managed to survive all these four centuries, but you say age is winning?"

"Yes, my lord. With her withcraft, Darvula lasted a mere seventy-five years after you left us that first time. Somehow, through her alchemy, I imagine, Ujuvary has managed to sustain life but has not remained constant in her status." Elizabeth smiled.

"Ujuvary is of no consequence," he said reaching out to stroke the countess' arm and shoulder. "It is you three who are my concern."

"What of money, my Lord Thorko?" Elizabeth asked.

"Has not Ujuvary provided you with stones and gold of great value over the years?"

Elizabeth nodded.

"When last I was here, you had an immense fortune. At that time you had more wealth than twelve people could spend in twelve lifetimes—money enough to last for over ten thousand years. Is that not enough?''

"Of course, my lord. By that time, you will rule the planet, and all will be yours as I am yours.''

"And I, my lord," Ida said.

"And I," Aleigha added.

The women bowed their heads when Thorko smiled at them.

"Do not concern yourselves for Ujuvary. If she dies, she dies. I do not care. Do you?"

They shook their heads, agreeing with the sorcerer. A sudden whimsical attitude seized them, and they burst into a bubbling laugh.

"Come, my sweet lady," Thorko said, offering his arm to Elizabeth. As they started up the steps, Thorko stopped to face the two women behind them.

Arm in arm, Aleigha smiling broadly, the two women came to a halt when they looked up at Thorko. "What is it, my lord?" Ida asked.

"There is a problem. One or both of you have been careless. If it weren't such, you could frolic the night away, but you have work.''

"Work? We do not understand, my lord," Aleigha said.

"Go back to the dungeon. Hurry! *The girls are almost loose.*"

Ida and Aleigha stared at each other for a full second.

"Hurry!" Thorko waved them away.

Turning, they bolted for the back of the

house and the stairs that led to the dungeon.

Rushing down the first flight of steps, Aleigha slowed. "I'm angry, Ida. Why did he wait? Did he know of this earlier? Are they actually getting loose, as he said?"

"Do not be foolish, little one. You're angry because you wanted to make love with me. Am I right?"

Aleigha nodded.

"If they are loose, we will handle the situation. If they are not, we will retire, and you may do with me, to a point, what you will."

Aleigha started toward the door that led to the next flight of steps, grumbling under her breath.

"Aleigha!" Ida called.

She spun around. "What?"

"Do not be so foolish as to throw away the opportunity offered by Thorko this night—eternal life for subservience. He *will* rule the world, and we *will* be with him."

"Eternal *existence*. Remember? He reminded us that we only exist and do not have life."

"It is better than rotting in a grave or being blown about the earth as dust."

Aleigha turned once more and opened the heavy wooden door. Ida followed her down the shadowy steps. Aleigha turned on the gas and waited for several minutes for the girls to succumb. Pulling open the heavy door, they entered after turning on the lights.

"Look! Thorko was right. Some of them are loose. How could this have happened?" Ida said, glaring at Aleigha who was in charge of the girls both here and in the laboratories.

Shrugging, Aleigha stepped forward. The knife lay between the girls, mere inches from the hand of the one whose belt was still in place, held there by a fraction of an inch of leather. The naked girl on the other side of the blade had cut through her belt and lay sprawled on the cement floor. The blonde with long hair was still tethered to the wall but the rope had been cut while the rest of the girls had either freed themselves or were about to when Aleigha had turned on the gas.

"This blade!" Aleigha said, "Where did it come from? Who gave it to them?"

"It's from the kitchen, isn't it?"

Aleigha nodded. "On occasion it was brought down to cut a length of rope for a new girl. Edward! It has to be Edward who was so careless. He must have laid it on the shelf here," she said, pointing to the small platform, "and they somehow found it in the dark."

"What can we do? Do you have more belts?"

Aleigha shook her head. "We'll have to have new ones fashioned. Until then, we'll have to keep them under the gas."

"Won't that mean gassing them every three hours or so?"

Aleigha nodded.

"We won't get much sleep that way."

Aleigha smiled. "Sleep? Do you want sleep?"

"No, I want you."

Ida stepped closer to Aleigha and they kissed, their tongues promising more when they reached the upstairs.

Picking up the knife, Aleigha followed Ida to the outer chamber and closed the door behind her. Turning the gas valve, she let it open for two minutes. That would be a sufficient amount for now. In three hours, they'd come down and repeat the dosage.

The two women made their way to the first floor and then to Ida's bedroom.

Friday - 3:03 a.m.

Elizabeth Browne Nargella stood nude in the center of her bedroom, her head bowed.

Thorko sat in a chair near the bed, admiring the woman's firm body. Her breasts rose and fell with her breathing while she awaited his command.

"Go to the bed, Elizabeth," he said quietly.

She walked across the room and lay down on the canopied bed, silk sheets gently cooling her body.

A slight rustling brought her attention to the foot of the bed, and she saw Thorko, stripped naked, approaching her.

His thin body was etched with the same miniscule lines of age, covering it in its entirety. His massive penis, already engourged with blood, bounced gently as he climbed onto the bed next to her.

A raging passion tore at her loins, anticipating Thorko's lovemaking. His sexuality equaled hers on the occasions when he was with her, but his sex drive was such that once or twice during a visit would be the extent of their lovemaking. She anticipated his organ being thrust into her body. It was lovely and fulfilling when Ida administered her charms to Elizabeth, and Aleigha, although rough by comparison, was able to arouse an animalistic reaction within her breast.

But it was Thorko whom she loved. It was Thorko who had made the overture to her that Ferencz, her husband, was in the way. It was Thorko who suggested that Ferencz do battle with the invaders, and it was Thorko who arranged her husband's death during the fighting.

Thorko lay full upon her, his tongue exploring her face and neck while she lay back enjoying his touch. He lightly ran his tongue over a small scar on her neck, kissing it, nibbling it.

Her temperature rose as her instincts awakened. She wanted him, but she knew it would be when he was ready and not an instant before. She desperately needed the satisfaction Thorko could give, but she would be patient, knowing full well that he would enter her at the proper time.

His mouth closed on hers, her tongue invading the dark confines of his mouth, caressing, investigating, probing. She anticipated his penis thrusting in and out of her body until both of them would climax.

When she withdrew her tongue, she tasted his entering her mouth. His tongue, longer than any she'd ever encountered, explored the interior of her mouth before reaching toward the opening of her throat. She wished it were even longer, long enough to send it down her throat and into her body.

Thorko rolled off but kept his mouth tightly clamped on hers. Resting on one elbow, he slowly, tantalizingly brought his free hand to her breasts. Gently kneading them, he squeezed with more authority, and she arched her back as gyrating sensations grew to a swirling, rolling seizure of pleasure. Arching her back farther, she raised her body higher, offering her breasts to him.

Trailing one hand down her front, he homed in on her navel, teasing with concentric circles which grew smaller as he neared the center of her birth cup.

A moan escaped her lips, and she cried out. Ecstasy, sheer ecstasy! Her body

burned. The flames of her sexuality, fanned
into an inferno, roared in her hips. Thorko's
finger rammed into her midsection, gently
then roughly, carefully yet carelessly.

Tears of sheer animal pleasure
squeezed from her closed eyes. Every
square inch of her body quivered, anticipating the next thing he'd do. Her skin
seemed alive with a will of its own, reacting
in any way it wanted. When his finger left
her navel, it moved erratically down, down
toward her pubic hair. The hair seemed
more like live nerve endings, and each one
reacted accordingly as his finger passed
through until it reached her clitoris. Barely
touching it, he moved it from one side to the
other.

Elizabeth quaked, the fires raging
within her, consuming her, flooding her sensitive skin from within, while she tingled
insanely, each hair follicle shaking
violently. When would he do it? When?

Thorko lowered his head to her breasts,
and that long tongue snaked out. She knew
that tongue and claimed it as her own
possession. The wet, soft surface licked
over her skin, sending new waves of sweet
torture tearing through her ready body. His
mouth locked onto one nipple, pulling,
sucking, biting, releasing only to repeat the
procedure over and over. When he finished
with it, the aureole glowed with blood
surging beneath the surface. His lips moved
away, toward the other mound of white flesh

and the throbbing bud waiting at its peak. Hardly touching her skin, he clamped onto the other nipple, mouthing it, biting, nuzzling, teasing in the same way.

Little by little, he explored her entire body with his tongue, licking, touching, sampling the taste of her skin.

Elizabeth knew she could tolerate no more of the delightful torture and raised her head. Her arms reached out grabbing Thorko around the neck. Pulling him down to her, she kissed him and whispered, "Now, my darling. Now!"

Thorko raised his lower body as she spread her legs. When the tip of his penis brushed her sensitive pubic hair, she screamed as the sensation drove home the message of pleasure to come. As his gigantic organ passed through, penetrating her lower body, it roughly grazed the clitoris and she bit her tongue. The feeling over-whelmed her, washing to every corner of her body, filling every orifice of her being. Lost in the undulating waves of passion as Thorko pounded at her body, her head spun.

Muttering over and over as her lover continued his ministrations, her voice rose in praise of him. "Fuck me. Fuck me, my lord and master, Thorko. Fuck me, Thorko!"

Her mind and body, intertwining as one, climbed the heights of physical pleasure, as she and Thorko neared their climaxes. Twisting her head to one side, she exposed more of her neck and closed her eyes when she saw his face nearing hers.

Thorko did not kiss her but slipped his lips along her jawline, toward the windpipe and river of life that flowed so close to the surface. Opening his mouth, his teeth bit onto her skin, holding tightly as he chewed back and forth on the scar tissue he had tenderly kissed earlier. When the coppery taste of blood filled his mouth, his body went rigid and his ancient seed spewed into the countess's body.

Elizabeth, aware of the new taunting of her senses, reveled in her spiraling feelings as Thorko's teeth clenched the flesh on her neck. Writhing with the ultimate giving and pleasure she derived from it, she felt his body stiffen at the same time her middle seemed to explode.

After a few minutes, her passion ebbed to a more tolerable level, and when Thorko lay still, she embraced him, tears running down the sides of her face.

Then they slept.

                   Friday - 4:30 a.m.

Ida lay in Aleigha's arms, each exploring the other's body.

Thorko had rolled off the countess, but they slept in each other's embrace.

The girls in the dungeon sprawled where they had fallen earlier in the morning hours, gassed into a deep sleep, totally oblivious of their escape plan's failure.

On the first floor, a shadow, darker than the dark engulfing the house, moved quietly from room to room.

15

Friday - 7:45 a.m.

Gus looked over the rim of his coffee cup, studying his partner who held his head down, eyes fixed on an open folder. "You and Ellie have a fight?"

Jerry jerked up to stare at him. "No. Why?"

"You're really lost in that file. I just thought you might be trying to get your mind off another sort of problem." Gus smiled broadly. He knew full well that Ellie and Jerry had not, in their short marriage, even had a cross word pass between them. If he were ever to consider marriage it would have to be a girl like Ellie Hewlett, but as far as Gus knew, there weren't anymore like her around.

"No. Nothing like that, Gus. It's this case. I was sort of airing out different aspects of it last night with Ellie. Not everything—just the high spots. You know the maddening thing about it?"

Gus shook his head, and drained his cup in one swallow.

"Everything—and nothing."

"What the hell is that supposed to mean?"

Jerry stood up and came around his desk to sit on the edge of Gus'. "I'll grant you I haven't been a detective all that long, but from what I've studied and heard and been taught, there should be some sort of thread to hang different leads on?"

"Thread?" Gus asked, wrinkling his forehead.

"My way of saying it, Gus, but have you ever seen a case with so much in the way of files and missing persons with absolutely no leads other than this Kingston gal? It was her folder I was going through now."

Gus nodded, "I know where you're coming from. We don't have much choice as to what we should be doing, do we? Did you come up with anything new in her folder?"

Jerry shook his head, standing up to go around to the other side of the double desk area and sitting down heavily. "I'm not all the way through it yet. What are we doing today?"

Gus shrugged. "I guess the only option we have is to return to the North Duluth Avenue area and pick up where we left off yesterday. I think that's the only place we'll find anything, if there's anything to find."

"Wrong!" Jerry jumped from his seat and came around the desks to throw an advertising pamphlet on Gus's blotter. "Take a look at this."

Gus picked up the folder and opened it. "What should I be looking for?"

"This." Jerry pointed to the front of it.

"What's so interesting about that? It's just a folder for the company Daun Kingston worked for."

"That's right. You were talking to the kid's mother."

"What kid's mother? What in hell are you talking about?"

"Yesterday on North Duluth. The run-down place where the little blonde bellowed louder'n a bull moose in heat."

Gus nodded. "What about it?"

"While you were talking with the mother, I spoke with her eight year-old son for a minute. He had a valise, remember?"

Gus frowned. "Yeah. She was going to clobber him for having taken it out of someone's trash barrel or something. What about it?"

"This." Jerry pointed to the words, emblazoned in bright, red ink across the front of the brochure:

MAGAZINES
GLAMOUR
The HELPER
Leisureading, Inc.
Dallas, Texas

"So? Don't play games with me so early

in the morning, Jerry. Spit it out. What in hell are you trying to tell me?"

"I don't think you looked at the bag closely. I did when I talked with the boy. I was just trying to make conversation. I asked him if the letters on the valise were the name of his company. He said they were, and I asked him what they meant. He said he didn't know."

"What the fuck are you driving at?" Gus impatiently chewed his lower lip.

"This," Jerry said triumphantly and picked up a piece of memo paper from Gus' desk. He laid it over the brochure in such a way that the only thing left showing were the letters "es" on the top line, "r" on the second, "er" on the third and "Inc." on the bottom. "Those are the letters that were on the kid's valise."

"Are you positive?"

"I'd bet *my* first-born on it."

"Is Ellie . . . ?"

"No, just a figure of speech, Gus." Jerry smiled sheepishly. "I think we should get the hell out there right now and ask the kid where he found it."

"I think you've hit on something, Jerry," Gus said flatly, standing to slip into his jacket which he had hung across the back of his chair.

Jerry cocked an eyebrow and frowned at him. "You don't sound all that enthusiastic."

"I am about what you learned but not

about going back to that house. Those kids are real brats."

"It goes with the job. How many times have you told me that? The bad goes with the good, day in and day out. I think those were your exact words."

Blushing, Gus stepped away from his desk. "Why? Why do I have to be saddled with a guy who can remember conversations word for word?" He started toward the door and stopped for an instant. He turned to find Jerry grinning broadly, shaking his head. "Come on, 'Rookie!' "

Jerry followed his partner from the day room.

Friday - 9:00 a.m.

Darcy Blake opened the door. Her expression changed immediately from the frown she had had on her face to one of smiling attentiveness when she saw who stood on the rickety front porch.

"Well, good morning, officers. How are you two this morning?"

"Very good, Mrs. Blake," Jerry said. "Could we see Mickey for a moment?"

She made a half-hearted attempt to button the top button on her blouse, which hung away from her chest, partially displaying her small breasts. "You want to see Mickey?"

"That's right," Gus said.

"You really want to see Mickey?"

Both men nodded.

"He is here, isn't he?" Jerry asked.

"He's all right, isn't he?" Gus added.

She nodded absently. "Huh? Sure, he's here, and he's fine. I just didn't think you two policemen had come back here to see him, that's all."

Jerry frowned, turning to Gus.

Gus coughed and said, " 'Nother time perhaps."

She smiled at Gus, nodding. "I understand. You're busy, right?"

"You got it," Gus said, glancing at his partner.

She turned and left the hallway.

"You'll learn a come-on when it's thrown in the form of a curve ball, Jerry."

Jerry shook his head, inhaling deeply. The stench of urine and days-old garbage assailed his nostrils.

"Don't breathe too deeply either," Gus said, holding a finger to his lips when he heard a commotion from the back of the house.

"I don't care if you are busy playing," Darcy screamed. "You're coming in here and talking to the police. I don't know what you did, but whatever it was, you're going to get it good when they leave."

"Awww, Ma," Mickey bellowed as she pulled him by his ear into the hallway from the kitchen.

"Easy, Mrs. Blake."

Blushing, she released Mickey's ear, which he rubbed vigorously.

"I didn't do nothin'," he wailed. "I didn't. Really."

Jerry dropped to his haunches, crouching to look into the eight year-old's eyes. "Remember when we were here yesterday, Mickey?"

The boy nodded, looking up at Gus and then back to Jerry.

"Remember your business case?"

He nodded again.

"Could I see it again?" Jerry felt Darcy's eyes on him, and when he looked up, he found her studying him with a confused look furrowed into her pretty features.

Without waiting, Mickey spun about and ran to the kitchen. They heard a cabinet door opening and then banged shut.

"Goddamnit, Mickey, how many times have I told you not to slam doors?" Darcy caught herself and instantly lowered her voice. "I'm sorry, gentlemen."

Gus could see the red creeping onto her face when she lowered it.

Mickey ran back into the hallway. "D'you say somethin', Ma?"

"I said you shouldn't slam doors so hard, Mickey." Embarrassed, she coughed and turned partially away.

Handing the valise to Jerry, Mickey said, "Here."

Jerry took it and held it up for Gus to

peruse. Reaching into his inner coat pocket, Jerry withdrew the folder he had discovered in the Kingston file. The letters and their respective positions matched.

"Where did you find this, son?" Gus crouched down next to Jerry.

"I dunno. I don't 'member."

Gus stood, turning to Darcy. "Ma'am, if your son can tell us, we'll finally be getting someplace with this case."

"Is there a reward or anything?"

Gus shook his head. "It's an opportunity to show him how a good citizen helps the police. Let's say the reward would be a civics lesson well learned."

Darcy looked back at Gus as though he were crazy. "Tell 'em what they want to know, Mickey."

"You'll hit me, Ma."

"I won't."

"Will, too. You always do."

"I do not, but I will this time if you don't tell them what they want to know."

"In the alley," the boy mumbled.

Gus looked past the boy into the living room. Rundown furniture and torn upholstery proclaimed the family's poverty.

"Where?" Jerry asked, standing up.

"In the alley," Mickey said, raising his voice.

"That's better," Darcy said.

"Can you show us where, Mickey? Can you show us where you found it?" Jerry patted the boy on the head.

Mickey nodded.

"Would you like to go for a ride in our car? Then you can show us where you found the bag. Okay? Would you like that?"

Mickey nodded again.

"Will you bring him back here?" Darcy asked, patting a wayward hair into place.

"Of course, we will," Jerry said, ushering Mickey through the front door.

Gus followed but stopped at the doorway. Bending down, he picked something up and turned to face Darcy. "You shouldn't be so careless with your money, ma'am." He held out a crumpled $20 bill.

"That's not—mine," she said hesitantly.

"Well, it was laying there in the corner. If one of your kids had found it, they'd have lost it or gone to the store and bought candy with it. It's yours all right."

"No strings?" she asked, ignoring what he had just said.

Gus shook his head. "No strings."

Darcy smiled. "You come back anytime you want. Hear?"

Friday - 9:20 a.m.

"It was along here someplace," Mickey said, standing between Gus' legs in the front seat of the Chevrolet.

"Do you think you can remember right where it was when you found it?"

"I . . . I think so." He peered at the rows

of garages on either side and wrinkled his face.

Jerry, behind the wheel, allowed the idling motor to pull the car through the alley. He watched the boy's face for some sign of recognition.

"Was it just laying out in the alley, Mickey?" Gus asked. "Or was it close to one of these buildings?"

"It was in a box. Next to some barrels, I think."

"Was it in someone's rubbish pile?"

Mickey didn't answer.

Gus repeated the question.

"You'll tell my ma, then she'll hit me."

"Hey, come on, Mickey, would we do something like that?"

Mickey shrugged.

Jerry put his foot on the brake pedal as he came to the end of the alley. "You're sure it was in this block?"

Mickey nodded. "Uh-huh. It was right there, between that fence and the garage."

Jerry didn't stop but pulled out of the alley, turned the corner and drove away from the building to which Mickey had pointed. "Are you really certain, Mickey?"

"Yup, that's the place all right. Best thing I ever found there, too."

"What else have you found?" Gus asked, rolling down the window on his side.

"Nothing much. Some broken glass tubes or something and some real sharp little knives. I cut myself on one once, but I didn't show Ma. She'd'a' hit me."

Jerry looked across to Gus, and they frowned at each other.

"We're going to take you home now, Mickey. You've been a real big help. You tell your mother that you really helped us a lot. Okay?" Jerry smiled at him.

When Jerry pulled to a stop, Gus opened the car door and helped the boy out. Mickey ran full tilt up the old sidewalk and into the house, slamming the door behind him.

They could hear Darcy scream at him and then silence.

"I hope the kid can talk fast enough so she knows he's been helpful and won't hit him," Jerry said, frowning through the window.

"That's one big trouble of yours that you'll have to overcome if you want to make it as a detective, Jerry. Get rid of that soft spot in your heart."

Gus glared at him before turning to look out his window. "Go around the block. We'll park in front and go to the house."

Friday - 9:35 a.m.

"Hey, this is the house where we quit yesterday," Jerry said, looking at the gray, somber stone mansion.

"You're right. I wonder if we'd have looked on it differently yesterday from the way we are now?" Gus opened his car door and got out. He waited until Jerry came around to the sidewalk.

"Pretty ironic, if you ask me," Jerry said. "We could have gone in here yesterday and asked routine questions and left. Today we'll handle it differently."

"How?" Gus asked, taking the lead as they walked up the long bush-lined path. Huge trees stood guard in the front yard, guaranteeing shade all day long. Poplars lined the property on both sides. Gus turned to Jerry. For some reason he felt the house was examining them as much as they were examining it.

"Well, we'll ask what they know about the valise for one thing, won't we?"

"Nope. No way. Anything but. We'll ask the same questions and see how they react. We can always come back. Right now, we don't have too much to talk about with them. I want to see if they're going to admit that the Kingston gal got this far and what their reaction is to the fact that she's missing."

"You going to talk?"

"If you want me to," Gus said.

"I think you should. I might screw it up good."

"Hey, you've done all right so far. Besides, it was your finding the connection between the valise and Kingston that's given us our first solid lead."

"Regardless, you do the talking."

"Gotcha," Gus said, thrusting out his fist, one finger poised to ring the bell.

A faint buzzing sounded, and after several minutes footsteps clicked on a bare floor as someone approached the front of the house. The knob turned, and the heavy paneled door swung open.

"Yes?"

Gus studied the short woman for a moment before speaking. She appeared to be in her early to mid-thirties, with short dark hair and eyes that looked directly at him. "Are you the lady of the house?" He held up his badge.

"No sir."

"Is she in? I'm Detective Gus Weaver, and this is Detective Jerry Hewlett."

"Yes sir, she's in."

"May I speak with her?"

Aleigha stepped back, allowing the two men to enter. "I'm not certain if she's available. If she isn't, you can speak with her secretary."

She stepped to a door and opened it, swinging it back on noiseless hinges. "If you gentlemen will step in here and wait, I'll get one of them for you. Make yourselves comfortable."

Once the door was closed, Jerry looked at Gus and whistled softly. "Wow! Just like in the movies. Maid and everything."

Gus nodded, scanning the room quickly. Ceilings that he estimated to be 12 feet high seemed to disappear in the gloom

of the dimly lighted room. Large pieces of
furniture huddled here and there in the 40
foot long parlor. A fireplace at the end
caught his attention, and he motioned for
Jerry to follow him.

"I don't think I could live in a
mausoleum like this," Gus said quietly.
"Look at this." He pointed to the plaque
hanging over the fireplace. "A coat of arms.
You know anything about coats of arms?"

"Where would I have learned about
coats of arms?" Jerry said, stepping around
him to peer intently at the symbol.

"As I understand it," Gus said, "they
have their own language. A guy could tell
who was on whose side by just looking at
their shield."

"Why didn't they just look at their
faces?"

"They had armour on—helmets and
face coverings. At any rate, everything
means something on a coat of arms like
that."

"Really?"

"Yeah. You should study up on it sometime."

Jerry dutifully pulled out a small notebook and pencil, continuing to study the
large circular piece of armor.

Gus ambled about the huge room,
glancing at portraits, antique furniture and
accoutrements here and there. One portrait
in particular held his attention longer than
the others. A woman, her oval face peering

down at the room, held her painted gaze on
him. He moved to his right, then to his left,
but the eyes didn't leave him. The white lace
collar and flared skirt must have been the
latest style in their day.

Turning, he saw Jerry at the fireplace.
"What are you doing?"

"Detecting, Detective Weaver. Why?"

Gus nodded but didn't smile. Something about this room bothered him, but he
had no idea what it might be. Probably just
the thought of a few people living in a hotel
like this, being waited on hand and foot,
was enough to gall him. Still he was philo-
sophical enough to know that not everyone
could handle life in the same way. It'd be
boring as hell if such were the case.

"Hey, Gus, what do you suppose these
three things are?"

Gus went to his partner's side and
followed his outstretched arm designating
three, ivory colored items that were pointed
to the left. "Damned if I know. What're you
doing?"

"Jotting down what's written on it. I
don't know why, so don't ask me. It's just a
hunch—and curiosity."

"I know what you mean."

"What?"

"Do you feel strange in here?"

"Now that you mention it, I do. What do
you suppose is causing us to react like
that?"

Gus shrugged. "It's a creepy room—

dark, big furniture, big paintings. Christ, everything's big in here, isn't it?"

"You're right about that," Jerry said. "Shh, I think I hear someone coming."

Like two school boys caught doing something they shouldn't, they took several large steps to the middle of the room, away from the fireplace and the coat of arms that had held their attention.

The door through which the maid had ushered them opened, and she reentered. "I'm sorry but my employer seldom if ever receives anyone. I've spoken with her secretary, and she will be here in a moment or so. Her name is Ida Chewell. Continue to make yourselves comfortable, gentlemen."

Aleigha closed the door.

Gus looked at Jerry. "If her employer seldom receives visitors, it's highly unlikely that she talked with Daun Kingston."

Jerry nodded and turned back to the door when it opened.

The tall, elegant woman closed the door behind her and seemed to glide across the room. Her high-necked dress emphasized her height even more, and when she confronted them she said, "My name is Ida Chewell. I'm secretary to E.B. Nargella. How may I be of help?"

Gus and Jerry pulled out their shields and flashed them at her.

"Aleigha said you were from the police. What is it you want?"

Gus went through the same approach

they had used the previous day. When he finished, he said, "Did you by chance have Miss Kingston call on you?"

"As a matter of fact, she did. I remember her quite clearly. She was quite lovely to look at." Ida sat down in a large chair, indicating the two men should sit on a nearby couch.

Jerry shot a quick, furtive glance at Gus who focused his attention on the woman. After they were seated, Gus continued with the usual questions.

"It's not important as to whether you purchased anything or not. Did she by chance say anything about her day's work, like which direction she was moving that day, anything?"

"Now that you mention it, she did say something about being unhappy with the job. I imagine," Ida said, leaning back in the chair, "such a life would be filled with hazards. She complained of not making much money. I bought a rather large order of magazine subscriptions to help her out."

"I see," Gus said, jotting information into his notebook. "That's very interesting. I'm glad you remembered her."

Ida smiled and stood. "I'm glad I could be of help. Perhaps I will recall more. Shall I call you if I do?"

"By all means," Gus said, handing her a card after he and Jerry had stood. They followed her to the door and stepped into the front hall.

"This is a lovely house," Jerry said, looking around the entryway. "When was it built?"

"Around the turn of the century," Ida said, smiling pleasantly.

Jerry leaned closer to the wall. "What sort of covering is that?"

"That?" Ida said. "That is leather. It's quite different. It seldom if ever gets dirty and needs little maintenance. It's quite original."

While Jerry and the woman talked, Gus peered around the hallway that led to the back of the house. At the end, a door opened and an ancient looking woman stepped into the hall. Glancing up, she saw Gus and shuffled back, retracing her steps. One large crescent earring swung from her left ear. Gus was about to ask the secretary if that might be her employer when he heard the door behind him open.

Swinging around, he found Jerry opening the front entrance. He hurriedly stepped around the woman. After thanking her again, they returned to the Chevrolet parked at the curb.

After they had pulled away, Gus said, "I think we'd better check them out pretty good."

"Why?"

"Daun Kingston was one of the better salespeople Leisureading ever had. This was her third or fourth year of doing it. I don't think she'd have complained about not making any money, do you?"

"I caught that," Jerry said.

"Of course," Gus said, "she might have used that as a ploy to make sales."

"I sort of doubt that. If she was as good a sales representative as the records indicate, she probably used good sales technique. I think we should assume that for the time being and go accordingly."

"Let's not assume anything. Remember what you get when you assume."

"What?" Jerry asked, turning the car from North Duluth.

"An *ass* with *u* and *me*."

Jerry chuckled.

"Seriously, I think we should get back to the station. I want to run a full check on this Ida Chewell and her employer, this Nargella woman."

16

Ida closed the front door and turned around. Her face twisted into an outraged mask when she saw the figure at the end of the hall. Ujuvary stood, humped over, her long, unkempt gray-white hair hanging across her shoulders. The aged woman looked up, her toothless mouth splitting into a grotesque smile. She cackled, walking toward Ida.

"You fool!" Ida stepped forward to block her way. "What are you doing down here?"

"I had business in the kitchen," Ujuvary said in a tired voice, labored by the exertion of walking.

"Did those men see you?"

"Maybe. Maybe not."

"How many times have we told you to stay out of sight, even when we're here alone? Do you realize how ugly you are, you old . . ."

"Shh," Ujuvary cautioned, holding a bent, gnarled finger to her lips. "They'll hear you." She motioned up the wide staircase.

"I hope they do. If they get angry enough, maybe they'll do something about you."

"The countess has taken my offerings all these years. I don't think she'll be so quick to rid herself of me as you'd have her."

Ida snarled, kicking out with her foot when the aged alchemist walked past. "Ugly old witch."

"You have me confused, Ilona Joo," Ujuvary said quietly, "with Darvula. Darvula was the witch. I'm the alchemist. Remember?"

"Don't make light of me, Ujuvary. I'll get rid of you yet."

The old woman laboriously made her way toward the second floor, one step at a time, pausing to rest on each. Ida hated her. She was old. Her skin sagged, and her yellowed eyes watered all of the time. Ujuvary had refused for some reason to allow Thorko to grant her eternal life and youth. Although the alchemist had never admitted it, Ida thought that perhaps there was a sort of professional jealousy brooding within Ujuvary, and for that reason the woman had decided to use her own means to preserve her beauty and youth. It hadn't

worked, and although she still lived, the
years, decades and centuries had not been
kind to her. Ida was youthful in appearance.
With modern makeup she looked stunning.
She had been in her 36th year when she had
been beheaded. When Thorko had restored
her, she had retained the appearance she
had enjoyed prior to her death. The same
held true for Aleigha.

Aleigha, with her large breasts and slim
waist and firm buttocks, was pretty. Her
strange appetites, when it came to torture
and lovemaking, didn't always appeal to
Ida. Nevertheless, Ida enjoyed Aleigha's
body and attention whenever time per-
mitted.

A noise from above brought Ida back to
the entryway. Looking up the steps, she saw
Thorko, standing at the head of the stairs.
An angry grimace held his thin, narrow face.

"What have you done?" He pointed a
long, thin finger at Ujuvary.

The old hag stopped, looking upward.
"What?"

"What have you done? Who was here,
Ida?"

"The police, Lord Thorko."

"What did they want?"

"They are asking questions about a
young woman who sold magazine subscriptions."

"Do you know anything about her?"

Ida dropped her gaze to the floor, her
face flushing. She nodded slowly.

"Is she here—in the house?"

"Yes, my lord. She is in one of the labs at the present time."

"What did you tell the police?"

"I lied. I told them of a conversation the girl and I were to have had. They seemed satisfied."

"What has Ujuvary done?"

"The police saw her."

"So?"

"She is ugly, Lord Thorko."

"I know that. Why does the fact that the police saw her upset you?"

"Ujuvary, my lord, is not an asset to us. She is not your friend. She does what she does only out of necessity to stay alive."

"I do not understand you, Ida. Explain yourself." Thorko glared at her.

"My lady, the countess, is beautiful. Aleigha is youthful and attractive. I am not without beauty myself, my lord. Darvula and Ujuvary both rejected your plan of eternal youth and beauty, thinking that their own powers were sufficient to carry them through the years. Darvula is long dead. Ujuvary should be dead—just look at her. She looks like a walking cadaver."

Thorko smiled without taking his eyes from Ida. "And what are you, my dear, if not a walking cadaver?"

Ida looked at the floor, turning half away from the stairs. "You are right, of course, my lord."

"However," Thorko said, raising his

voice, "what you say is not to be ignored. Ujuvary—the way she is now—is definitely no longer an asset."

"Not an asset?" Ujuvary's voice cracked from the strain of speaking so loudly. "Not an asset? Who will provide for the countess? I have given her gold and jewels and things of value to convert to currency over the years. She needs me."

Thorko threw his head back, his laugh echoing through the house. "Do you think I couldn't provide her with funds? Fool! I should have done something about you a long time ago."

"Stop!" Ujuvary grabbed for the railing, holding one hand over her heart, gasping from the effort of shouting the single word.

"You dare order me?" Thorko took one step down the stairway and stopped.

"You should know what will happen if you harm me."

Thorko glared at her. There were certain things Ujuvary could hide from him, and she had apparently succeeded in concealing some sort of protective threat. "And what is that?"

Ujuvary laughed quietly. "If you harm me—kill me—my lady's jewels and gold will revert back to the base material from which they were made. Do you understand what that would do?"

Thorko laughed again, his high-pitched humorless tones ringing throughout the mansion. "Fool!" He pointed at her, a reddish glow emanating from his finger. When he voiced the single word, a bolt zig-zagged down the staircase paralyzing the old lady.

Ujuvary grabbed her heart and, after teetering for a few seconds, retained her balance and stood still. Ida glared at her. Raising her attention to Thorko, she cleared her throat. "It is better, my lord. We'll all be better off if Ujuvary is . . ."

Thorko ignored her, raising his arms above his head. The robe he wore fell open, and she saw his penis hanging down limply. Offended at the sight of his manhood, Ida fixed her eyes upon his face. She worshipped Thorko's power—not his penis.

A crackling filled the air, growing louder with each swing of the grandfather clock's pendulum. When it reached unbearable proportions, Thorko dropped his arms. "The old hag's threat is nonexistent. I have seen to it that the countess' wealth is secure and have doubled it in size."

"How . . . ?" Ida started but stopped. If Thorko wanted her to know, he'd tell her.

"I probed the hag's mind. She's bereft of her faculties, and her threat is hollow. She is without such power."

"It will be better if . . ." Ida said softly, but with a note of determination. "We'll all be safer if she . . . What good is she? You yourself said the countess has wealth enough to last over ten thousand years. Now you have doubled it."

"True, Ida. Perhaps your inner desires should be satisfied—the ones you could not bring yourself to finish. '. . . better if Ujuvary were dead.' What good is she? None!" He snapped his fingers at Ujuvary who regained control of her body and faculties.

Cackling, she turned, half-running, half-falling down the stairs. When she reached the bottom, she hurried past Ida and limped toward the kitchen and the back of the house.

"Kill her, Thorko. She's getting away," Ida screamed but stopped when she heard a growl on the stairs. Looking up, she sucked in her breath. A large, canine beast stood on the steps, yellow eyes glowing hungrily. Frothy saliva dripped from the blue-black lips, which rolled back over huge, gleaming fangs. After making its way down the stairs, the beast stopped, glowering at Ida, who stood speechless. The animal shook its head around in a circle, giving voice to a throaty roar that shook the house.

Movement overhead caught Ida's attention out of the corner of her eye. Looking up, she saw a white-faced countess and Aleigha standing at the railing, peering down at the strange animal. Raising a finger to her lips, Ida cautioned them to silence. She returned her attention to the beast and mouthed the words, "Kill her, my Lord Thorko."

The monster turned, stalking the hallway through which the old woman had just passed to reach the kitchen. Rearing up, when it confronted the door, a powerful paw and foreleg shot out, knocking it from its moorings. More pale than ever, Ujuvary stood in the middle of the large kitchen, a butcher knife in hand. Her rheumy eyes stared at the monstrous apparition entering the room. She raised the knife to defend herself but did not fall back.

Not unlike a cat playing with a trapped victim, the beast inched its way into the kitchen, riveting its attention on the hag. When a mere three feet separated them, Ujuvary took a step back. The monster stopped. Ujuvary took another step back, then another.

After several seconds passed, the monster leaped, its fangs gleaming in the morning sunlight pouring through the window over the sink. Jaws that would not be denied closed on the old woman's windpipe and jugular vein. The animal tore the throat out, shaking its head. A small amount of blood erupted for a second or two and then stopped. The beast stood still, an unusual quiet filling the house. Rearing up, it placed its front paws on the work table and hung its head down.

Slowly, the animal changed shape, resuming the body and appearance of Thorko. When the transmogrification was complete, he stood up straight. Ida entered

the kitchen and stopped inside the doorway.

"Is it over, my lord?"

"Yes." He turned to face Ida. "You are a
fool, Ida. You try to make trouble for
Aleigha with me, but it is you who took the
Kingston woman in. Even now while she
hangs, giving her blood for your mistress,
the situation could be dangerous if I weren't
here."

"I do not understand, my lord." Ida
lowered her eyes. She hadn't expected any
sort of reprimand.

"You couldn't resist having her in the
stable of girls, could you? Now the police
have been here. If I hadn't been here, there's
no telling what might have transpired."

Ida shook her head but said nothing.

"If the police are satisfied with your
story, they won't be back. Ujuvary is dead,
and she'll no longer be a questionable item
in this house, in the event someone would
come around."

"I feel so safe, my lord, now that you are
here and have taken command."

"You have nothing to worry about, dear
Ida. I will renew the spell over the house to
ensure the safety of everyone in it while I am
gone. Ever since I put this house here, anyone seeing it or even coming into it accepts
it as real and believes it to be real. Why
should the stupid police be any different
and suspect something?"

"But the police came, my lord. Why did they come now?"

"Only because of your stupidity."

Thorko put his hand on Ida's shoulder, turning her toward the front of the house. When they reached the foot of the steps, Aleigha and the countess stood side by side, waiting for them.

"Is Ujuvary dead?" Elizabeth asked.

Ida nodded and turned to Thorko. "What of her body?"

"Ujuvary is gone."

"I know, my lord, but her body should be disposed of, and the lime pit has not yet been enlarged."

Turning to fix a baleful glare on Ida, he said, "I said she is *gone*."

Ida turned, looking toward the kitchen, from where she stood, the body should have been clearly visible. The room was empty.

Friday - 10:33 a.m.

The alleyway near the side of the old Egyptian Theater was deserted. Without warning, the body of an old woman suddenly appeared, propped against the brick wall between two large trash containers.

Two boys, 12 years of age, hurried along the alley. "Come on, Johnny. We can get to the hobby shop a lot quicker this way than going around the block."

"Right behind you, Al," Johnny said.

"You got hobby shops in Dubuque?"

"Yeah, there's a couple. Why?"

"Just wondering, that's all."

Al stopped walking, and Johnny bumped into him.

"What'd you stop for?"

"Look," Al said, holding up a shaky finger. He pointed at the old woman leaning against the wall, her eyes closed.

"Is . . . is she dead?" Johnny asked.

Al shrugged. "Dunno. Maybe. I think we'd better get the hell outta here. Come on."

"Wait a minute. What you running for? We didn't do anything."

"I know that. What do you want to do?"

"We'd better call the cops. She might be alive yet. I say we call the cops."

"Whatever," Al said, grabbing his cousin's hand and yanking him toward the end of the alley. There had to be a cop around someplace.

Friday - 11:11 a.m.

With the telephone crooked between his head and shoulder, Jerry wrote down information on the pad in front of him. "Okay. Thank you, Doctor Hyberger." He hung up and turned his attention to Gus, who had just entered the office.

"Where you been?" Jerry asked.

"I went to City Hall. You'll never believe the goof-up I found."

"What?"

"Well, first of all let me explain. I ran routine checks on Chewell and Nargella, and I drew a zero. Nothing. Blank. Nobody's ever heard of them."

"That's strange, isn't it?"

"In this day and age, you'd better believe it. I'll grant you I only checked on the surface, and I'm sure we'll eventually come up with something. So far, I found nothing at D.M.V., court records, or tax records, and that's where I discovered the big goof-up."

"What's that?"

"City Hall has no indication that that house was ever built. They've been getting away without paying taxes of any kind. See, they say there's no house at that address."

"That's impossible," Jerry said.

"I know that. You know that. The tax assessor, if he believed me, knows that. But nevertheless, that's the way it is. Just to make certain, I went to the public library and checked out directories that go back a long time. They don't show anything about a house at that address either."

Jerry ran a hand through his hair. "Maybe it's a good thing I copied the stuff off that coat of arms. I called a friend of mine at the college, and I'm going over to see him after lunch."

"Let me see what you copied," Gus said.

Jerry handed him his notebook.

Gus flipped it open and read:

*Cross at the top—Maltese? Sigis-
mundus—Bathori—two blotches
that could be letters—Dux—Transylvania—what could be three
worn letters—shield in center with
what looks like club on it with
three sharp, curved things pointing to left. Inner circle with series
of repeated symbols or letters on
it. None too clear.*

Gus looked up at Jerry. "You've gotta
be kidding. Transylvania? Bela Lugosi's
stomping ground? Was that really on
there?"

Jerry nodded. "And don't forget that
Janet Mulrooney's body had very little blood
left in it."

Gus looked up, half-expecting to see his
partner grinning or making a grimace. Instead, he found him serious. Then the full
realization of what Jerry had said just
struck home.

Friday - 12:10 p.m.

Detective Rick Wolper turned the corner
of the hall, hurrying toward his desk. The
eight by ten photos in his hand were still
damp from the developing process. *Why'd
we have to draw the assignment of handling
the death of some old bag lady?* True, there
weren't too many derelicts in Sioux Falls,

but surely there wasn't any foul play involved. There wasn't a mark on the body.
More than likely, she'd suffered a heart
attack and simply died. The county would
bury her, and that would be that. He had
enough of a work load without having to fill
out the forms that went with this sort of
thing.

After entering the office, he walked by
Gus Weaver's desk.

Gus looked up. "Hey, Rick, how's it
going?"

"Could be better." He stopped, grateful
for the chance to talk with Gus for a
minute.

Jerry Hewlett looked up from his desk,
nodding to Rick.

"You guys sure got it made," Rick said.

"How do you figure?" Jerry asked.

"Well, first you were working the streets
without any formal case load. Then the captain pulls you in and gives you one case to
work on. It isn't very fair if you ask me."

"First," Gus said, "nobody's asking you.
Second, we don't have just one case. We've
got a shitpot full. They're all the same type,
but we got a bunch."

"How's it going?" Rick asked. "Anything turning up?"

"We got lucky, if you want to call it that,
when we got a hit on the prints of the girl
whose body was found at that construction
site. They matched with one of the missing

girls, but not one of those in our case load. Now, she's included."

"Where'd they match?" Rick asked, idly looking at the photos.

"The kid was picked up as a hooker before she was reported missing. What you got there?" Gus asked, pointing toward the eight by tens.

"Oh, these? Nothing. They're of an old bag lady that croaked downtown. See what I mean when I say you've got it made?"

"How's that?" Jerry asked.

"You get to go out looking for young girls who are missing while I get stuck with old bags like this." Rick threw the photos on Gus' desk.

Gus and Jerry laughed, glancing at the pictures.

"You're sure to be pitied," Gus said, idly picking up the photos. "At least you don't have to look for them. You've found yours." He handed them back to Rick and stopped. Turning them around he studied them again. "Where'd you say she was found?"

"Downtown. In an alley close to the mall. Why?"

Gus said nothing, peering intently at the eight by tens. "Jerry, look at this. Familiar?"

Jerry turned over the picture and looked at it. "From where?"

"This morning. At Count Dracula's castle. Remember?"

Rick stared at Gus as if he'd lost his mind. "Count Dracula's castle?"

Jerry stared at the picture. "What the hell you talking about?"

"When we were leaving, I saw an old lady for an instant at the back of the hall. I'd swear it was this bag lady right here."

Jerry shook his head. "I didn't see anybody like that. I was talking to the Chewell woman. You sure?"

Gus nodded, taking the picture from Jerry to examine them again.

"Count Dracula's castle?" Rick repeated.

"What time was she found?" Gus asked.

"A little after ten-thirty," Rick said.

"Who found her?"

"Two kids. One's visiting from Iowa." Rick looked first at Gus, then Jerry. "Count Dracula's castle? What the hell are you two talking about?"

"What time was it when we left there?" Gus asked, ignoring Rick.

Jerry shrugged. "A minute or so after ten. Maybe five after or so. Why?"

"If we left North Duluth Avenue at—let's say five past ten—how'd the old lady get all the way downtown in an alley and die by ten-thirty or so?"

"Hey, you're not certain if it's the same woman, are you?"

"I wasn't at first, but I am now. Look at this." Gus stood up, moving around his desk to go to Jerry's. Pointing at the picture, he indicated the large earring shaped like a crescent moon hanging from her left ear.

"So?"

"So, the woman I saw had an earring just like this on, and it was on her left ear, and she didn't have one on her right. Old—long white hair—one oddball earring on the left ear. I'll bet pizza and beer that I'm right."

"You got a bet, but then, I'm a sucker for pizza and beer, no matter who buys," Jerry said.

"What time do we have the appointment at the college?"

"Right after lunch."

"Okay. Between now and then we'd better get over to records and make certain that there's no data whatsoever on that mausoleum of a house."

"What do you think we got going, Gus?" Jerry asked, standing.

Gus shrugged. "I don't have the slightest idea. Well, that's a lie. I do have an idea, but I'm not saying it to anyone—not even you."

"That's okay, Gus. I think I've been thinking something like it for the last hour or so."

Jerry followed Gus from the room.

Rick scratched his head, calling after them, "Count Dracula's castle? Mausoleum for a house? What the hell are you two talking about?"

Gus stepped back into the room. "Catch you later, Rick. Then we'll fill you in. Okay?" Gus disappeared around the frame of the door and ran to catch up with Jerry.

Rick shook his head. Police work had to be getting to them; that was all there was to it.

17

Friday - 12:31 p.m.

Gus looked over the empty desks. It was a rotten time to try to find anything out at the tax assessor's office, but it seemed to be the most logical step to take at the time. He had been standing in the same spot before within the last few hours and had been asked to be shown the records for the large graystone mansion on the North Duluth. There had been no record of it, which in turn had prompted him to go to the public library and look through the old city directories. He had found nothing there either.

When Jerry lighted up a cigarette, Gus turned to him. "You realize that's off-limits in here?"

Jerry looked at him, a little-boy guilty expression crossing his face. Dropping it to the floor, he stomped on the cigarette. "Sorry 'bout that."

"Hey, it's your life. Besides, if you hadn't put it out, as a good officer of the law, I would have had to arrest your ass for smoking."

"My ass doesn't smoke." Jerry turned when an attractive woman approached them.

"May I help you gentlemen?"

Gus noted the woman was in her late twenties or early thirties and had no ring on her left hand. Smiling, he lowered his voice. "I'm Detective Gus Weaver, and this is Detective Jerry Hewlett. I was in earlier this morning and took a peek at the assessor's records for taxes on a certain piece of property. Could I take another look?" He flashed his badge, keeping his attention riveted to her blue eyes.

"I guess you can." She glanced at Jerry before fixing her gaze on Gus. "What's the address?"

After Gus told her, he watched her walk away then turned to his partner.

"Nice legs," Jerry said.

"You're not supposed to notice things like that anymore. You're married."

"Hey, I'm a cop. I've got to be observant."

Gus smiled broadly and leaned on the counter. After a few minutes passed, he approached the woman walking toward him as she returned with the computer print-out.

"Here you are, Detective Weaver," she said.

Gus took the sheet without taking his eyes from her. When she turned to leave, he dropped his attention to the sheet. "I don't believe this."

"What?" Jerry asked, stepping closer to his partner.

"The address is here. Hey, miss, can you please come back here?"

"Yes?" she said, returning to the counter.

"Is this for real?"

"I don't understand."

"This print-out. Where'd you get it?"

"Where'd I . . .? From the computer. Why, for heaven's sake?"

"This morning I was in here and asked for the same address. The print-out I was given then didn't have the address. The lot was listed as being vacant."

"I don't think so," she said.

"Don't call me a liar, lady." Gus glared at the woman.

"I'm not calling anyone a liar. The fact is, if I just withdrew that information from the computer and someone else did it for you this morning, I promise you the address was on it. You just overlooked it."

"If you're right, then both your boss and the woman who got it for me missed it as

well. They looked and didn't see it, either."
Gus pointed to the mansion's address. "See.
It's right there. *Now*, it's right there. This
morning, it wasn't. Is your boss in?"

She half-turned, making a sweeping
gesture with her arm. "You can see that
most of the people are gone for lunch. Mr.
English and I are the only two in the department during the noon hour."

"What's his capacity?"

"He's an assistant manager. What did
you do with the print-out from this
morning?"

Gus palmed his forehead and said,
"Why didn't I think of that? I threw it
away—in the wastebasket over there." He
pointed to the green square can standing in
the corner. Gus and Jerry crossed to it and
took off the lid. Halfway down, they found
the only computer print-out sheet in the
canvas bag. While Jerry dumped the
contents back in, Gus walked over to the
counter, opening the crumpled paper.

"You better get it all cleaned up, or I'll
be in dutch with the boss when he gets
back," the woman said. She took the
proffered sheet from Gus and glanced down
the list. Her eyes widened. Then she picked
up the sheet she had just printed out herself.

Jerry stepped to the counter. "He was
right, right?"

"I don't understand this," she said
quietly.

"Could someone have been tampering with the computer?" Gus leaned forward, taking the two sheets from her.

"I don't see how. My desk is right next to the door that opens into the computer room. No one went in who didn't have business in there this morning."

"Yeah," Gus said, "and it had to have been sometime this morning—after I was here. You're absolutely certain?"

She nodded. "Of course someone could have tapped into the system, but that doesn't make much sense either."

"Why?" Gus asked. "It sounds as if somebody's trying to pull a fast one on the city and state."

"I suppose that the old records wouldn't show it either?" she said.

"City directories in the library didn't carry it," Gus said, turning to Jerry. "It doesn't make sense."

Jerry nodded.

"If somebody tapped into the computer, it would have to be someone who has an interest in the house. But why would they put the address *in* if they've gotten away without paying taxes all this time?" The woman looked directly at Gus, as if expecting an answer.

"That seems to be the big question of the day, Miss—er?"

"Dorothy—Dorothy Allison, Detective Weaver."

"Make it 'Gus', Dorothy."

"Dottie to my friends."

"I'd like to apply for friendship, Dottie."

"You got it, Gus."

A different sort of silence filled the reception area, and Jerry coughed. "It's getting late, Gus. We've got to get over to the college. Remember?"

"Right. I'll get back to you, Dottie," he said, turning to follow Jerry out of the office.

"What time is our appointment?" Gus asked, hurrying to catch up.

"One-thirty. Why? You in a hurry to get back to Dottie, lover boy?"

"Very funny. Since we've got some time, let's stop at the public library on the way. This address thing makes no sense whatsoever."

A few minutes later, they reached the public library. Gus led the way to the reference shelves where he had found the directories earlier.

Pulling down the books for 1975, 1970, 1960 and 1950, he handed two to Jerry and sat down at a long table. "Look in the pink section. That's where the streets and addresses are listed."

After thumbing through the thick books, Jerry stopped. "It's here."

Gus looked up. "Jesus, I think I'm losing it. It's in here, too."

"Did you look at these same books this morning? Maybe it was omitted in the ones you looked in."

Gus frowned. "No way. I started with the most recent one. When I didn't find it in there, I checked each year for ten or twelve years. Then I started jumping back until I got to 1960, then 1950."

"Is that where you stopped?"

"Yeah."

"How old would you say that house is?"

"Why?"

"It wasn't built in the forties, was it?"

"I doubt it."

"Turn of the century?"

"I guess you might say that," Gus said, a look of puzzlement crossing his face.

"Probably even before, considering the height of the ceilings. See, the Chewell woman told me it was built around the turn of the century."

"What are you driving at?"

Jerry stood up. "We're wasting our time with the sixties and seventies. Let's go back as far as we can in the directories."

Following his partner's lead, Gus walked around the table at which they had been sitting. In each city directory they found the address and name of the owner.

"This is crazy," Jerry said. "How could the same person own that property from 1898 until today?"

"Yeah. And how does one go about inserting a name into books that are years old without leaving a clue as to how it was done?" Gus frowned again. "Who the hell is this Elizabeth Browne Nargella? How many

Elizabeth Browne Nargellas have there been?''

"How many?''

"Yeah,'' Gus said, slamming the book back onto the shelf. "How many? I'm not going to buy the fact that it's the same person, are you?''

"Look, Gus, you thought a few minutes before that you were losing it. No way are you doing that. You're a good cop and—''

"I don't know where you're going with that line of bullshit but I'm not buying one owner for that house since 1898. Forget it. I'm not that much of a romantic, and my imagination doesn't work that good either.''

"What I was going to say,'' Jerry said, placing the rest of the books back in place, "is simply that you're a good cop and a trained observer. If you say they weren't in the books before, I believe you. After all, I did see the computer print-outs at the assessor's office. Right?''

"So what in hell's the bottom line?'' Gus' voice carried, and a stern, thin woman who was seated at the next table glared at them over her glasses.

"We're up against something that's out of the ordinary.''

"That's a bit of understatement if I ever heard it.''

Jerry grinned sheepishly. "The thing I'm wondering is this. Does this Nargella woman have anything to do with the missing girls?''

"Good question. Got an answer?"

Jerry shook his head and headed out-side. The sun poured heat and light down on Sioux Falls, while birds sang their songs in the shade of nearby trees. People strolled along, passing the two plainclothesmen and ignoring them.

"I wish I did," Jerry said. "Maybe we'll find out something at the college."

"Remember what you said about the Mulrooney girl not having much blood?"

"Yeah."

"Were you kidding?"

"Hell no. That was in the medical report."

"That's not what I mean. When I made mention of the fact that Transylvania was in your notes, you brought up the fact of the low amount of blood."

"So?"

"The way you said it, I half-expected you to say we were after a vampire."

Jerry opened the car door and peered at Gus across the roof. "I think we should keep our options open, don't you?"

Gus studied Jerry—earnest, sincere, and not the sort to go off half-cocked with a theory that came right out of nineteenth century literature.

"Yeah, I guess maybe we should," Gus said and got into the car. "Let's keep the talk about vampires and such to a minimum though. All right?"

"Sure. I don't want anybody saying

we're a couple of nuts on the loose."

Gus smiled and leaned back in the seat.

Friday - 1:32 p.m.

Jerry pushed open the door to the office of Thomas Weber, Ph.D., chairman of the history department.

"Yes?" the matronly woman asked, looking up from the stack of papers in front of her.

"I'm Detective Jerry Hewlett. I have an appointment with Doctor Weber at 1:30."

"Oh, yes, Officer Hewlett. Doctor Weber told me you were coming in. Unfortunately, he was called away this morning, right before lunch."

"When will he be back?" Jerry glanced at Gus, who didn't react.

"I'm not certain. However he did make arrangements with Professor Fedders to answer your questions."

"Where'll I find him?"

"His office is just down the hall to your left."

"Thank you. Is he expecting us at this time?"

"Yes sir."

Jerry turned, leading Gus out of the office and started to his left. Five doors down the hall they found Professor Fedder's office, the door standing open.

"Come in, gentlemen," the tall, lanky man said, thrusting out his hand.

After the introductions, Fedders offered them seats. "Now, what can I do for you? How can I help?"

"Did Doctor Weber tell you anything?"

"Just something about a family of nobles, which I have looked up to refresh my memory. How may I help?"

"It has to do with a coat of arms."

"Ah, yes. He's the expert in that field. What about it?"

Jerry reached into his jacket pocket and withdrew his leather-bound notebook. Opening it, he handed it to Fedders.

Fedders face brightened the instant he saw the notes. "Bathory? Bathory? I don't believe it. Where'd you get this?"

"Like I told Doctor Weber, I copied as much as I could from this old coat of arms. We'd like you to tell us what it means, if you can."

Fedders chuckled. "Now I see why Tom referred you to me. I wrote a thesis on Transylvania a few years ago as part of my Masters work. Sure, I can tell you something about it. What do you want to know?"

"What's it mean? The writing?"

"Although I'm not acquainted *per se* with the Bathory coat of arms, I can tell you who Sigismundus Bathory was. The Bathorys were a strange bunch to say the least. Sigismundus inherited the title of prince from his father, Christopher Bathory. Christopher ruled Transylvania for a few years during the Turkish reign of Eastern

Europe. Sigismundus went insane and
abdicated about two years after assuming
his title and position. Somehow, he returned
to power as a tool of the Sultan a short while
later and then abdicated again in 1599. Two
years later, he definitely abdicated."

"If the guy was nuts," Gus asked, "how
did he get into a position of power?"

"By the order of King Rudolf II of
Hungary. You see, Hungary, Rumania, Transylvania and those other principalities were
shoved from pillar to post by religious
forces and warring kings. The Bathorys can
be traced back to Transylvania to the year
1529 or somewhere about that time.
Stephen Bathory was the voivode of Transylvania."

"Voivode?"

"Royal governor. His son, King Stephen
Bathory ruled Poland for eleven years. He
and his branch of the family seem to have
been quite all right."

"But these other two?" Gus asked. "The
first two men you mentioned were nuts,
right?"

"Yes. Am I helping you?"

Gus shrugged and looked at Jerry. "I'm
not certain. Keep going for a few more
minutes."

Fedders smiled shyly. "To use your
term, 'nuts,' let's take a look at Sigismundus' sister and his son. His son,
Gabriel, ruled Transylvania for five years
before he was murdered by rebellious

nobles. His sister seems to sum up the in-
sanity in the family."

"How's that, Professor?" Jerry asked.

"Elisabeth Bathory was tried and con-
victed on grounds that she was a werewolf
and was found guilty of murdering over six
hundred young girls." Fedders paused for
dramatic effect but fell back when he saw
the reaction of the policemen.

"Say that again, Prof," Gus said, sitting
up in his chair.

Fedders repeated the charges as
handed down through history.

"What happened to her?" Jerry asked,
sharing Gus' excitement.

"She was found guilty and sentenced to
be walled up in a room of her castle. You
see, since she was of noble rank, they
decided to do that rather than publicly
execute her."

"Why'd she rate so high?" Gus asked.
"Didn't you say that one of them was
murdered by other nobles?"

"Yes, I did. But that was more in
keeping with a *coup d'état*. A political
murder is different from an execution for
murder."

"Do you know why she killed the girls?"

"As a matter of fact, I do, and that's the
crux of the whole matter. You see, she
contended that the blood of young girls—
virgins, maidens—would sustain her own
youth and vitality."

"How'd she do it?" Jerry asked, his

throat dry.

"I've read accounts of the night she was arrested and the awful things that were found. One room had bodies heaped in it—bodies that had been drained of their blood and which were covered with bite marks. In other rooms, girls were found hanging, being drained of their blood by some madwoman named Szentes. They found the countess in her bath of blood in a bedroom upstairs with her lesbian lover, Ilona Joo."

"Christ," Gus breathed softly. "And I thought *we* dealt with a lot of nuts."

Fedders smiled wanly.

"I'm sorry I couldn't make out all of the words on the coat of arms," Jerry said, taking the notebook back from Fedders. "What's this mean? D-V-X?"

"It's really a 'u' instead of a 'v.' It's Latin. Means leader. *Dux, ducis.* Remember your World War II history? Il Duce? The leader? Comes from the same word."

"And what is the club with the three things coming out of it?" Jerry asked, looking up at Fedders.

"Believe it or not," Fedders said, "the club is a club, and the three projectiles are wolves' teeth."

"Did the line stop there, or were there more of the Bathorys?"

"It's not known for certain if Gabriel had children. He was only twenty-four when he died. Elisabeth Bathory married around the age of fifteen and had four children. They apparently didn't amount to much, since the Nadasdy line for all practical purposes disappeared from history with the death of Elisabeth." Fedder's patted a stray hair in place.

"Elisabeth Bathory Nadasdy?" Gus mumbled.

"Yes," Fedders said, ready to continue the dissertation. "The man she married, Count Ferencz Nadasdy, was a warrior. Shortly after the birth of their last child, he found no battles to fight and bored with the life of being a mere husband, he began to delve into the black arts."

"Black arts?" Jerry asked, looking up first at Fedders, then at Gus.

"Witchcraft. Satanic worship and rites. His wife, I guess, was right next to him when he did this."

"Why would they turn to that?" Gus asked.

"Well, let's face it, gentlemen, they didn't have TV or radio or movies to entertain themselves. The printing press was barely a hundred years old. So, after the wars were fought and once one had four children, if a bit of curiosity was present, one could almost be expected to turn to something a bit out of the ordinary."

"You sound as if you almost approve, Professor," Gus said.

"Not approve as such. Merely understand."

Gus looked at Jerry. "How long did this countess live after she was walled up?"

"That's a matter of speculation. Most accounts say for a period of four years. I've read of how she would laugh and scream in her madness at night and how the sound would carry across the countryside. Then, one night, it simply stopped. After a few days, when no more noise came from the walled-up room, the guards were taken away and the food was no longer taken to the castle."

"One more question, Professor?" Jerry said, standing. "How old was she when she died? Do you know?"

"Pretty close. She was born around 1570, married at fifteen, had four children, so probably by that time she was twenty or so. Naturally, she had help in raising the children, and during the lull between wars, when she and her husband turned to the black arts, another ten years or so passed. She conducted her own war against the populace of the countryside for eleven years, which would have made her about thirty-nine or forty at the time of the trial. She died four years later, thus she would have been somewhere around forty-three or forty-four years of age. Why?"

Jerry turned away, to find Gus standing near the door. "No reason, I guess. Just curious. Thanks a whole lot for your time and the information, Professor."

"History can make a person curious when a little information is gained. It seems one fact leads to another and another, and pretty soon the individual is caught up in searching out the most minute details. Let me show you what I mean." Fedders turned to the bookcase, searching for a volume. "Yes, here it is. I think you'll find this interesting."

When the professor turned back, he found the room empty.

Friday - 3:09 p.m.

Jerry backed out of the parking place. Turning to Gus, he said, "You tell me what you think."

"I think the professor has one helluva imagination."

"You mean about why people did what they did and so on?"

Gus nodded. "There are a few things really bugging me though. The coat of arms. The name Bathory—Elisabeth Bathory Nadasdy—Elizabeth Browne Nargella. Same initials. Same first name. The one killed six hundred girls and—"

"He said over six hundred," Jerry said.

"When it's that many, who counts? Now we have young girls being reported missing by their families. We've found one body which had little blood in it and had been bitten all over. What do you think?"

"I'm waiting for you to say it first," Jerry said.

"Say what?"

"You aren't going to trick me like that,"

Jerry said, a short, gruff laugh punctuating the statement.

"Okay, smart ass, what do we do? Go to the captain and tell him we want a warrant because we think we're onto some woman who sucked dry *over* six hundred young girls four hundred years ago? Is that what you want?"

Jerry shrugged.

"All right," Gus continued, "let me fly this one up the flagpole. Somehow we're facing a bunch of really old farts who are still doing what they got punished for four hundred years ago. Will you buy that?"

Jerry shrugged again.

"I'm out of ideas."

"Let's go tell the captain exactly everything we know and everything the professor told us. Let's dump it in his lap."

"Sounds good to me." Gus frowned.

Both men fell silent as Jerry drove back toward the police station. Both thought of the information they had just acquired and wondered what the real answer might be to the question of the missing girls. Were the missing girls and the mansion somehow connected? One thing they did know. Somehow the mansion and its inhabitants had to be doing something out of the ordinary. One of the women had lied to them. Another, the old lady, was seen by them in the mansion and then minutes later turned up dead in an alley behind an old theater.

In a short time, they'd be facing Captain Lord, and then they'd brainstorm some direction on this case.

18

Friday - 6:00 p.m.

Aleigha closed the door to the basement behind her. She was getting tired of gassing the girls every three hours. It was almost like a ritual. Still, she knew they had to be kept under the influence of the drug. The new belts wouldn't be ready until Monday. Why Thorko couldn't just snap his fingers and have new ones at their disposal was beyond her. The state of suspended animation the girls endured when the gas was turned on did not harm their overall well-being or health, but she knew she and Ida couldn't keep it up indefinitely either.

After checking the condition of the girls hanging in the labs, she went to the kitchen.

Ida, who stood at the counter, turned. "How are the girls in the labs?"

"Most of them are getting comatose.

The last two or three we brought up are doing well, naturally." Aleigha chuckled.

"What's funny?" Ida glared at her friend and lover. She could never quite understand Aleigha's elation at bleeding young girls to death.

"I was just thinking about the old days—when we first came together and began serving the countess."

"And that makes you laugh?"

"I was thinking of the crude ways in which we bled the girls then. They died all too quickly, didn't they?"

Ida nodded.

"But today," Aleigha said, her voice rising excitedly, "we have a good diet for them that enriches their blood. We can control the flow of blood with valves. Because we build up their blood reserves before we tap into them, they last much longer."

Ida crossed the room. "That pleases you, Aleigha?"

Aleigha nodded, feeling her sensuality growing as Ida neared her. She reached out, touching the taller woman on the hand. As if a spark of electricity passed between them, both reacted. Embracing, they kissed lustily.

Friday - 7:51 p.m.

Gus stretched his legs. "I hate stake-outs with a passion."

"Next time, don't tell the captain everything." Jerry grinned boyishly at his
partner.

"Well, what were we supposed to do?
Lie? Omit some of the details? What would
have happened then?"

"At least he didn't yank us off the case."

"That's a consolation? Christ! We're
looking for missing girls and stumble
across what could be a real weird situation,
something completely out of the ordinary.
And you want to stay on it?"

"Why not? We gotta do something to
earn our bread, right?"

Gus laughed and wiped a hand across
his face, stifling a yawn at the same time. "If
I live to be a hundred, I don't think I'll ever
forget the look on Lord's face when we told
him about our primary conclusions."

Jerry grinned. "Yeah. I thought he'd
blow a gasket when we didn't answer his
question right away about if we thought we
were dealing with a vampire."

Gus shook his head and looked out the
windshield at the huge gray mansion
hidden among the trees, half a block away.
"About the only consolation I can draw from
this is the fact he didn't have us go see the
shrink. Think about it, Jerry. Two grown
men walking into their superior's office and
saying something like: 'We think the girls
who are missing might be the victims of
someone drinking their blood.' "

Jerry nodded solemnly. "I don't know

what else we can think at this time. We've got one body—real low on blood, bite marks all over, and a weight gain that doesn't figure in when the other facts are considered. Then there's the old woman's body in the alley. How'd she get there so goddamn fast? Are the two cases related?"

"In a way, I wish we could have gotten a search warrant. Sure would make the whole thing a lot easier."

"That takes time, and we sure as hell don't have enough evidence or witnesses to support us going in front of a judge asking for a warrant."

"Lord sure goes by the book though. 'Stake the place out and see if you can spot anything out of the ordinary, then we'll think about a search warrant.' God, sometimes I wish I had been a cop thirty or forty years ago. At least then a guy didn't have that much red tape to worry about."

Nodding in agreement, Jerry glanced at the large house. "Sure is a moody looking place."

"And it won't get any cheerier as it gets darker," Gus said, stretching and giving vent to the yawn which he had felt growing.

"Maybe we'll hit something tonight. Who knows?"

"I'm willing to wait, Jerry. If we do, we do. If we don't and have to continue this lousy stakeout, I'm going to appreciate it even more that I'm not married."

"Huh?" Jerry grunted, turning to look at Gus.

"Your wife isn't going to dig you being away from home this much, is she?"

"Hey, she understands."

"You hope."

Jerry reached over, lightly punching Gus in the ribs.

Friday - 8:58 p.m.

Thorko swept down the wide staircase, Elizabeth Browne Nargella behind him. "Where are they?" he asked.

"I suppose they might be in the back of the house performing their duties," the countess said.

"I imagine they are at each other again." Thorko's voice rang with sarcasm.

"Do not let them upset you, my lord."

"Why do you insist on defending them? They are unnatural. They like each other in a way that only man and woman should."

"They are of great service to me," she said, stopping at the bottom step.

Thorko whirled around. "I know that you use them whenever I'm not around. Why, I don't understand."

"You are gone so often and for such long periods of time, my lord."

"And you cannot control your urges during that time?"

Elizabeth dropped her gaze from his all

encompassing, piercing eyes. Her face flushed. "No, my lord."

"In many ways, you are as unnatural as they. I should have put a stop to it a long time ago. Come."

"Where are we going, my lord?"

"To find them. It is time I confront the issue."

Friday - 8:59 p.m.

Aleigha finished putting the last dish away. She enjoyed those times when Ida and she could work together, even if it were only something as mundane as cleaning a room or washing dishes.

Ida untied the apron she had donned to clean the kitchen and hung it in a small closet. Turning, she found Aleigha smiling at her. Just as she was about to speak, the door to the kitchen burst open.

"So, there you are, you followers of Sappho!" Thorko loomed in the doorway, pointing an accusing finger at the two women.

Caught off guard, Ida and Aleigha stared at him and then at each other.

"What is it, my Lord Thorko?" Ida asked.

"What is it, indeed? I find the behavior of you two most abominable. Unsavory at the least."

"Do we not serve our lady and you to the best of our abilities? Is this no longer satisfactory, my Lord Thorko?" Ida asked, raising her eyes to meet his.

"What the two of you do with each other is most distasteful to me. I should have stopped it long, long ago."

"Then neither of us would have anyone to love, my lord," Aleigha said quietly.

"What difference does that make? When I spared your life hundreds of years ago, Szentes, it was not to be as you are now. You and Ilona Joo are both unnatural abominations. I should withdraw my spell from both of you."

Aleigha glanced fearfully at Ida. He had never, in the centuries since fleeing Hungary, made such an overt threat. What if he did withdraw it? They'd both be dead again. Aleigha feared that. She and Ida had discussed it many times once they realized what had happened after Thorko had brought them back from the dead.

"We do not wish to offend you, Lord Thorko," Ida said soothingly.

Aleigha smiled inwardly. She knew if anyone could pacify Thorko's anger, it would be Ida—Ilona Joo—mistress of the exotic.

"Do not placate me, woman," Thorko roared. "I could destroy you now with a snap of my fingers."

Elizabeth placed a hand on Thorko's arm. "Please, Thorko, don't. I need them when you are not here. I love only you, Thorko, but the fire of my lust needs tending constantly, whether you are here or not. Would it be your wish that I go to another man for satisfaction?''

Ida and Aleigha sighed silently. If the countess held her ground, they'd be safe.

''These two women are lovers. You use them and they use you, but they *love* one another. This is useless. Wasted energy. I should eradicate them both this instant.'' Thorko turned, fixing his burning eyes on the two women.

''Do that and your lady love suffers, Thorko,'' Ida said. ''If you are so powerful, why not provide us with belts for the sluts in the dungeon? I don't believe you can.''

Ida stormed past the amazed sorcerer and countess. Aleigha closely following her. They rushed through the hall toward the living room.

Elizabeth put a restraining hand on Thorko's arm once more.

''That is the second time you have restrained me since we came into this room,'' he said evenly. ''What is it you're trying to tell me?''

''Nothing that would upset you, my lord. It is simply that without them, I shall surely die. We cannot find anyone to replace them. Who could we get? Because of the age in which we find ourselves, it would be impossible to discover anyone who would be as subservient as they. It gives you the necessary freedom to roam the earth, establishing the outposts of your future reign. If you wish me to be at your side

throughout the ages, spare them or I shall
not survive."

Thorko pulled her into his arms and
kissed her. Then he turned, leading her
toward the hallway that would take them to
the front of the house.

Friday - 9:09 p.m.

Aleigha followed Ida up the wide staircase. She half-expected to be struck down
any second. Never in the four hundred plus
years since she had been resurrected had
she ever heard anyone, much less Ida, talk
back to Thorko. She watched Ida's narrow
hips sway as she walked up the stairs. Perhaps Ida had been influenced by the times
they lived in. Aleigha had no idea, but she
feared change. She feared the conse-
quences that would surely follow Ida's
remarks.

"Wait!" Thorko's voice echoed through
the house as he entered the front hall.

Aleigha and Ida stopped, turning slowly
to look down at him. This would be their last
moment on earth together. In a second,
Thorko would withdraw the spell, and they'd
be dead once more.

"Yes, my lord?" Ida's voice icily rang
through the high-ceilinged entryway.

"Perhaps I was hasty. Perhaps you serve
best in the manner in which you do now.
After all, it has worked for over four
centuries, has it not?"

Aleigha looked up at Ida who stood several steps higher than she. She didn't believe what she had just heard. Thorko was giving in? It couldn't be. She'd never seen him do that to anyone—not even the countess. At least, she'd never witnessed him relinquishing a point so easily.

"Is there anything else, my Lord Thorko?" Ida asked.

"I believe we should talk more. Come down." He gestured with one arm and stepped back.

Aleigha watched Ida come down one step. She saw victory in Ida's eyes and turned, waiting for Ida to step down even with her. When they stood side by side, they walked down the stairs.

Friday - 9:09 p.m.

Judy yawned. Where was she?

"Jude?" The voice came out of the dark.

"Yeah, Rhon. What's up?"

"My head hurts a little."

"Mine does, too. I wonder why?"

One by one the girls regained consciousness, all complaining of headaches. "Forget the headache," Coral yelped. "My belt is still cut. Why? What happened? Didn't anyone come in here?"

Each girl had cut her belt to the point of freedom or had nothing more than a mere shred of leather holding the harness in place.

"I'm going to stand up," Judy said. Struggling to her feet, she leaned against the wall for support. Her legs tingled, hurting painfully for the first few minutes that she stood. "Be careful," she warned. "My legs are real weak and rubbery. It'll take a few minutes to get used to standing up. Hang onto the wall. It's tough keeping balance in the dark."

The girls got to their feet, bending down after a moment or two to rub their legs, helping to increase the circulation.

"Hey, Linda," Coral said.

"What?"

"Have you got the knife?"

"Just a minute." Linda swept her hands over her head. "It's not on the shelf."

"Remember? The gas came on and whoever had the knife dropped it," Margaret said.

"Quick. Find the knife," someone said.

"Wait a minute," Linda said. "How many are loose?"

They quickly took roll call and learned that they were all free, including Linda who had cut the rope tethering her to the wall before giving up the knife the last time.

"Then what in hell are we waiting for?" Coral asked. "Let's see if we can get the door open."

When the girls stood huddled together by the door, Linda ran her hand over the smooth, cold surface. "There's no knob."

"Fine."

"Shit!"

"Push it once."

Linda leaned against the door and it swung outward. "It's opening.

"It is?"

"Why?"

"What do you mean, why?"

"Why wasn't it locked?"

"We were tied up to the wall. They figured we'd never get loose and be able to get away."

"Makes sense."

"Where are we?"

"It sure is dark. See if anyone can find a light switch," Judy said. "I remember a lot of light coming through the door when I saw it that once."

"I got it," Margaret yelped excitedly.

The narrow room exploded with light. The girls closed their eyes, rubbing them to ease the brightness. When their eyes had adjusted somewhat, they found it necessary to squint at the glare of the single 100 watt bulb.

Unashamed of being naked and only wishing to be free of the dark room, they found the steps leading upward and, in single file, mounted them.

"Shh," Judy hissed. "We don't want them to know that we're free. Let's get the hell outta here and away. That's all I'm hoping for."

"Me, too," several of the others sighed.

When they reached the top of the stairs,

they listened intently at the heavy, wooden door blocking their path.

Friday - 9:12 p.m.

Aleigha and Ida stepped from the last riser and looked at Thorko and the countess.

"Come into the parlor," Thorko said, quietly and evenly.

When they were in the large room, barely illuminated by one lamp, he gestured for them to sit down.

"First, let me tell you of my unrest. The last hour or so I have had the strangest feeling. It is not unlike the quiet before a summer storm. I believe it is because of this apprehensiveness that I was ill-tempered with you in the kitchen. Of course I really do not care what the two of you do and what the two of you are. My pettiness is gone. My goal for world domination is all that counts. I hope the two of you realize that you are involved with a great movement, and once we accomplish our goals, our reward will be domination over the entire world and the people therein." He fell silent for a moment, letting the statement sink in.

"It is good, Lord Thorko," Ida said. "Your plan and goals must take precedent over all."

Aleigha bowed her head, agreeing with Ida, not quite certain what to believe. She had to know. "My Lord Thorko?"

"Yes?"

"You are no longer angry at Ida and me because of our love?"

"No. I wasn't really angry. It is this sensation that I do not fully understand. It will pass, and then all will be well. When this happens, I usually sleep, and then after it passes, I am in full control of my faculties once more. Everything is well where you are concerned." He bowed toward Aleigha and then to Ida.

Aleigha relaxed.

Thorko stood up and offered his hand to the countess. "Come, my dear, we shall retire."

Elizabeth stood, accepting his arm, and they left the drawing room.

Friday - 9:13 p.m.

Judy and Linda eased the heavy, oak door open, barely cracking the space between door and jamb. Judy pressed her head to the crack, peering into the gloom of the hallway where doors lined either side. When she was positive no one was about, she inched the door open wider. Putting a finger to her lips, she stepped into the narrow hallway. The girls followed her, and when the last one came through the door, she closed it without making a sound.

Judy held up a hand and whispered, "What are these doors?" She pointed to them, each separated by three or four feet.

Shushing her companions, she reached out and turned a knob. When it gave, she pulled on the door and entered the barely lighted room. When Judy saw the girl hanging from the ceiling, she clamped a hand over her mouth to keep from screaming.

Friday - 9:14 p.m.

Gus stretched. "I wish to hell something would happen," he said, groaning from his stiffness.

"Yeah, me too," Jerry said. Unscrewing the cap from a thermos, he poured some coffee into a cup. "Coffee?"

"Why not? I need something to keep me from falling asleep."

Jerry handed him the cup and said, "Shit! Looks like they're going to bed." He pointed through the trees at a second floor window in the mansion, which had just been illuminated.

"Not everybody. I think there's still a light on in the front of the house. I hope to hell they don't leave lights on all night. Otherwise we're sitting out here watching a sleeping house."

"Whatever," Jerry said. "At any rate, we don't have much choice, do we?"

"I guess not. We watch and wait some more." He sipped his coffee. "Tastes like battery acid."

Friday - 9:14 p.m.

Thorko slipped from his robe and
watched Elizabeth undress. When they
stood nude, next to the bed, they embraced,
running their hands over each other's body.
Easing her back onto the bed, Thorko held
himself up for a moment, admiring her
breasts in the soft, subdued light he had
turned on a moment before. Lowering himself, he plunged his erect penis into her
body.

Friday - 9:14 p.m.

Aleigha smiled at Ida. They had won. At
least they had been spared and were still
included in Thorko's overall plan. Since the
sorcerer and the countess had gone
upstairs, she and Ida had simply sat in the
living room, thankful to have been spared
Thorko's wrath.

"Why do you suppose Thorko is upset?"
Aleigha stood, crossing over to Ida, who sat
at the end of a couch.

"I have no idea. The thing I'm thankful
for is the fact that it was something other
than our relationship that had set him off."

Holding out her hand, Aleigha said,
"Come. We'll make coffee before we retire."

Ida stood, and the two women walked
back toward the kitchen. Halfway there
Aleigha stopped short. "I just thought of
something. The girls!"

"What about . . . ? They weren't gassed, were they?"

"No. Come on." Aleigha hurried down the hall toward the kitchen and the corridor beyond.

Friday - 9:14 p.m.

"What is it?" Rhonda asked.

"Don't look. It's awful." Judy barred the way into the room.

"What is?"

"There's a girl hanging in there."

"What?" Rhonda asked.

"You heard me."

"Listen," Coral whispered. "I hear someone coming."

"Hide in there," Rhonda said, pointing beyond Judy.

"Be quiet. Don't look at the girl," Judy whispered hoarsely and stepped back.

The girls quickly filed into the dim room and closed the door.

Huddling against the door to secure it, the girls held their breath. Judy turned, peering at the face of the hanging girl.

"Help me," she murmured.

"Who are you?" Judy asked, working her way closer to the girl.

A long minute passed before an answer was forthcoming. "Daun. Daun Kingston."

"Daun? Help me, somebody. It's Daun. We've got to get her down."

Four of the girls hurried over and gently

released Daun's feet, lifting her at the same time to keep her weight from pulling on her arms. Several attempts at freeing her bound wrists failed until the girls managed to slip the loop from the hook.

"Oh, my leg," Daun cried.

"What is it?" Judy asked.

Precious seconds passed until Daun could speak. "There's something sticking my leg."

Judy looked down, gasping. The valve attached to the needle had been twisted. Reaching out, Judy was about to pull the needle out when Daun moaned.

Mustering every ounce of mental prowess, she spoke more quickly. "Don't pull—it—out. I'll bleed—to—death."

"Stand her up. One on either side. We've gotta get out of here—now!" Judy went back to the door. Pressing her ear next to the wood, she heard footsteps approaching. Quickly receding in the distance, they stopped for a moment. Judy heard a door open and close. "Come on." She threw open the door and stepped into the hall. "Check those other doors. See if there are more girls hanging like Daun was."

The girls opened the doors to find girls too weak to respond to their questions. Freeing them, they let them lay on the floor. Of the twelve hanging victims, four were strong enough to respond and were helped to their feet, supported between two of the other girls.

"Listen," Judy whispered. "Listen. Somebody else is coming.

Friday - 9:18 p.m.

"They're gone!" Ida gasped as she looked into the empty room. "Where could they have gone?"

"We didn't see them at all," Aleigha said, holding up one of the cut belts.

"We've got to find them. They have to be in the house someplace. They couldn't have gotten out without us knowing."

The two women turned, running up the steps to the basement level. Once there, they ran the full length of the house to the staircase that would take them to the first floor.

"We'd best check the labs. Perhaps they're hiding in one of them," Ida said, puffing.

Friday - 9:18 p.m.

"Get back and close the door," Judy ordered, pulling the door shut herself. "Don't make a sound."

They heard the sound of running feet coming nearer. Then the sound of a door closing filled the room. Silence. Muffled voices, and a door opened and closed. Then another. And another. Each sound inexorably moved closer and closer.

Then muffled voices were right outside in the hall. Each girl held her breath. They watched, horrified, as the knob slowly turned.

19

Aleigha pursed her lips, touching them with a forefinger, and reached out to turn the knob. Slowly moving the brass fixture, she freed the latch of its hold and pushed the door in. For a long second, she and Ida stared at the naked girls before them.

"Well, here you are, my pets," she said softly. "They'll be stiff from inactivity, Ida. Don't be concerned with—"

Aleigha never had a chance to finish the sentence.

The captives looked at the two women for a long moment, appraising their number and size. Two of them. One was short with huge breasts, the other tall and rather thin.

As one, the girls reacted to Judy's cry. "Get 'em!"

Charging forward, the wave of nude bodies caught the two women off guard, and they were quickly knocked from their feet. Without thought or consideration, the girls ran over them. Freedom! They could taste it. They could smell it. They could almost touch it. They were going to get out of that house of horrors one way or another.

Linda and Margaret half-carried, half-dragged Daun through the hallway to the kitchen. Each of the girls from the dungeon helped those from the labs where they had been found hanging. Instinctively, Judy and Rhonda, helping a girl, dashed as fast as they could through the kitchen into the hall that would lead them to the front of the house. Could they find their way out? Would any door leading outside be locked or barred?

Ahead, Rhonda saw a gigantic oak door, standing at least ten feet high and topped with a frosted transom window. If the door were locked and they couldn't open it, the window overhead was too high for them to reach.

Judy reached out with a shaky hand. Freedom was right on the other side. Someplace on the other side of that door were her parents and Rhonda's parents; the families and friends of all of them waited. Her hand closed on the knob, and she turned it. Nothing happened. Though it turned, the door didn't budge. Jerking and pulling, she did her best but nothing happened.

"Wait," Linda cried, stepping forward. She reached out, turning a dead bolt whose handle was right above the knob. "Now."

"Stop!" Ida screamed from behind. "Don't go through that door. If you do, you'll die."

"Don't take another step," Aleigha growled from Ida's side. "I want all of you. Don't move."

"Fuck you two!" Coral's fist blazed through the air. Catching Ida on the point of her chin, she fell backward and sideways into Aleigha who lost her footing. Both women went to the floor.

"Come on, girls! Let's go!" Judy threw open the door, and the cool, June night air swept over them, washing away the days and weeks of captivity in a refreshing shower of cleansing freedom.

One after another, they charged into the night.

Friday - 9:20 p.m.

Gus and Jerry lolled in the front seat of their unmarked patrol car.

"Do you know what I'd rather be doing right now?" Gus asked.

Before Jerry could hazard a guess, the night was suddenly filled with the cries and screams of women.

"What the hell is that?" Jerry asked, sitting up. "Look! Look for Christ's sake! Girls! Naked girls! Coming out of the mansion!"

"My wish has been granted," Gus said, reaching for the microphone. "I'll be right behind you, Jerry. I'll call for backup."

Jerry jumped from the car, hurrying around the front and dashing toward the mansion. The girls had slowed down once they had descended the broad stairs from the wide veranda and had disappeared behind the tree trunks and hedges. He could hear Gus' footsteps running up behind him and half-turned to ask, "What do you suppose the hell's going on?"

"You've got me. Who's to say who they are or what they're doing or . . . Hey, there, hold on. We're the police. Stop right where you are."

At first when they reached the sidewalk, the girls didn't react immediately. Then the words registered, Police! They were safe.

Gus and Jerry ran up to the girls huddled together near a large shrub where they had retreated.

"Who are you? What's the idea of running around like the day you were born?" Gus asked curtly.

"I'm Judy Merton. This is Rhonda Gordon."

"I'm Daun Kingston," Daun managed weakly.

The names came pouring out, one after the other, bringing to the fore with each policeman the files they had practically memorized.

"Where've you girls been?"

"In there," Coral said, nodding over her shoulder and rubbing her right hand.

Gus and Jerry looked over their heads at the mansion. A wolf whistle from the street brought both men around to find cars slowing and gapers hanging out the windows.

"Get back into the yard and out of sight. We'll have a riot here in a minute if we don't get you girls off the street."

"I won't go back in there," Sherry Blaine cried. "I won't. They'll hurt me. They'll kill us."

"It's all right, honey," Jerry said, looking down at the frightened 12 year-old. "We understand. You've all been through a lot, but Officer Weaver and I will protect you. We've sent for help, and all of you will be with your folks real soon."

Sherry looked up. "Promise?"

"I promise." Jerry made a quick motion with his hands, and the girls ducked out of sight.

"What the hell was going on in there?" Gus asked.

"Most of us were being held in a dark room."

"Do you know why?"

"I think I do," Judy said, stepping forward, unmindful of her nakedness for a moment. Then modestly covering her breasts and lower body as best she could, she crouched down.

The other girls did the same, lessening Jerry and Gus' initial feeling of embarrassment.

"What?" Jerry asked.

"I think they were feeding us well to keep us healthy so they could kill us—for our blood. I know that sounds crazy, but so help me, it's the truth. I swear."

Gus shot a quick look at Jerry before turning back to Judy. "What makes you say that?"

"Look at these four girls. What the hell's hanging out of their legs?" She pointed to Daun's inner thigh when the girl thrust her leg out.

Gus dropped to his haunches and, after pulling a pen light out of his shirt pocket, played the beam on the valve. He whistled softly. "Are you girls the only ones in there?"

"No," Rhonda said without moving. "There are at least seven or eight more in there. They were hanging up like meat in a packing house. They were draining blood from them."

"We'd better wait until the backup unit gets here," Gus said, looking at Jerry. Turning back to Rhonda and the others, he said, "How many people are in there?"

"We only saw two, other than those still captive. Coral knocked them on their ass right before we came out," Judy said.

"Well, you girls are safe now."

"All right, girls," a woman's voice cried out from the porch. Aleigha and Ida started down the steps and slowed down when they saw the two men standing near their

captives. "Enough is enough. We can't have
you girls running around the city without
your clothing. You men, there, get off this
property at once. Do you hear me?" Ida
angrily snapped out the words.

Gus and Jerry watched them approach.
"Are these the two you saw in there?"

"Yes," the girls chorused.

"Hold it right there, ma'am," Gus said.
"We're the police. I believe these young
ladies would like to sign a complaint
against you. You're both under arrest."

Aleigha stared at Gus, then burst into
laughter. "You can't do that. This is an
institution for disturbed girls."

"It's nothing of the kind," Jerry said,
"and you know it. We've been looking for
these girls, and they've all identified themselves by name. Their parents will be
delighted to have them back."

Ida raised her chin in a haughty
manner. "You two dolts have no idea with
whom you're dealing. Unless you leave this
property instantly, you'll never live to regret
your error."

"That may be, lady," Gus said, "but in
the meantime I'd like to inform you of your
rights. You have the right . . ." Gus intoned
their lawful rights while Jerry pulled out his
handcuffs, slapping them onto Aleigha's
wrists. Then Gus pulled his out and cuffed
Ida, who continued holding her chin high.

"You girls stay low and out of sight,"
Jerry said. "Gus and I'll take care of these

two.''

Off in the distance a siren wailed through the night as a backup unit raced to the scene.

Friday - 9:24 p.m.

Thorko pumped lustily at Elizabeth's body, their passion swelling to a bursting point. When they both climaxed, shudders of relief swept over him, washing away the tension he had felt earlier.

As his penis withered inside her and he leaned down to kiss her on the mouth, he suddenly froze. Something was wrong. Something was drastically wrong. Why hadn't he noticed it before this instant? The sensation of anger and trepidation that had filled his entire being earlier in the evening—that which had made him so volatile with Ida and Aleigha—suddenly hammered at him even harder. What was wrong? Why couldn't he put his finger on it? The police! The police were nearby, threatening him and his people. He had to do something. He had to get the countess and Ida and Aleigha away from the police. Why had they come? What had put them onto this place?

Ujuvary!

It had been his own fault. Why hadn't he simply disintegrated her body? Why had he merely transported her to someplace where she could be found? He recalled that Ida had

been angry with the old woman because one
of the policemen who had been at the house
that morning had apparently seen her. The
fight with the alchemist had ensued, and
he'd killed her.

Leaping from the bed, he cried,
"Quickly! Dress! We must flee at once."

Elizabeth looked at him, dumbfounded.
She could still feel his large member in her
body and wanted to relish his semen
gushing into her. She loved that sensation.
Now he wanted her to get up and move
about? That wasn't fair. She wanted to lie
there without moving for as long as possible
and maintain that full feeling he always
gave her.

"Now!" he screamed. "The police are
close by. That is why I was so unsettled
earlier this evening. They must have been
lurking about someplace, watching us."

Elizabeth rolled off the bed and quickly
dressed. "Where are we going?"

"We'll find a place. Another small city
like this one. It's amazing how one can do
things in a town this size and seldom if ever
arouse suspicion."

When they were both dressed, he
opened the door and pushed her through.
"We'll get Edward and leave."

Running down the staircase, their footsteps echoed hollowly as if there were
nothing else in the building. "Aleigha?
Ida?" he cried out, but the sound of his
voice danced from wall to wall, mocking

him. Then he knew. "The police have them. Come, there's no time to lose."

Grabbing the countess' hand, he dragged her through the house toward the garage and the small room used by Edward. Throwing open the door, he found the chauffeur lying on the bed, passed out. The syringe, spoon and tourniquet on the table next to the candle told the story all too well.

"Fool!" Thorko growled. "Awaken!" He spread his arms, and Edward sat up, his eyes clear and alert.

"Yes? What is it, my lord?"

"Come. You must drive us away from this place this instant."

Edward swung off the bed and led them to the garage, the limousine glistened in the dim light of the single bulb overhead.

Once they were ensconced in the back seat, Elizabeth turned to Thorko. "Why don't you simply whisk us away from here. Then we'd be safe."

"You forgot I cannot do that with living matter. Ujuvary was dead when I transported her away. Do not worry. We will be all right. Edward, go as fast as you can. I'll protect us from the police."

"Where to?"

"To the interstate north of the city. We'll head east for the time being."

Edward turned the key, and the engine roared to life, purring with its own energy. Pressing the button to open the garage door, he put the car in gear and floored the accelerator.

Friday - 9:30 p.m.

The wail of the siren had died down when the second unit arrived. Two uniformed policemen waved the traffic on past the mansion. Once they had help, Gus and Jerry radioed in for one or two policewomen to come to the scene.

"You might help things if you tell us who is in the house," Gus said to Ida.

"You fool!" Her eyes glowered at him, her hatred spilled over. "Don't you realize that all of this is beyond your ken? Beyond your scope?"

"Play it any way you want, lady. We've got you at least, you and your friend over there." He nodded toward Aleigha and caught sight of the blinking beacon light on St. Joseph's Cathedral several blocks away.

The roar of a motor brought his head around, and then—he froze in motion. Everyone froze—unmoving, standing or sitting, exactly as they had been when the sound of the car motor first became audible.

Gus could see the long, black car zooming down the driveway, but he couldn't move a muscle. What was wrong? What had happened? Why couldn't he move? From his position he could see some of the others, including Jerry, simply standing there, doing what they had been doing but not moving at all.

The limousine bounced out of the driveway and turned to its left, charging away into the night.

Gus had to call headquarters, but how? Now that he thought about it, he could hear nothing either—no traffic sounds, no night noises, no conversation. Jerry had been asking the tall woman about who else might be in the mansion.

The way his head was positioned, Gus could still see the woman, and she wasn't moving either. Up high, a single orange-red light shone steadily. What the hell was that? Then he realized it was one of the beacons on the Catholic Cathedral shining brightly —but not blinking.

What the hell had happened?

Friday - 9:31 p.m.

When Edward gunned the engine and the limousine shot out of the garage and down the driveway, Thorko pointed at the people on the lawn, muttering some unintelligible words. When he saw them all freeze, he smiled confidently. They'd make it.

"Do hurry, Edward. I want to get away from here as quickly as possible."

"What of Aleigha and Ida?" Elizabeth

asked, looking through the rear window as the car rifled past the huge cathedral.

"We may have to sacrifice them. If we must lose them, we will find others who will do for you as nicely."

"You seem to forget, Lord Thorko, that they have been with me since the beginning."

"*I* have been with you since the beginning. I made them for what they are, when I freed you from your prison. You forget your obligations too quickly, my dear."

Edward swung hard to the right and screeched to a halt at the intersection with Minnesota Avenue. The cars on the busy thoroughfare all held their places. Thorko's energy had permeated the entire city. Ducking around automobiles, Edward wound through them. When he came to a traffic light intersection, he roared through until he came to North Drive, where he turned hard to the right once more.

The limousine hurtled along at 90 miles an hour, past cars, their drivers and passengers frozen, up the curving road, past the prison.

When the car passed a cemetery, Edward floored the accelerator, sending the speedometer needle past 100.

Thorko leaned back, relaxing. His sorcery would win. It always did.

The car rapidly approached a tight

curve to the left, and in preparing to make the turn, Edward slammed his foot on the brake pedal but it slipped off, striking the accelerator. The car, not unlike an un-leashed wild animal, leaped forward even faster, jumping across the curb and plowing through a wire fence heading straight at a high voltage tower.

The front of the limousine struck the leg of the tower with the impact of a battering ram, sending a shock wave through it. Edward's head struck the windshield, cracking it, while the steering column pushed back, crushing his chest. Blood spurted from his mouth as his eyes stared sightlessly through the window at the high tension line that had broken loose.

Elizabeth and Thorko smashed their heads against the padded back of the front seat, sprawling onto the floor in a heap. Dazed but not unconscious, Thorko waited a minute before moving to make sure nothing was wrong with his body.

"Are you all right?" he asked.

"I . . . I'm shaken but I think I'm fine," Elizabeth managed in a whisper.

Thorko sat up and helped her to the seat.

Outside the broken power line whipped about like an angry snake, sparking, flashing, arcing to the ground as it danced closer to the car. The air, singed with burning ozone, crackled like frying bacon,

the sound quickly reaching a deafening
cacophony. The ground smoked, sending
blue tendrils into the dark night, which was
lighted spasmodically by the sparks and
secondary arcs.

Thorko gasped when he realized what
was happening. Cowering back in the seat,
he whimpered.

"My Lord Thorko, what is it? What is the
matter?"

Holding up a shaky finger, he pointed at
the blue snakes darting along the ground
toward the limo. Surrounding the car, the
crackling grew even louder. "Electricity.
I . . . I don't know it. I . . . I can't control it.
We've got to get out of here. Follow me."

Reaching for her hand, he grabbed it
and opened the door. Blue-white arcs of
lightning leaped from the swinging line to
the tower itself, to the ground, to the
limousine.

Thorko stepped out, and before his foot
touched the ground, an arc of electricity
shot from his shoe to the ground, hurtling
him back against the car and into Elizabeth.
The man and woman remained there, held
fast against the car, acting as a positive
ground for much of the 7,500 volts from the
loose line.

Arcs several inches thick danced from
Thorko's and Elizabeth's hands and arms.
They jerked violently, blue-black smoke
curling up from their feet, while new arcs of

electricity escaped from their hips, elbows and hands, seeking contact with the automobile behind them and the tower legs on either side.

Thorko and Elizabeth writhed in a bluish-white dance of death while the arcs darted about, sputtering and snapping not unlike a thousand bullwhips, detouring through the dying bodies of the sorcerer and the countess. Their clothing burned away, and bare flesh quickly cooked, searing to the metal of the car's body, adhering and smouldering. Curls of smoke wound their way up from the hair of the couple, while the burned areas of their bodies grew and spread quickly. The stench of charred flesh filled the air with the stink of cooked ozone.

When there was nothing left for the electricity to pass through other than the car, the ashes and chunks of scorched and blackened human flesh fell away to the ground.

Friday - 9:40 p.m.

The mansion on North Duluth wavered for a moment and then disappeared.

Gus blinked his eyes. The chatter of people suddenly filled the air along with the sounds of traffic filtering up from Minnesota Avenue and the cars passing by on North Duluth.

"Hey, Jerry, what the hell happened?"

Jerry walked over, shaking his head. "You've got me. Hey, where the hell is the mansion?" He stared wide-eyed at the vacant lot that had held the graystone mansion a few minutes earlier.

Gus whirled around and looked. The trees had changed. Instead of stately oaks and walnuts, scrubby willows and several birch trees stood by themselves. The house was gone!

"Did you see the limo take off?"

Jerry nodded. "Yeah. I heard it more than I saw it. I turned and just caught a glimpse of it. Who was in it?"

"You've got me. Maybe the two we cuffed can tell us." Gus slowly turned back, away from where the mansion had been. The girls who had run out of the house were still trying to figure out what had happened, but there was no sign of the two women they had arrested.

One of the girls, screaming, brought Gus and Jerry running to her side. "What's wrong?" Jerry asked.

The girl, unable to speak, pointed at the ground behind one of the other girls. When that girl turned, she jumped and screamed, too.

Gus and Jerry stepped forward and looked. An aged cadaver lay on the ground without its head. The skull lay several feet away. Shiny handcuffs held the skeletal wrists together.

"Hey, what's this?" Coral yelled from a few feet away, keeping her eyes fixed on the ground.

Gus and Jerry went to the girl's side. A pile of gray ashes lay in a small pool of light filtering through the willow tree blocking the street light. Half-covered by the ash, a pair of handcuffs gleamed brightly.

Gus stepped closer to Jerry. "What the fuck's going on? Where's the goddamn house? What happened? Why'd we find ourselves suddenly incapable of moving for a while? What happened to the two women we cuffed?"

Jerry shook his head. "I don't know, Gus. I really don't know."

Suddenly Gus broke into laughter, shaking his head.

"What's so funny?" Jerry asked.

"I was just thinking about Captain Lord. If he had a tough time with our vampire theory this afternoon, imagine what he'll say when he hears about this."

Jerry grinned. "At least we have some witnesses to back up what happened here tonight."

"Right. Let's get them downtown. We'll be up all night trying to write this little adventure up so that it makes some sense."

The girls were put in police cars and vans and taken to the hospital while Gus and Jerry went to the station to write up their reports.

On North Duluth Avenue, the twin beacons of St. Joseph's Cathedral blinked merrily.

EPILOGUE

Friday 10:00 p.m.

The program director pointed to Al Richards, the news anchorman for KFLL-TV.

"Good evening. I'm Les Richards. Authorities are still trying to come up with some sort of explanation for the loss of nine minutes tonight. KFLL and its sister radio station, as well as police and other news media, were swamped with calls beginning at 9:40 this evening. People were asking what had happened to cause an apparent nine minute blackout of sorts. Reports from people prompted a primary investigation, and it does seem as if nine minutes were taken out of existence in the Sioux Falls area this evening. Our own newscast is nine minutes late tonight, which we learned when we checked with the network. When we have a more in-depth report, we will bring it to you.

"In an unrelated matter, a limousine

crashed into a high voltage tower this evening, killing the driver who has not been identified and electrocuting two other people whose remains were found outside the car. We don't have a full report on it, but Michael O'Rourke is on the scene. Michael?"

"This is Michael O'Rourke reporting. Two people died this evening because they were either thrown from their wrecked auto or because they tried to get out once the accident had taken place. According to Fire-chief Fred Enesco, when they touched the ground, they were struck by the electricity and probably died instantly."

Firemen in the background behind the reporter were zipping up black plastic bags containing the remains of Thorko, the sorcerer, and the Countess Elisabeth Bathory Nadasdy.

From the poison pen of
JOHN TIGGES

Novels of horror that will haunt your dreams.

VENOM. Horrifying nightmares crowded her mind—images of frenzied natives writhing to the music of an ancient ceremony, of a little girl strapped to an altar, and of a huge king cobra, its fangs dripping with venom, poised to strike . . . .

_____2602-3 $3.95 US/$4.95 CAN

AS EVIL DOES. From beyond the grave he perceived a presence so powerful, an entity so evil, that it filled his heart with icy dread. Still, he could not let the dead rest in peace until he had discovered secrets no man was meant to know.

_____2521-3 $3.95 US/$4.95 CAN

BONE-CHILLING HORROR FROM EDMUND PLANTE

SEED OF EVIL. A savage union with a strange man left Patty, a divorced mother of two, with a child she couldn't bring herself to abort—or love. He looked like a normal boy, but when "accidents" began to happen—murderous, violent occurrences—Patty knew that this child was nothing less than the spawn of the devil.

____2581-7 $3.95US/$4.95CAN

TRANSFORMATION. Sally Martin was changing. Her body had become pale and bloated, her lustrous hair had fallen out, her jaundiced eyes were no longer able to bear sunlight. Meanwhile, ripening inside her, a hideous pulsing organism was waiting to burst upon an unsuspecting world, infecting all it touched.

____2490-X $3.95US/$4.95CAN